THE FOUR PATRIOTS

A graduate from IIT Kanpur, **Sumit Agarwal** is a successful businessman. He is also a music composer, lyricist, singer, actor and writer. His music videos can be viewed on his Youtube channel, or on his website www.sumitagarwal.net.

Sumit runs an NGO, Prerna (www.prernaa.org). Among its many social welfare initiatives, the NGO has adopted ten government primary schools, in order to facilitate best quality education. He is also the founder of Kasauti, a consortium of NGOs formed to aid clean and answerable politics.

Reach him at:
Facebook page: sumitsvoice
Twitter handle: sumitagarwal17
Email: info@mlagroup.com

Praise for the book

I'm confident that your book, *The Four Patriots*, will inspire the youth.
—**Akhilesh Yadav**, Hon'ble Chief Minister, Uttar Pradesh

Best of luck.
—**Ruskin Bond**

Reading the book was a breeze.
—**Semeen Ali**, author of *Broken Barriers, Transitions*

The novel leaves the reader with a heightened sense of patriotism. It is an enthralling read.
—**Saba Mahmood Bashir,** author of *I Swallowed the Moon: The Poetry of Gulzar*

If you want India to become *sone ki chiriya* (golden bird) again, then you must read this book and participate in the development of our country.
—**Om Puri**, veteran film actor

An amazing treatment of a subject which is India's need of the moment.
—**Abhijeet Bhattacharya**, renowned singer

It is an ethereal amalgamation of reality and fantasy. The book not only portrays the dismay among the youth of our country, but also shows them the path to glory for the country and themselves, in the most interesting and captivating way possible.
—**Pankaj Agarwal**, Chancellor, Shri Ramswaroop Memorial University, Uttar Pradesh

A must-read for people who love their country.
—**Bharat Kapoor**, film actor

It's an amazing book. It shows that if you seek despair, you get despair; but if you seek hope, you will find it in your heart.
—**Rakesh Bedi**, renowned film and television actor

An inspiring read.
—**Avtar Gill**, veteran film and television actor

An interesting story of four successful politicians and their journey
— **Aanjjan Srivastava,** veteran film and television actor

The Four Patriots is a gripping story of four individuals, deftly woven into a patriotic theme. It is a great read.
—**Rajat Malhotra**, Engineering Director, Twitter

Each page keeps you craving for more.
>—**Pulkit Trivedi**, Head of Ecommerce Business, Google India

This book is about youngsters and the fire within them to make this country a better place. Very touching and motivating.
>—**Aseem Trivedi**, political cartoonist and activist

The narration is amazing. The book re-ignites the spirit of patriotism and nationalism.
>—**Bhuwan Chaturvedi**. CEO, Paharpur Cooling Towers Group

A superb portrayal of reality, this book will not only be a hit commercially, but also guide the youth to create a bright future for India.
>—**C.M. Bhandari**, former Indian Ambassador to Cambodia, UAE, Poland and Lithuania; and yoga guru

The book would surely inspire the youth of today and instil a feeling of nationalism
>—**A.K. Chaturvedi**, retired IAS officer

This book gives us hope that our nation can be transformed.
>—**Akash Tripathi**, Managing Director, M.P Power Corporation

Sumit's prose is filled with positivity and wit. His unique story-telling style will keep you hooked till the last page.
>—**Dr R.N Trivedi**, retired IAS officer

You cannot miss this if you are a patriot yourself. I wish Sumit great success in what I can already foresee as an extraordinary writing career.
>—**Geeta Kapoor**, former international table tennis player

THE FOUR PATRIOTS

Sumit Agarwal

RUPA

Published by
Rupa Publications India Pvt. Ltd 2016
7/16, Ansari Road, Daryaganj
New Delhi 110002

Sales Centres:
Allahabad Bengaluru Chennai
Hyderabad Jaipur Kathmandu
Kolkata Mumbai

Copyright © Sumit Agarwal 2016

This is a work of fiction. Names, characters, places and incidents are
either the product of the author's imagination or are used fictitiously,
and any resemblance to any actual persons, living or dead,
events or locales is entirely coincidental.

All rights reserved.

No part of this publication may be reproduced, transmitted,
or stored in a retrieval system, in any form or by any means, electronic,
mechanical, photocopying, recording or otherwise,
without the prior permission of the publisher.

ISBN: 978-81-291-4204-7

First impression 2016

10 9 8 7 6 5 4 3 2 1

The moral right of the author has been asserted.

Printed at Parksons Graphics Pvt. Ltd, Mumbai

This book is sold subject to the condition that it shall not, by way of trade or
otherwise, be lent, resold, hired out, or otherwise circulated,
without the publisher's prior consent, in any form of binding
or cover other than that in which it is published.

Contents

Acknowledgements	*ix*
Prologue	*x*

BOOK 1

1.	Aditya and Elena	3
2.	Varun and Alisha	9
3.	Salman and Mahi	28
4.	Raghav vs Teachers' Association	40
5.	Aditya on Star Cruise	49
6.	Varun and Radhika	66
7.	Salman Antagonizes Ganesh	72
8.	Raghav, the Prince of Sumerpur	79
9.	Aditya Meets the Mayor	90
10.	Varun and the JPC	99
11.	Salman Quits his Job	105
12.	Raghav Quits Indian National Front	109
13.	Kali Zabaan Works in Aditya's Favour	120

BOOK 2

14.	Naya Bharat Comes to Power	131
15.	The Planning Commission—The Quadro vs Oldies	143
16.	Varun's Operation Colonoscope	158
17.	Jatin and Gang at Macau	168
18.	Gold Strikes Salman	178
19.	Oggy and the Cockroaches	190
20.	Raghav at Tokyo	202
21.	Operation*	224

22.	Aditya and Mrs Parker	238
23.	The Youngest Prime Minister	252
24.	The Incineration Plan for the Superbugs	261
25.	The Prime Minister's Development Fund	267
26.	Dekhna Nahin…Karna hai	277
27.	The Reunion	284

Epilogue   291
Author's Note   295

Acknowledgements

First and foremost, I would like to thank my motherland India, for providing the backdrop for this story. You will find this more apt, as you come across the many 'it happens only in India' moments during your journey through the book.

This story is not totally fictional; a large part of it is real life happenings. The characters of the four protagonists are also drawn largely from real people. Without naming I thank them for adding life and soul to the characters.

I would like to thank my father, who allows me to pursue my artistic interests like music and writing, while we struggle to manage our chemicals manufacturing business. My mother, who is always there for me. My wife, for always supporting and inspiring me to follow my dreams, and for her unconditional and unabated love.

Thank you IIT-Kanpur for shaping me into what I am. From Sumit to Summy and then 'Chummi'. Miss you all guys!

Thank you Riya Agarwal, Amarjeet Neogy, Richa Agarwal, Kushagra, Chhavi Saraf, Prashant Garg, Rammohan Agarwal, Mohini Saraf, Kritika di, Ratnesh Sagar, Alok Kumar, Deepak Naragund, Jaspreet Singh for being my in-house board of editors/critics.

Lastly and most importantly, Bajrang Baliji. I am fortunate enough to be born intact, no organs or body parts missing. I live a prosperous life with a full family. My God has given me a better life than I could ever ask for and I hope this first pen-work of mine, shall have his blessings too.

PROLOGUE

NEW DELHI, RED FORT, 15 AUGUST 2022

Patriotism was in the air. Thousands of performers and spectators had assembled at the historic Red Fort to display their solidarity to the new superpower, their very own nation, India. Much had happened over the past few years that made India's story seem more like a Hollywood thriller than a real set of events.

The Prime Minister of India was addressing the nation on the occasion of its 75th independence day. This address was special and had people across the country glued to their television screens, because on this day he gave something very unique to the nation. Something that made people wonder at his intelligence and wisdom.

'It's so thrilling to listen to our Prime Minister! God only knows what announcement he is going to make today,' said Sumit Bakshi, the most popular news reporter from Indian TV, twitching his lips and eyebrows in a peculiar way that the audience loved.

'Yes, aren't we all excited!' agreed Jagat Bindra from ABCD News, moving his hands in his typical choral director style. 'Remember! He scrapped reservation! The reservation law was nothing but a vote earner – another version of the divide and rule policy of the British. This man seemed to be different – someone who saw beyond vote-bank politics.'

The camera shifted focus from the area that seated the guests just in front of the podium from where the PM was speaking to the wide road behind it, now blocked by security on either side, and finally to the rectangular area, proudly displaying the figure '75' in saffon, white and green, with a sky blue background. The sight was fascinating. Thousands of children were there, the synchronized colours of their caps and dresses facilitating the graceful display.

'The last five years have been no less than a miracle for India. The world has begun to envy us. The Naya Bharat government, under the leadership of Dr Sabbarwal and his four patriots, has transformed the nation. There is security, well-being, development and positivity,' said Sumit Bakshi.

'No way? How embarrassing James! Just hold on for half an hour,' the annoyed teacher scolded the pleading skinny boy with untidy hair, in a hushed voice. 'Okay, come, I will speak to the security. Just don't sit there for an hour like you do at school.

'"The four patriots"—a nice way to address the quadro, Sumit!' said Jagat, adding, 'They have changed the mindset of the common Indian. *"Iss desh ka kuch nahin ho sakta"* has been replaced with pride and faith in the system. They have been through hell to make it happen.'

Both the reporters had closely covered each move of Dr Sabbarwal's team over the past five years.

The tall green-eyed boy rushed to the toilet adjacent to the children's area with a continuous wall of brightly painted blue metallic sheets behind it, separating the premises of the event from the rest of the ground.

As the PM rose to the podium, the crowd broke into frenzy, cheering for the country and their leader.

'Today, my friends, I will tell you about a decision of mine, which maybe the most controversial decisions that I have taken for the progress of our country. One, for which we may even have to amend with the Constitution. But I am sure it will have a long-lasting positive impact,' said the PM.

He looked around and could sense the crowd's excitement. 'Okay, I will give you a hint. After this is implemented, there will be little need for "Right to Recall",' he added.

The boy was back sooner than his teacher would have expected, not intending to miss the action and in the least, going back to the open seating area in the scorching sun.

The crowd roared and cheered.

'We are going to reduce the tenure of our elected representatives, the MPs and MLAs from five years to two years,' said the PM.

The crowd rumbled as if India had just hit a six on the last decisive ball against Pakistan. Everybody looked at each other in amazement.

'This man is totally unpredictable!' said Sumit, 'The media had explored all possible options, no one dreamt of something so drastic!'

The green eyed boy was now climbing to a high point in a dense tree with monkey-like adeptness. He removed his blazer, pushed back his hair to a neat stack behind his forehead, then drew a cardboard box from a concealed location and opened it. He took out a carbine and assembled it. He placed the gun on a wooden plank fixed between two strong branches and aimed at his target. The non-flowering tree was carefully chosen so that it was not inhabited by birds. This place was ideal for him. He had a clear view of his target, yet was invisible to anyone looking towards the tree. Finally he took off his spectacles and put on a pair of dark anti-glare glasses. Now, he looked like a trained assassin. Through the lens on the head of carbine he could see clearly the forehead of the Prime Minister.

"It was not easy for me, my friends, to take this decision. The politics of looting in the first four years and doling out lollipops in the last year has to stop. The system has to be designed to be performance driven. This change will, for sure, spur the elected representatives to start working from day one,' he said.

The killer pulled the trigger. His work was not very hard, as the PM was not reading out from notes on the desk, his speech was extempore. His head did not move up and down. The sound from the gun drowned in the cacophony of the crowd.

The bullet seemed to have hit right on mark. The killer saw him fall and immediately started to pack his stuff. He left his ammunition where it was. He converted his looks back to that of the untidy schoolboy and slowly climbed down to a lower branch.

By now the crowd had realized that something dreadful had happened. Amongst the pandemonium of children shouting and running helter-skelter and with his looks changed back to the untidy school boy, he easily managed to get mix into the crowd.

'Where are you Mr Mistry? What, still with the Russians? The task here has been accomplished. It's in our best interest that you all take off immediately,' Avinash Singh, Officer on Special Duty, National Investigation Agency, spoke loudly over his mobile to be audible amidst the noise at the parade ground, as he rushed to the parking lot. He was dressed in a white uniform with a chauffer's cap. Mr Mistry was an MP from the left wing of the opposition. Avinash wanted to make sure this job was perfectly executed. No footprints, no evidences! He was happy that things had moved as per plan so far. Had it not been for Mr Mistry and his strong alliance with the Russians, it would have been impossible to carry out the operation at hand.

He rushed to the parking spot where Mr Mistry had advised him to park the car.

Dr Sabbarwal watched his dream being shattered. A tear trickled down his cheek. He knew death was inching in on him. He could not die in peace now. He picked up his mobile. He was worried about the safety of his four disciples. Varun, Salman, Raghav and Aditya, the four pillars to the shimmering edifice of Indian glory. And now one pillar had been brutally razed to the ground. If fate had it, he would have faced the bullet today. How he wished he could have done so!

The killer walked away with an expression of tremendous satisfaction. He had never imagined the first step of the operation would be this easy. He had put an end to a saga of glory that this traditionally chaotic country was moving towards. His masters would be very pleased indeed! He wondered what interest the Russians could possibly have had in eliminating one of the most powerful persons in the system. He quickly discarded these thoughts. He had a lot more to accomplish within the next few hours…

Jagat and Sumit looked at each other in shock and despair. They could not believe their eyes. The damage they had just witnessed was an irreversible one. Had the four patriots finally been defeated? Was this the end of their story and that of India's rise to glory as well?

BOOK 1

Aditya and Elena
Kanpur, 2006

It was the convocation day at IIT Kanpur. Those who had passed had assembled in the auditorium with their parents. The chief guest, Dr Manmohan Singh, Prime Minister of India would soon be arriving. Aditya looked at his father who was enthusiastically talking to his mother and sister about how they would plan a grand marriage for their son, whom they considered to be the most eligible bachelor in the city. It would be the next important milestone in his life after the convocation. Often when Aditya would visit home on weekends, his father would tell him about the rishtas pouring in from far and wide.

His mother was wearing a pastel green and purple kanjivaram silk saree with at least a kilogram of gold on her neck and her hair drenched in chameli oil were tied in a tight bun, holding every strand in discipline. His thoughts shifted to Elena, who was sitting with her parents just two rows ahead, soberly waiting in anticipation. He couldn't help but notice the stark contrast between their mothers. Elena's mother wore a smart summer suit with a Rolex watch and a Burberry purse. Her coiffured auburn hair gracefully relished the freedom conferred upon them.

There had never been an inter-caste marriage in Aditya's family—a conservative one. But this would not be strictly inter-caste, it would be an inter-country marriage. A good step towards world peace and harmony, and manageable, he convinced himself.

They had been taught that an engineer can solve any problem by approaching it in a logical way, listing the various ways to solve it, and then choosing the best alternative. He had done the same and concluded that he would not risk introducing the newly formed 'two-member alliance for world-peace' to both the families at one go. Later this evening, they would first talk to Elena's parents and after a few days, to his family.

Aditya vividly remembered his first encounter with Elena. It was his first week at the Institute. They were made to wake up at 5 am every morning and an instructor would lead them to a ground opposite the Student Activity Centre (SAC) for jogging and exercise.

The boys had already scanned each face appearing from the girl's hostel by this time of the 'physical training' week. They met during classes and at the SAC for Fresher's Day preparations. Thirty-nine girls in a batch of 680 was a dismal ratio. Most of them looked studious and the glamour quotient was zero. There were just three decent-looking girls and all the boys kept trying to cross their paths.

A marathon was organized on the last day of the physical training week. It spanned several rounds of the Institute around the air-strip, the wind tunnel and the adjoining Nankari village. At school, Aditya had tried hard, but could never win a medal. He had practiced mostly for the 1,600 metres event during those days and hence, developed a good stamina. It was the last lap and most of the runners had dropped out. Around forty were still there, most of them ahead of him.

'Holy smokes!' he muttered to himself, blinking his eyes in disbelief, as he overtook a girl. It was a new face. He slowed down. Her attire indicated her foreign origin. She looked like Drew Barrymore, her pinkish-white complexion glowing in the morning light. She nodded her head and smiled at him slightly, not intending to give away a single ounce of valuable energy at this juncture. Aditya smiled back and offered her a scented wet tissue from his pocket. Aditya was fair, athletic, simple, unassuming and usually smartly dressed. Round-neck T-shirts and denims were his favourite. His curly hair had earned him the title 'Copper Turnings'—a nickname lovingly endowed upon him by his wing mates. This happened after they saw the lathe machine in the science lab digging out curly shavings of copper. His heart-warming smile was probably his greatest asset and, like always, it worked here too. They jogged together to finish at 4th and 5th places, respectively.

Elena was from Austria and had enrolled for aeronautical engineering course under the foreign-national student's quota. Since Aditya's branch was chemical engineering they didn't meet that often. But they became close friends during the second year, when they teamed up for the inter-hostel contest 'Galaxy'. Aditya was the cultural secretary of his hostel, a good singer and a rhythm guitarist as well. Elena was the Hostel Secretary for the girls' hostel and participated in dramatics and debate. Their troop won the contest and beginning then, they spent most of their time together—in the canteen, library and the common lectures. She meant everything to him. He would often think that she would adjust well with his folks as she had a close-knit family like theirs. Aditya finally proposed to her during the fifth semester and she took almost another semester to accept it.

After the convocation, Aditya made an excuse to his parents saying that his project guide, Professor Manogaran, had invited him for dinner.

Aditya joined Elena's family for dinner and they made small talk about the weather, the Institute, and the economy of Europe. Aditya gathered his courage, turned to her father, and said, 'Sir, I am sure Elena must have told you about us. We would like to get married with your permission.' A moment of awkward silence followed. Her father looked at her mother, as Elena and Aditya exchanged glances.

'Sorry son. No!' said her father sternly, then trying to change the topic, he said, 'I heard you play the guitar. Must be quite a stress buster?'

'Yes, Sir, I do. But I am more interested in learning about your concerns regarding our marriage... It is extremely important for us!' said Aditya.

'I would rather not discuss this any further,' he said as he got up to leave.

Aditya looked at Elena, who seemed equally anxious, but did not dare to speak against her father. Aditya weighed his options of pressing this further now vis-à-vis coming back the next morning to discuss this again. They had a flight in the afternoon. He couldn't afford to lose any time.

'I love your daughter and she loves me too. Please tell me why do you disapprove of our marriage,' Aditya insisted.

'There is only one way this can happen...if you come to live with us in Vienna,' the man said.

Aditya took a deep breath, gathered his thoughts and spoke after a few seconds, 'I surely would, Sir, but I am the only son of my parents. My father has toiled day and night to build his little empire. He would need me here. I know you love your daughter and would like to see her more often. I can promise that we will be there whenever you want to see us.'

'You are getting me wrong son! If missing her was the only problem, I would not have sent her here for four years,' said her father.

'This morning Elena took us to a tea stall and I saw a small child washing utensils there. She told me there is no social security system here. Besides, the crime rate is quite high. The newspapers are full of such instances. I am worried about her security,' he added.

'It's not so bad, Sir. Nothing like that will happen, I guarantee. My family has been here since ages...'

Elena's father ignored Aditya and said, 'No, I can't close my eyes on this. The environment at the Institute may be safe and protected, but outside it's very different. We went to the banks of the river Ganga, your so-called holy river. It was almost dry. Heaps of garbage and plastic were everywhere and the water smelled like sewage. Few years from now, your people will be killing each other for water, food and other things. It's going to be really bad. There is no future here. I can see this... Besides, the mindset of the people is twisted. We are not used to all this. How can I leave my daughter in this jungle?'

'It's only a cultural difference, Sir. We are a developing country. Things are changing very fast. I will take good care of Elena,' said Aditya. Now, he wished Elena was not so submissive to her parents.

'No!' he replied calmly but went on saying dismal things about India, including the laxity of the administration and pollution. Aditya looked towards Elena for support but her gaze was fixed at the ground and her mother nodded from time to time in agreement with her father.

'You would not let us marry because this country is misgoverned? Seriously?' said Aditya.

'Unfortunately, yes,' replied Elena's father.

Varun and Alisha

Los Angeles, 2010

'"Let them know how you felt" was a funny name for a grocery store,' thought Varun as he stepped out of his Audi—sports version. He was dressed in a smart black suit. He was five feet eight inches tall, fair and lean. His soft black hair had a full bounce, making him look a bit taller than he actually was. A short Chinese man behind the counter smiled and handed him an envelope. Varun scanned the paper inside carefully, pushed it back into the envelope and handed it to the shopkeeper with a bunch of 100-dollar bills. The shopkeeper sealed the envelope and placed it in a wooden box, locked and placed it back amongst scores of similar wooden boxes stacked neatly on the shelves behind the counter.

'*Jhakaas!*' the Anil Kapoor inside him exclaimed. He was a hard-core fan of the actor, having watched all his movies from 'Mashaal' to 'Slumdog Millionaire'.

He drove to his office, pushed up the knot of his tie, and mumbled the *Hanuman Chalisa* as he ascended the stairs of Pinktouch Softwares, located in uptown New York City. Today was his appraisal interview and his boss Mark—a bald, nasty man in his sixties, was a twisted fellow who didn't particularly approve of his quick wit.

'There aren't many takers outside this company for average performers. I would advise you to stop pushing your resume around and focus on your starving performance here,' said Mark, barely allowing Varun to settle down.

'Shit! How did he know?' thought Varun, feeling almost punched on the nose. Without allowing the slightest change of expression, he said confidently, 'I have to keep checking what the market is offering to good developers and managers, Sir. As a Senior Team Leader at Pinktouch, I need to keep abreast, so that I may expand my team neither throwing peanuts, which will get us monkeys, nor meatloaves fetching us overambitious hounds.'

'Even if I were to believe you Varun, I understand your sales figures are 20 per cent lower this year. How far do you think we can go like this?' said Mark.

'Sir, Pinktouch's total revenues are down 32 per cent and the industry average is 45 per cent, the recession is all around. You know the product designed by my team is one of our bestsellers… We could have done better, but I did not get the required support. All my requests for the ad campaigns, dealer schemes and incentives were turned down on the grounds of recession. Pinktouch has internal accruals to support itself for at least eight years, though it's only five years since our inception. Recession is the time when we can become stronger than competition but we have to be aggressive. But the management must have taken a better decision and I am looking forward to better results in the coming financial year from my team.' He wanted to say a lot of things, but decided to surrender.

'Varun, we have a complaint from your wife…err… ex-wife alleging that you physically assaulted her. You know our company has a zero tolerance to violence against women,' said Hillary, the HR manager, a pleasant faced yet stern lady in her late fifties.

'I have read the company's code of conduct Ma'am. It deals with the workplace, not the employees' homes. There are issues in one's personal life that deserve some privacy,' Varun retorted as his thoughts drifted to his home.

◆

Varun's father was a retired professor and was now working as a Dean at a private engineering college in Indore. He remembered his evening walks with Papa and mummy. His father used to carry a small baton to ward off stray dogs. They would talk about everything, from what happened at Varun's school to campus gossip about the cold war between North Indian and South Indian professors. It was a close-knit family.

With all the security and love at home, Varun grew up to be a cheerful, exuberant and charming man with strong family values. When it was time for him to get married, a number of proposals were turned down by his family. The wish-list for the bride-to-be was a long one. After all, a good looking, virtuous Brahmin boy from the highest gotra, graduated from the best engineering institute of the country, was not something any sundry girl deserved. She had to be beautiful, fair, educated, homely, vegetarian (strictly), a culinary wizard, an early riser, obedient, willing-to-stay at home type… and the list was endless. Every once in a while, he would be fascinated by the good looks of a prospective girl, but callously turned the proposal down on the slightest shortfall.

On one occasion, when Varun came home, his parents went out for their usual evening walk without informing him as he was asleep. He woke up to the sound of the doorbell ringing for the third time. He made his way to the door with eyes half closed still battling the jet lag. The girl at the door gave him a cursory smile and started saying something but he could not register anything. His gaze was fixed on those perfectly crafted lips. She wore a maroon muslin saree and her black hair were loosely tied with a broad hairclip. She was fairly tall—about five feet seven inches, with a perfectly balanced figure. Her expression was as innocent as a child's. She handed him a pamphlet and started to walk away. There was something magical about her. Varun was mesmerised by her charms. He regretted not having asked her name or having talked to her. He regretted being in just a vest and jockeys even more. He read the pamphlet which suggested it was from an NGO that aimed at educating daily-wage workers in the locality.

He returned to his room but could not sleep. He kept thinking about how he could meet her again. The next day, he went to meet his best friend, Madhav Singhal. They had been schoolmates. He narrated the incident to him and they decided to became members of the NGO. They started participating in its events. They gained tremendous satisfaction interacting with the workers and educating them. However, for Varun, the real motivation was Alisha, the chance to see her, to talk to her someday.

'You hardly talk to her, except for the perfunctory greetings you people exchange. I have never seen you like this... Just go and talk to her,' said Madhav.

'I will. For now just being in her proximity is enough,' said Varun, running his fingers through his soft hair.

'Stop acting like a Majnu! It is sad to see my engineer friend, the epitome of rationality, fall into this one-sided blind love that knows no logic. What are you thinking?'

'I hope she doesn't already have a boyfriend…' was all Varun managed to say, dreamily. He used to compare Alisha's smile with the cine divas, with the most fascinating faces he had seen, but found hers the cutest.

Gradually, his friends at the NGO came to know that he had a crush on Alisha. Alisha too, if she had not already realized this from the unusually frequent stares he gave her, got to know about it. He used to hear Alisha and her friends giggle as he passed by and would ask Madhav, 'Do you think they are laughing at me?'

It had almost been a fortnight since he had joined the NGO. He had already extended his leave by a week and would have to fly back soon.

'I would never have thought twice if she was a tentative match. I would have asked her scores of questions, from her aim in life, to her views about live-in relationships. And here I am! Not even having talked to her properly. Am I in love or is this just infatuation?' Varun asked Madhav as they walked the long cobble-stoned path.

'That's what I am trying to tell you my Gadadhaari Bheem from LA! Don't feel so powerless. Just go and talk to her,' said Madhav.

It was to be Varun's last day at the NGO, so he resolved to talk to Alisha. He tried to rehearse his lines, but wasn't satisfied.

During the break, she was standing with her group, her usual happy self. As Varun walked up to them, he heard the giggling stop.

'Can I talk to you for a moment, Alisha?'

'Yes, sure! Please tell me Varun,' she said politely.

'It's something private. If you don't mind, can I have a

minute alone?' he said.

He heard suppressed giggles. It made him slightly nervous, but he was determined to speak his mind before leaving.

'Okay,' Alisha said and they took a side trail that led to a giant banyan tree.

'You know, I have always loved you.' Varun regretted his words as soon as they came out.

'"Always?"—You have hardly known her for a fortnight! "Loved you?"—Aren't you being too abrupt? True, you feel like you have loved her for ages…you infatuated, abnormal, lovelorn majnu. But how is a decent girl supposed to react if you tell her you love her, the first time you properly speak to her? You have messed it up, you idiot!' Varun thought.

'I am sorry. I mean it was like love at first sight for me. You know I joined the NGO for you.' She was listening with a glazed expression. He eagerly waited for a reaction from her, but there was none. He was, however, determined to vent his heart out today.

'I wish I could spend more time here, with you. Just getting to see you every day makes me happy, not to mention the immense additional pleasure I get from teaching these people.' He waited for a smile, a kind acknowledgement or an understanding nod of the head, but nothing seemed forthcoming. It seemed she was not taking this well and maybe had not expected this abrupt conversation. An awkward silence followed.

Finally, he spoke again. 'I am sorry if I have bothered you in any way during all these days. But I had to tell you this today, since I shall be leaving for the USA and I don't want to regret later in life, that I couldn't even tell the girl I loved, how I felt for her. So the next time we cross paths, we can at least smile at each other and say "hello".'

She was smiling now. He was relaxed that at least she was not mad at him for being such a freak. He figured out the faint smile was just meant to keep him from feeling hurt. She was being nice to the tortured soul that was bidding farewell. Probably she was feeling relaxed that there would be no more creepy staring from him.

He extended his hand to mark the departing goodbye. The touch of her soft palm sent electric waves through his body. It was divine. One-sided-love has a strange worship-like feel attached to it. He would never regret having this parting conversation. He looked at her in the eye, smiled and said 'bye'.

He turned back and started walking towards his home, happy and lost in the sensation.

'Stop, Mr Varun!'

So this was not going to be that simple. How could he have assumed that he would deliver his ego-massaging monologue and walk away? This was going to get awkward. His self-designed happy ending was not going to work.

'We approached you looking for financial support for our NGO, but you…'

'Have you been able to impress a girl half as beautiful as her, even with all your charms put together?' Varun scolded himself. 'How could you assume that she would not have a boyfriend already? A beautiful girl like her cannot be single!' he thought.

'Oh! Sorry. I know I have behaved like a stalker. I never realized you were being tolerant towards my behaviour just because I was a possible patron for the NGO. You people are doing a wonderful job. I will send a cheque through Madhav,' he said.

She was laughing hysterically now.

'What happened?' he asked, thinking almost simultaneously

'I have made such a fool of myself, what am I blabbering?'

She raised her hand and put her soft palm on his lips, literally shutting him up. Her touch was heavenly.

'My God! I never thought you could talk that much! At least let me complete...' she said.

'Oh! Sorry. Yes, please.'

'I was saying that we approached you expecting a small donation, but you went to the extent of giving your personal time, which very few people would do, and I was impressed. Slowly, however, I also came to know there was this something else that made you come to the NGO every day. I was under the impression that you were too shy to speak. I didn't know you could speak this much. At least you should have tried... asked me what I feet...proposed to me...'

'What? Is this really true? She has feelings for me? *Jhakaas*!' This was one of the happiest moments in Varun's life. In his mind, Anil Kapoor had even started shaking his leg to his signature *dhina-dhin-dha* dance move. A new wave of confidence swept over him. His exuberance and cheerfulness that seemed to have deserted him over the last week, were back.

'How could I have been such a fool? I am the campus's most eligible bachelor after all, "the Varun Pandey",' he thought.

He walked towards Alisha, looking at her in the eyes, a smile on his face.

'Friends?' he held out his hand towards her.

'Yes, Mr Give-up from the USA!' she laughed at him extending hers.

His hand engulfed hers fully, not leaving an inch of her tender fingers and palm out of contact. There was something magical about it and now, sensuous too, even in a simple shake of hand.

He kept looking into her beautiful hazel eyes for a few seconds, as if lost in deep thought and then asked, 'Are you a vegetarian?'

◆

Varun was jolted back to reality by the sharp voice of the HR Manager, 'But what if it affects the company's goodwill, don't you think some of our stakeholders may have read about it?'

'Oh God! Am I still in front of the appraisal panel?' He cursed them for bringing him back from the sweet reverie of his courtship days with Alisha and questioning him about the dispute with his wife that had led to police intervention.

Raman Singh, Varun's immediate boss and Senior Marketing Manager at Pinktouch, said, 'Hillary, I know all about this and it was not Varun's fault, this could happen to anyone. It has been only two months since his marriage and he is having a hard time. He is in no way an under performer! I think we need to support him. Think of our clients like Bigboy Securities, Henry and Morgan Associates, Bluebell Finance… They had all been on our wish-list until Varun bagged their contracts with his relationship-building skills.' He looked at Mark and Hillary to see if they had softened.

Varun knew it was time to strike the emotional cord. 'There have been only three passions in my life—my work, my family and my country. I have tried to do justice to all three… Trust me and I will prove to be the company's most valuable asset. Please don't take it as my request or connivance to get a good appraisal. I am confident of my abilities and I respect my employers as we consider them to be "annadatas", according to the Indian culture.'

'Providers of livelihood,' explained Raman to the others.

'Should I understand that as a refined furtherance of your loan request pending with the company? From what I understand, we gave you good stock options and incentives before the current recession,' said Mark, apparently unmoved by Varun's attempt to touch his feelings.

'Shit! No effect at all! It's time to make my final move,' Varun thought.

'Mark, I know about the other property you have in Kentucky, I have heard you need a baby sitter there. I have a friend there, whose sister needs odd jobs. Please let me know!' said Varun, and watched Mark turn pale and rejoiced within.

'Lastly, I wish to inform you gentlemen that I have managed to sustain my losses with help from my family and I won't need the loan anymore. Rest assured, my company as well as the bosses can trust my maturity in safeguarding their best interests,' Varun said and ran his fingers through his hair, as he watched the stunned expression on Mark's face, enjoying the pin-drop silence.

Hillary wanted to react to this comment, normally a taboo in such 'meant to screw H-1Bs' settings, however, watching Mark's crestfallen face, unable to understand what had hit him, she chose to keep silent. 'Of course, one is over-sensitive when it comes to grandchildren. This guy must have touched Mark somewhere deep down with his benign offer,' she thought.

Varun felt like a golf player, standing in profile, holding his club up in the air after striking the blow, watching the airborne ball proudly as it approached the target.

Raman looked at Varun with an expression that said, 'What did you just do?' He was sure that Varun's statement could not be what it sounded like—an offer to help. He must have thrown back some offence. He would now be suspended, demoted, sacked for his atrocity. True, Mark and Hillary had got personal during the interview, which they should not have, but that didn't mean an H1-B work-visa holder could retaliate in such a way. This time he had taken it a bit too far.

While Mark and Hillary were busy frantically discussing what punishment was to be rendered to the arrogant pawn, Raman intently tried to overhear their hushed conversation. It was evident that there was a difference of opinion amongst them, as Hillary was unable to reconcile with Mark's judgement. Raman was sure he would not see Varun in the office now. It seemed like an eternity before Mark finally spoke.

'Mr Varun, notwithstanding the merciless grilling we have to subject our managers to, a necessary part of appraisal process ('Liar, this is not my first interview' thought Varun), both of us...I mean all three of us ('Hypocrites, they had hardly consulted Raman during the discussions.') agree that you are an asset to Pinktouch. We award you a 25 per cent increase in remuneration and stock options worth $200,000.'

'Homework, homework and homework! My three keys to success,' rejoiced Varun.

Raman and Varun were walking towards the canteen. 'What the fish? Varun 'Panga' Pandey, what was this baby sitter thing with Mark? Why mention his grandchildren at an appraisal meeting?'

'Children, not grandchildren! He has a mistress and a parallel family in Kentucky,' said Varun.

'Oh! I did not go that far. But how the hell did you come to know about it?' asked Raman.

Varun laughed and put an arm around Raman's shoulder, 'Look, I know it may sound weird, but I had an inkling that Mark would unnecessarily screw my appraisal. You know he doesn't like me much as I have been opposing his conservative strategy against recession for several months. He is an egotistic bastard, isn't he?'

'Yes, he is... So?' retorted Raman.

'So, I hired a detective who had been working on finding his Achilles' heel for the past two months, but couldn't discover anything. But two days back, he spotted mark entering a Grocery-store cum Confession-Archive owned by a Chinese man. Strange are the ways of these civilizations! What they don't have the courage to tell their loved ones while they are alive, they pay agencies to do it after their death. All the agency has to do is make sure that the emotionally-wrought confession in the sealed envelope handed over to them by their client, reaches the nominee at the right time. This morning, I dropped by and read the note. Fortunately, for me, the Chinese turned out to be a compulsive gambler in desperate need of money to pay his installments. My detective had everything fixed. Mark had written a message for his family owning up the mess he had created. "Let them know how you felt" is the name of the shop.'

'You are really "param" Varun,' exclaimed Raman in sheer awe. 'Who hires a detective to spy on his boss?'

'I am only your shagird! Tell me, was it not a worthy investment? A few thousand dollars versus 25 per cent raise and stock options?' he chucked.

'Hmmm...' Raman shook his head.

'Did you talk to your cousin to get my appointment fixed with the Minister?' said Varun, adding, 'I have also talked to the Supreme Court judge. Let this job be done and I will be so relieved. I have to go to India and tie some loose ends.'

'Don't you feel scared Varun?' asked Raman.

He was really concerned for Varun. His appetite for risk was scary.

◆

'Yes, I feel scared, but not from these heights. I feel scared that I may also become a permanent NRI, like so many of our batch mates. I had thought that I would make a handsome saving in five years and return to do business in India,' said Varun, who had arrived at Indore the previous day and was sitting with Madhav at the Institute library, at a secluded corner table on the 3rd floor. The students normally swarmed the lower floors that had more course-related books. After finishing three pints of beer each, Varun and Madhav would come to the library, pick up the latest arrivals from the journals or encyclopedia section and head straight for their corner of tranquillity. Both of them had their heads down, snugly resting between the smooth white pages of the thick newly-printed books spread-eagled beneath their cheeks. They loved the smooth feel of the high quality paper rubbing against their cheeks and the smell of ink emanating from the fresh print.

'I really wonder what is there in that country that even patriots like you can't let go. At least I was sure about you, that you would return!' said Madhav.

'It's so difficult to survive here and it is so much easier there,' he answered.

'Hmm... I see, twenty-two years you thrived here, and just three years there changed things so much!' exclaimed Madhav.'

'No, seriously. The cost of living is much cheaper there as compared to India. For what you can get a row house there, you would barely get a studio flat here. Car, TV, mobile phone, food, everything is so much more affordable in the USA,' he explained.

'Oh shit! And we all live with the belief that developed

countries like the USA must be deadly expensive,' said Madhav.

'Not really! Everything is cheaper there, comparatively. What is expensive is only what really should be expensive... time. Doctors, lawyers, barbers and other service providers are very expensive there. Don't know what has infested our country, the cost of the things necessary for survival is increasing,' he said.

'We deserve much better than this, yaar! Look at the roads. They are always dug up, it's so dusty,' he added.

'Yeah, whichever department has some job to do, digs it up and forgets about it. The common man suffers. Our health, our life, has no value,' Madhav said. 'With each passing year, the belief that this country cannot be helped is growing deeper and deeper.'

'When they can do any kind of underground line or road repairs overnight there, without leaving a sign, what stops our government from adopting the same procedures here?' Varun said, thoughtfully.

'I think we are equally to be blamed,' said Madhav. 'We have become so tolerant that we accept whatever is thrust upon us silently and carry on with our lives. I was in Delhi a few days back. There was a strike of municipal sweepers and the whole city was literally sitting on garbage and plastic waste. Not a single protest rally or mass agitation was reported. People are happy as long as their houses are clean. Can you even imagine something like that happening in the USA? They would screw the people in power left, right and centre, isn't it?'

'And then we talk about quality of life being low in our country,' said Varun. 'But what right do I have to crib about all this? I am living there comfortably.'

'Our people and our country do not deserve what we are being put through. Sometimes I feel guilty not to be doing anything about it,' he said wistfully.

'I know you will do it…something for the country…but what about your personal life? Where did it go wrong? After meeting Alisha during your trip to India, early last year, I was surprised when you came back the very next month for marriage. Of course, I knew you both were madly in love, but I was not expecting Uncle to agree for the inter-caste marriage so soon. Everything seemed picture perfect…an arranged marriage, banna-banni songs, the yellow-orange-white-red floral theme, meticulously performed rituals, and of course the grand dinner. Both the families were so happy, though I remember there were hardly any relatives from Alisha's side, mostly just friends,' said Madhav.

'It was the worst phase of my life. Don't remind me about it,' said Varun.

'No worries. Maybe later,' said Madhav, trying to comfort him.

'No, I will tell you,' said Varun.

◆

Immediately after marriage we left for the USA. We went to the Bahamas for honeymoon. It was like I was living my dream with an angel—chirpy, lively and bubbling with love. The only thing that disturbed me a little was her inclination to stay connected to her friends. She would sit for unusually long hours on the net, doing God knows what! She had Yahoo chat and Orkut accounts, with a formidable friend count. We reached back home and I re-joined office. After about a month, things started turning around.

'Varoo darling, what do you think of this?' she asked, pushing a newspaper classified page towards me, on the breakfast table. It had an advertisement for the post of a counsellor, circled with a red sketch pen.

'But...we had agreed on certain things. I would not like my wife to go out and do a job. I can earn enough.'

'The house really closes in on me when you are not here Varoo,' she said, putting her hand over mine. I withdrew my hand, indignant. Promises are meant to be honoured. I had made my list of requisites clear to her well in time.

As the momentary surge of anger subsided, I realized I could be hurting my angel. 'I understand Alisha,' I said and put my hand back on hers, to comfort her. 'You could do a lot of constructive things from home, to keep you busy.'

'Like?' she raised her eyebrows and looked at me.

'Like decorating the house for instance, it's still bare... or do a correspondence course on any subject of your choice. Write a book, maybe...'

'You don't understand...' she interrupted me, impatiently. 'I said, I need to go out, I can't stay within these four walls the whole day.'

'But I told you very clearly that I wanted a home-maker, not a working wife.'

'I know, and I thought I would manage. But it's killing me. What's the big issue with letting me work?'

'I don't believe this...' I said, and got up and walked out. How could I let her go out all alone, that too in a land of strangers? It was not only about family values, I think I was too possessive. Somewhere deep inside, her pro-activeness in the virtual world made me feel all the more insecure. Sometimes I would see her chat with old friends. As long as they were girls, I had no issues. But I didn't like her interacting with men. I don't know if she would have found it acceptable if I chatted with girls too. I would often tease her, sourly, that if I found time, I too would make a lot of female friends on her godforsaken Yahoo chat messenger.

Our lives became a roller-coaster ride with periods of harmony and discord. She always had some new demands, most of which I thought were devised to poke at my peace. Since I had refused her the freedom she wanted, she would vent out her frustration in different ways. She asked me to set up a boutique of designer clothes for her, which probably would have cost me all my savings and also necessitated some borrowings. On another occasion, she wanted me to buy a lavish row house with an exquisite garden in the front and a wooden deck in the backyard with barbeque, recliners and a high-end Bose sound system. The installments would have cost me half my salary for the next ten years.

I still loved her. Somewhere she was successful in making me feel guilty of confining her to the house and continuously declining her needs. Now she would continue to chat even after I reached home from office. She would immediately switch windows on the screen when I entered the room, but I could make out two names on her screen on several occasions—'coolstud_farzan' and 'machoman_foryou'. It made me suspicious and angry.

'You will not allow me to go out to work, nor help me set up anything to work from home, or let me participate in decisions about where to invest…and now you want me to stop interacting with my friends. I will go mad Varun,' she would snap back at me.

If as a child I would have seen this situation in a movie, I would have scorned the hero for putting up with such non-sense. It's funny how things that seem so simple during childhood, become complicated as we grow older. Or maybe one has to be in a situation to understand it completely. How one becomes a 'fool in love'! How a man's worst fear is to imagine another man touching his woman. This is probably the one fear that brings him back to the woman he loves even when she acts like a vamp. How he wishes he lives just long enough for his woman to gather some wrinkles on her face and not be attractive enough to find another man after his death.

I found her chatting quite counter-productive and wondered why she couldn't do anything constructive to keep herself busy. One day, when I returned from office, I found her chatting with 'machoman_foryou' and in a fit of rage I broke her CPU and monitor with my dumbbells. That's when she called the police. I was arrested and could be bailed out only after three days. I returned home to find a letter from her.

Varun,
We spent some really good time together. I never thought it would end this way.

I had shared with you how violence affected my childhood. After that, violence was the last thing I had expected from you.

We were not meant to be, and it's sad. I am leaving for India. I will not go back home. If you can do me a favour, please don't try to contact me or look for me. I have put all the papers you would require for a divorce in your drawer. I can be reached on my email id in case the authorities require to contact me for ensuring my consent.
Alisha

◆

'What? How could she just erase you from her life? Anybody

would react the way you did if their wives kept talking to strangers. I am sure it must have been very difficult for you, with the kind of emotional attachment you had... putting back all your pieces together and moving on in life,' said Madhav.

'Pretty much!' said Varun.

'Did you really not try to contact her after coming out?' he asked.

'I did, the only way I had was to try and find her on the same Orkut and Yahoo chat that were responsible for our separation. But she had closed all her accounts. There was no way I could find her. Slowly I reconciled myself to the fact that she had probably used my outburst as a cover up for something she had been wanting to do for quite some time...walk out of my life!'

'Do you still miss her sometimes?' asked Madhav.

'I don't know. But what I do know is that I will never fall in love again.'

Salman and Mahi

Mumbai, 2010

Salman was smartly dressed in a white shirt, blue denims and a dark grey waist-coat, with golden-rimmed Ray-ban glasses and his hair neatly combed backwards and gelled to a bright sheen. He wore a slight stubble. His well-chiselled features and muscular physique easily won him the title of the most handsome man amongst the girls in the locality. He stepped out from his black Eco Sport and walked towards the chawl.

He greeted a group of young boys hanging out near a paan shop and asked one of them, 'Did you meet Tarun Grover? I had spoken to him about your placement in his company.'

'He has called me tomorrow, Salman Bhaiya,' he replied cheerfully.

'Amit, how is Papa now?' He asked another one.

'The doctor says his tuberculosis is not going away. We have exhausted his entire retirement benefits as well as our savings. I don't know how we will manage now,' said Amit, with a grave expression.

'But, why? Uncle's name must be registered in the Employee State Insurance Scheme. He should get all medical expenses as well as a monthly allowance from there. After all, why do we deposit money to ESI all our lives?'

'I went there Bhaiya, but the Babu told me to bring ₹10,000 to start the treatment. From where would I get such a big amount all of a sudden?'

'Okay, let me come with you tomorrow. Meet me at the ESI hospital gate at 9 am,' said Salman...

Salman turned to the group of boys and said, 'Continue having fun guys! This is the age when you can hang out with friends, chill and enjoy life. But don't forget your responsibilities. You people have to change things around here.'

The boys in the group enthusiastically wished him 'Good night', as Salman waved at them and took the stairs to the first floor of the chawl. Although he could afford a penthouse with his hefty salary, he was emotionally attached to this place where he had spent his childhood.

'Looking so happy Maa!' Salman hugged his mother as soon as she opened the door. 'Babu ji, didn't I tell you the call would come today? See, it came, didn't it!' Salman was delighted to see the happiness on the faces of the elderly couple.

The old lady went in and brought a tiffin carrier filled with some mathris she had made. She got emotional and said, 'I had made these for Parag, he is so fond of them. He kept telling me to keep some ready-to-eat snacks in the cupboard, for his late night studies.' A tear flowed down her cheek.

'See, I used to tell you all the time, he is your only son, you should not have sent him away. But you always kept saying that his happiness is your happiness and you wanted to see him spread his wings and fly.'

'But we did not know that he would fly away to never come back,' the old lady wept.

'Now he has got married too, still he says let me enjoy life for two or three more years. Doesn't he miss us?' Babu ji said, his voice cracking.

Salman put his arm around the old lady's shoulder and said, 'He is an ass. Forgot his parents' love! He will feel your need soon. It is not only parents who need their children to take care of them when they grow old, the children also need them equally, for love, guidance and a sense of security. Who would know this better than me?'

He was lying in the old lady's lap now and she was running her fingers through his hair.

'After my father died, you have always been like Maa-Babu ji to me. It is with your blessings only that I am the all-India manager of Coffee Moments, today,' he said softly.

Over dinner, he planned a weekend trip to Mahalbaleshwar with his foster parents to cheer them up. As Salman performed Namaz in his well-furnished room before going to bed, he remembered being told how his mother had died while giving birth to him and his father had died of tuberculosis, unable to afford the expensive treatment. He was only eight years old, then.

Next day he drove to the ESI hospital where Amit was waiting for him with his father, who was sitting in a wheelchair and finding it difficult to breathe. Saliva trickled down from one side of his mouth. They rushed him in.

'Who is he?' asked the clerk, looking at Salman who looked better dressed and too well-off to be in the ESI hospital.

'Friend, Sir,' said Amit. 'My father is in a very bad shape... this is our last hope for his treatment. I am about to get a job and I promise to pay your ₹10,000 before anything else, but for now please admit him.'

The clerk was chewing paan like a cow, deeply engrossed in making entries in a register. He raised his head to spit the red juice in a dustbin placed on one side of his table, already mottled red all over. Amit's father folded his hands towards the clerk as he looked at him, while returning to the register. Babu ji lay pitifully in the chair, head hanging to one side and body sagged down.

The clerk swayed his head understandingly and said, 'Okay, bring him after two days, right now we are fully packed.'

'Then refer him to an affiliated private hospital,' Salman said. 'Employee State Insurance Scheme offers the best possible treatment. If it is not available in-house, the patient is to be referred to the nearest private hospital enlisted with you, for cashless treatment, isn't it? Can't you see the patient is critical?'

'No, we have TB treatment in-house, so we cannot refer to private hospitals. You can meet the doctor and he will write the medicines, which you can get issued, but we cannot admit him right now,' said the clerk.

'But there has to be some way…' Amit said desperately.

'I told you the way, but what can I do if you don't understand. How much better the old man would have been if you had got him admitted last week! Are you not spending on his treatment now? You should understand, we don't ask for ourselves, we have to send the account to the higher-ups,' he said.

'That's what we are trying to tell you, the man upstairs is watching everything. A person toils all his life, eats less but deposits a part of his hard-earned money here, so that in such times of illness, he does not have to beg, steal and borrow,' Salman said firmly.

'Is that all? Fine, now come day after tomorrow,' said the clerk, returning to his calligraphy over the shabby dusty register, hopeless at the lack of worldly wisdom in the generation he was confronted with.

'But I have brought Papa here with so much difficulty, I am afraid his condition may deteriorate further if we subject him to further strain by taking him all the way back now. Please don't do this, I will do what you say,' Amit begged.

'We watch the same drama every day. Keep your Papa on my head!' the clerk said, still not looking up, totally indifferent.

'We are talking to you with decency and you are misbehaving with us?' Salman said indignantly.

'Shut up now, creepy young chap. Go, do what you can! Just get lost now,' the clerk said arrogantly in a slightly louder voice, now looking straight at Salman, displeased at his audacity to speak to him in such a non-submissive tone.

A few peons from the office came closer as they heard the discussion heat up.

'*Ise prasaad chahiye*,' Salman said, looking at Amit.

Amit took a step back as he knew what was going to happen. It meant Salman could no longer control his temper. In a flash Salman held the clerk by his hair and banged his head on the table. 'Is this sufficient, or you need more?' he shouted, seething with anger at the inhuman treatment being meted out in the hospital. He had resolved that Amit would not lose his father the way he did.

Two colleagues of the clerk rushed towards Salman, one with an operation knife and the other with a staff. As soon as they came close, he punched one on the nose and kicked the other in the stomach, so that they instantly collapsed to the ground. There was a hue and cry; Salman and Amit were surrounded by the hospital staff and guards armed with lathis and knives. They closed in on them slowly. Salman took out his revolver and held it up in the air. The crowd stopped proceeding any further.

One man in the crowd shouted, 'Call the police!' The crowd was in frenzy but the revolver held them back. Salman also called a number and holding the mobile to his ear, slowly turned 180-degrees watching everyone carefully so that no one would come forward.

'Look, gentlemen, this is not my mistake. An old labourer is on the verge of dying and this bastard is negotiating his life for ten thousand rupees,' Salman spoke with pain and emotion in his voice. He still held the mobile to his ear, seemingly upset at not being able to connect to help. At the same time he kept turning slowly, keeping the crowd at bay. He could not see Amit anywhere. He had probably rushed out to get some help and the boys from the chawl would be here very soon.

'How dare you touch a government employee? Our union will not spare you, there is no way you can escape going to prison now,' the clerk said, the red juice dripping from the sides of his lips, his shirt speckled with red patches, like the dustbin he spat into. 'And if you are really so akin to them, why don't you advise them, this ten thousand does not go in my pocket, it's a requirement of the system. Everybody here knows!' While some in the crowd nodded their heads in agreement with the victimized clerk, some of them hurled nasty abuses and threats at Salman.

Salman now brought the phone down from his ears and pulled out a thick pen from his front pocket. 'This is a video pen. Whatever has happened here...its complete recording is there with my friends outside. If police will come, the press will also come and your entire department will be held to disgrace. I will file a suit against each one of you. Your friend just confessed that you all know about the bribes being taken in this hospital.'

The crowd suddenly lost its aggression and their postures

toned down to sheepish subdued ones. Some of them dropped their weapons and stepped back, trying to avoid the camera by getting lost in the crowd.

Salman continued, 'But I can forget all that, if you treat Babu ji well and send him back as a healthy man.'

Suddenly the room was filled with loud mourning as Amit wept, sitting on the floor, next to his father's wheelchair. 'See! You people killed my father...for just ten thousand rupees!'

The crowd turned to see that the old man had died in his chair.

The next day, the pictures and videos of the ESI incident were all over newspapers and the electronic media. Many of them were suspended owing to charges of corruption and carelessness leading to an old man's death. The Babu was sent to jail, as the matter had been highlighted too much on the media.

A week later, at the 'tribute-paying ceremony', Amit was telling Salman, 'Why are you so silent Bhaiya? It is only due to your courage that Papa's murderer is behind the bars today.'

'No, that doesn't comfort me anymore Amit. I can't get it out of my head...what the ESI Babu was saying again and again. Maybe he is not the real culprit. The real murderers are still out in the open, sitting very high!'

♦

'You're the best thing that has happened to me!' Salman said, tightening his grip around Mahi's waist, kissing her gently below the earlobe on her neck, exposed by her silky brown hair that had fallen to one side. The moistness rendered to her skin by the slight sweating from the heat of their bodies held against each other, made it even more desirable to him. Her delicate frame and pearl-smooth skin contrasted starkly with his stubble and muscular physique. She reciprocated by gently kissing him on the lips, but just couldn't bring herself to separate her lips from his. His stubble scratched her tender skin, but it was a sweet pain she had become addicted to. There was a magnetic attraction between them. Their lips were locked in what seemed to be an unending embrace.

Soon he was bearing her weight over him, their bodies wanting to maximize every inch of contact. She could feel his body as they held each other tighter and tighter. The kissing became more and more passionate...her nails burying into his shoulders...and suddenly Salman pulled back, throwing his head back to the pillow.

'Sorry, sorry...' said Mahi, as she saw blood ooze out from his lower lip, from a love bite. A tear rolled out of her eye in repentance. Salman's tongue arrested the precious pearl halfway down the cheek and they kissed again, this time more gently. The salty taste of her tear mingled with the sour iron-like taste of the blood from his lips, bringing their souls closer.

Mahi rolled over and lay on his side, her head resting on his biceps, her eyes closed, still upset at the pain she had inflicted. Salman, built like a soldier, handled her like a fragile doll, gentle with every move. Despite her delicate framework, she could dominate him in bed.

She turned and lay on her side, with her back to him, staring at the wall, blankly. Salman cuddled her, his hands caressing her, his breath warming her temples. Mahi turned her face back and they kissed. They found themselves, once again, at the vortex of this hurricane of passion that sucked them and churned them into one. They made love passionately. Their first time in this intimate spooning position!

'Why do you want to avoid my family? We have known each other for eight months now and you have not visited my home even once,' Mahi said wistfully.

'What's the point in meeting them, when I can't commit anything? I want you to work towards your dreams, become a successful Company Secretary. Moreover, I don't want you to be emotionally dependant on me.'

Mahi closed her eyes, breathing deeply, trying to cool herself. The long silence took Salman eight months back in time...

♦

Mahi was just nineteen, ten years younger than him. They had met at the Coffee Moments outlet at the City Centre Mall in Mumbai. Mahi was shouting at the man behind the counter, demanding to speak with the Manager. She and her five friends had come all the way from Mulund just to have their favourite 'chocolate mud delight' and it was not available. The Manager tried to calm her down, saying that it was an unusual circumstance and even offered them complimentary coffee.

'Spoiled brats!' Salman thought, as he witnessed the ruckus from his glass cabin behind the counter. 'If only this generation would have the guts to raise their voice for more meaningful causes!' The commotion did not seem to end. He banged shut the customer feedback register he had been trying to study, walked up to the girls and said courteously yet firmly, 'Please have a seat. You will get your chocomuds within fifteen minutes.'

'But who are you? When the manager says he can't arrange it?'

'Shaktiman...kids!' Salman smiled at them and walked out of the outlet, drove to the bakery from where they outsourced the pastries, taking the newly constructed flyover. He was back in fourteen minutes.

And thus, began Mahi's fascination for Salman. She started visiting the outlet daily. Salman stopped at this outlet for a few hours every day as it was his accounting hub. He used to ignore her glances, staring and chuckling with friends, considering it as mere kids' mischief.

One day when he reached home, he found a greeting card in his mail box. He opened it to find a beautiful handmade card wishing him 'Happy Birthday'. It was signed 'Yours, Mahi'. He was inadvertently touched as he himself didn't remember his birthday. He didn't have a family to remind him either.

'Thanks! How did you find out?' Salman asked her, as they sat at a corner table. He was actually sharing 'coffee moments' with someone for the first time in his tenure at Coffee Moments. He had never found the time or a reason to sit on the other side of the counter and taste at ease what he had been selling for years.

'Facebook!' she said raising her shoulders in a 'where-else' posture, tilting her head to one side.

That night Salman visited Facebook after six months and lo and behold! She was there waiting for him. 'Hey!!!' popped up the chat window. They started chatting every night and Mahi confided in him about almost everything. Salman, though a bit of an introvert, also opened up to her affection and shared how he had lost his parents, struggled to make a place for himself and how he felt that his purpose in life was not just to pursue money and success, but to do something for the people.

Mahi, for sure, was infatuated with him, not only for the 'macho' factor, but for the depth in his character and for the really nice person that he was. Salman considered her as his best friend—the only one he could share his feelings with, to some extent. He found her attractive but never thought about taking it further than that. She was too young.

It was a cold December night and Salman's chawl was facing an unusually long power-cut. Salman had just reached home and was having a shower when he heard a knock on the door. Pulling back his wet hair, he quickly wrapped a towel and put on a T-shirt. He was taken aback to see Mahi standing at the door as he opened it. She was wearing a red midi, with a belt around her waist. The dress clung to her body, already wet from the drizzle outside, her scooty hardly providing any cover against it. Tears started rolling down her eyes on seeing Salman.

'What happened?' he asked, making her sit on the sofa as he lit a candle.

'My father! He wants to send me to London for higher studies.'

'You are lucky, and you should be happy,' he said.

'But...' she said, as more tears started rolling down her cheeks. 'How can I stay away from you...you idiot! Don't you know I can't live without you?' she blurted out. She looked sweet and innocent, in the candle light. As Salman bent down to wipe her tears, she kissed him gently. He flinched backwards, but she clung to him and pressed her cheek against his, still moist from tears. The fragrance she wore and the touch of her skin were overpowering...

It was as if destiny wanted them to be together, at least for that night, and so it happened. It was a first for Mahi and for Salman too... being in love...

He was no longer uncomfortable with the so-called generation gap between them. In fact, their bond gave him a pervading sense of confidence and happiness.

◆

'Don't give me that emotional independence crap again,' Mahi shouted, bringing him back from flashback. 'When you love me and I love you, then, how the hell can we not be emotionally dependant? We are not friends with benefits, damn it!'

Salman kept quiet as he knew that logic and arguments would only lead to further quarrelling. She had already abjured the opportunity to study abroad because of him and he did not want her to make any more sacrifices. Salman's silence enraged Mahi further, who quickly got dressed, gathered her belongings and left, hurling curses at a reticent Salman. Their dates would often end like this, as Mahi could no longer live with this clandestine affair.

Salman would sit pensively whenever this happened, trying to reason with himself whether he was doing the right thing. 'I can't put her through any more torture. I have to tide over my insecurities and misgivings. She's all I have!' Salman said to himself. The vacuum that filled his mind every time this happened was making way for love...

'I will do something tomorrow itself, to put things in the right perspective,' he promised to himself as he rushed to attend the public address by one of the MLA candidates in his chawl. Something tickled inside his stomach as he imagined the reaction on Mahi's face when he would give her this surprise.

Raghav vs Teachers' Association
Lucknow, 2010

'There is something remarkable about this man. We must follow his every move. He is the face of the youth in the state, the nephew of Chief Minister Krishan Singh Chandel and cousin of State Home Minister Madhur Singh,' said Jagat Bindra, Chief Reporter on political affairs, addressing his team of reporters at Sahara, Uttar Pradesh.

'People consider his cousin, Madhur, as CM Krishan Singh's successor, but I somehow see in Raghav, all the qualities of a deserving young Chief Minister-to-be. He is modest, noble, determined, and balanced and precise in speech. He has an immaculate track record. Many a times I feel that although he is, by default, with the Krishan Singh–Madhur Singh camp, he is not happy with the congregation of the corrupt in this government,' Bindra added.

'But why doesn't he show his disagreement, then?' asked one of the reporters.

'He has done that a few times. That's why they made him Education Minister and thought they had sidetracked him. Education has been on the bottom rungs of this state's priority list for decades. But, ever since he has taken over this ministry, the picture has changed altogether. The same teachers who used to read newspapers and weave sweaters in schools, arrive half-an-hour early and stay back to check notebooks in fear of suspension. The quality of mid-day meal, teachers' absenteeism, the pitiful situation of studies…all the problems seem to have been tackled in a single sweep,' said Bindra.

'But Jagat Sir, I have studied in a government primary school. I know the teachers, there, won't teach. Corruption has eaten up the entire machinery. How can he set things right with the same machinery? I find it kind of unbelievable,' asked one of the team members.

'He has formed a committee in each city, comprising retired principals, retired military officers and social workers. If this committee inspects and finds any major non-conformity, the whole staff is suspended, including the teachers, assistant teachers and the principal of the school,' Bindra responded.

'But how did all this happen, did the system not pose any problem?' asked another curious reporter, who knew suspending government employees in the country was no cakewalk.

'Of course, it did. The Teachers' Association went on strike the very next month these committees were formed,' said Bindra, smiling.

◆

'The schools should not close down even for a single day! Call them for a meeting. I want to meet their top eight representatives. Fix up a time for tomorrow morning,' Raghav Singh Chandel told his deputy Ramdas.

Raghav was in his mid-thirties. The morning yoga sessions ensured that there was no flab anywhere. He wore a simple white shirt, neatly tucked in, with grey creaseless trousers. He was a good six feet tall, fair, wore a prince moustache and his face radiated a glow of confidence emanating positive vibes one could not miss...

'Sir, it has been tried many times earlier to purge the system, but these people go on strike every time, schools close down and then there is negotiation, mostly one-sided, to call off the new monitoring mechanisms,' replied a hopeless Ramdas.

But Raghav was hardly listening to him. His mind was at work. 'And arrange my telecon with the Assistant Teachers' Association right now! Don't forget to call the press tomorrow.'

◆

There was an air of rejoice in the Teachers' Association office. Javed, President of the Association was cheerfully telling Mr Bajpai, the Secretary, 'Bajpai ji, ultimately, it is our demand which they will have to comply with. Not only do thousands of our members run the government schools machinery in the state, but we also form a formidable vote bank. Inshallah, you will see our strength touching new heights, tomorrow!'

◆

Next morning, at the Conference Hall, Raghav gave a detailed presentation outlining his plans to revamp the education system of the state, explaining why primary education was so important. He said that it was the backbone of education. If the students' fundamentals would be weak, they would not be able to understand difficult concepts in higher classes. He made a sentimental appeal to the association leaders to join hands with him for the advancement of the education system.

'Raghavji, do you think we are fools? First you suspend our people without reason and then you give us this pep-talk about development and all. Development will happen only when you let schools run, isn't it?' asked Javed.

'Please restore our suspended brothers immediately and dissolve the inspection committees with immediate effect. Otherwise, the schools are not going to start,' added Ramakant Bajpai.

'And the rate at which prices are shooting up in your government's regime, we are not even able to make both ends meet. How can we focus on teaching, if we don't even get two proper meals? Our dearness allowance should be increased by at least 15 per cent,' Javed demanded.

Raghav was silent for a while. Javed and Bajpai looked at each other and smiled victoriously. Ramdas put his palm to his forehead, deploring within, the sadistic pleasures that cheap leaders derived from such situations. 'Why did Raghav Sir have to meet them personally, the education secretaries could have done it!' he thought.

Raghav got up from his seat, slowly walked a half-circle round the conference table, in deep thought. He stopped at the other end of the oval table where Javed was sitting. He spoke slowly as if speaking his thoughts aloud, 'If the twenty-four thousand rupees that you get in a month are not able to fetch you two proper meals, I think this job is not fit for you. Maybe you should look for another one. I shall arrange for your termination letter tomorrow. The government provided you assistant teachers so that the desired ratio of 35 students per teacher could be met, but most of your teachers left the teaching to these assistants, to do some other jobs or to simply sit at home!'

'Make up your mind Mantriji, no government has been able to withstand for long against our unity.' Javed got up and signalled the other leaders to end the meeting. 'Let us leave brothers as it seems we were called here just to be humiliated.'

'Fine, do as you wish, but take this last piece of advice from me. We have formed inspection committees as per the judgement of Allahbad High Court in favour of a public interest litigation and there is no way you can get them dissolved. The ministry has also filed a petition in the court under right to education, against government teachers, who go on repeated strikes and jeopardize the students' future. They should not only be removed but all their retirement benefits should go to the treasury, so that new teachers may be appointed. Besides we have talked to the Assistant Teachers' Association and they are not with you in this. After all they will get the opportunity to become teachers only if you leave!' said Raghav.

Javed and Bajpai exchanged glances again, but this time not so gleefully. They also looked at the other members to see if their reactions showed any nervousness.

Raghav continued, 'We have also discussed the matter with your opponent group in the Association led by Misraji and they will not support your strike this time. And lastly, we don't want to collaborate with you for your votes, but yes, if you feel that our philosophy and work will benefit the people of this country, we welcome you to join hands with us and write a new success story in the education department.'

Javed whispered to Bajpai, '*Launda unchee cheez hai*! Maybe we made a mistake in gauging this young boy, what do you say?' They discussed for two minutes before Javed said, 'We are with you Minister Sahab. It would be a pleasure to be part of the team led by a capable person like you. And we will take your mission to such great heights that Misra Group doesn't even have the capability to imagine.'

'Good! Let us get back to work then, right now!' said Raghav.

They folded their hands in 'Namaste' and bowed down, humbly reciprocated by the Minister, and left.

♦

'Sir, you will certainly laugh when you hear this one,' said Ramdas. 'Some teachers are giving upto one lakh rupees bribe to get themselves suspended!'

'What? Why would they do that?' asked Raghav.

'Some have to build their house, or arrange their daughter's marriage, or simply feel like relaxing for a few years. They keep getting half the salary during suspension period and later on, whenever they want, they go to court and get back the balance salary with interest and all other benefits.'

'But why have we not been able to control this, even after knowing it all the while?'

'We tried, Sir. We tried to take action against the officers who took bribes to suspend these teachers, but they too went to court, and you know how our courts work.'

'Fine, so this means that the department does not contest its cases well in the court. Please arrange my meeting tomorrow with the top three law firms in the city, we will ensure that the crooks don't get a walkover from us in the courts from now onwards.'

'Ramdas, please also arrange a meeting this Friday with the thirty people that I shortlisted for my back office secretariat. I also want zone-wise summary of online complaints coming to our website.'

'But Sir, there are hardly any complaints through the website!'

'That is because people think it's a waste of time and nothing will happen through this online system. Now onwards I want you to personally maintain an excel sheet of such complaints, forward them with a definite action plan to the concerned secretary or officer and submit a weekly summary of progress on each one to me, along with print-outs of the original complaint. Every last Saturday of the month, organize a meeting with all rank one officers, where I will personally discuss the statuses of these complaints. And also ensure that the progress on the complaint is updated regularly on the portal, so that the complainants may see it.'

'Sir, but don't you think you are giving too much time and importance to these complaints?'

'Importance, yes… but time, I shall in fact be saving through this exercise. Every complaint indicates some flaw in the system that we have forgotten to take care of. Without these complaints, I could take months or years to be able to detect those flaws. I look at problems, not as problems, but as opportunities.'

'Sir, what about Javed? Don't you think he will come back with more trouble soon?'

'No, he won't.'

'But how can you be so sure, Sir?'

'Because we have terminated him today.'

'On what grounds, Sir?'

'Contempt of court'

'How, Sir?'

'You remember…yesterday there was his interview in the Sahara, Uttar Pradesh Channel. In one of the questions the reporter asked Javed why he was calling a strike against the monitoring committees set up by us, even though he knew they had been formed by the order of the High Court. In his rage and arrogance he told the reporter that "The court can go to hell. What does the court know about ground realities?" He immediately realised his mistake and said, what was happening was against the self-respect of the teachers and they would not compromise on that. This remark about the court was edited before broadcasting, but I got an unedited copy from my sources.'

'But if you had to terminate him, why did you call today's meeting in the first place?'

'The message, Ramdas! How would the message reach out to the teachers across the cities, towns and villages? Do you think the other seven members who came with him would not have communicated each and every detail to the grapevine? By tomorrow most of the teachers will know what happened in the meeting and that we are not willing to negotiate on fundamentals. You know my philosophy—Be evil to some if you have to, for the greater good.'

'Right, Sir! That's what I admire the most about you,' said Ramdas, wondering at the energy, intelligence and commitment of this man. He was like an ace batsman playing a twenty-twenty match, hitting one six after the other, even on a rough and hazardous pitch. One miss and a bouncer could send him off to the deathbed. It was one of those moments that reminded him of the lyrics of his favourite song by Richard Marx 'One man stood tall, faced the devil with his back to the wall...'

'Don't take it as flattery, but I really admire your fearlessness, Sir. What gives you the drive to carry on so relentlessly?'

Ramdas watched as Raghav's expression suddenly changed to melancholy. 'No, Ramdas, I am not all that fearless. There are some dark pages in the book of my life, I would rather not have. I failed someone, failed miserably, irreparably...'

Ramdas walked behind him and kept a hand on his shoulder. 'I know you cannot fail anyone, Sir. I would not believe anyone, not you, not even god on that. I have seen you become sad like this on so many occasions. You have not shared with me but I would really give anything to purge your soul of this memory that brings you down.'

Raghav was staring blankly at a large portrait on his office wall, gazing inward. The portrait of a lady, who seemed to be of royal descent.

'Just hold my hand and I will lead you to safety, to glory!' The words kept echoing in his head.

Aditya on Star Cruise
Varanasi, 2011

A young man, wearing a tuxedo, stepped out of his Honda Accord on a lonely, secluded road in the middle of the night, holding a spade in his hand, headed somewhere with sinister motives. A small utility van was following him. He reached a dark strip of muddy land stretched along the road. He started digging, alone, sweating profusely. He obviously didn't want to take any chances; he had to be sure the work was done accurately. Who knows, a not-deep-enough hole, may mean a matter of life and death for someone. You could not afford to leave such things to others. Sweat dripped from his forehead incessantly as he continued to strike vehement blows at the soil below.

He straightened up and arched backwards to ease the stiffness, then signaled to his men in the van. A bald, dark stalky man with thick moustaches and a tall lanky one with long hair came out. They lifted the backdoor of the van upwards and pulled up their trousers at the waists, in preparation of the job they were about to do. The expression on their faces was cold and ruthless. They scuttled towards the pit he had dug, holding a mass wrapped in plastic. It was heavy and they dumped it into the pit, removing the plastic neatly. Then they shoved back the soil around the pit and quickly levelled the land. They did not want to leave any trace.

The man in the tuxedo was digging another pit, with the same wrath. Every drop of sweat that oozed out of his forehead seemed to add to his fury, and he kept striking one blow after the other with his sharp spade. Soon the second pit was ready, a bit broader and deeper than the first one. This was one of the reasons, he dug the pits personally. One could not dig same sized pits and expect the job to have been done safely. The soil was always prone to rainwater and wind, and slightest carelessness would expose what should not be.

He signalled again, and this time the two men trotted with even more speed towards the pit, holding an even heavier object wrapped in a different coloured plastic. They repeated the same activity as last time, very carefully.

Their boss dug eight more pits one after the other and they followed the same routine. Finally, they came out with a roll of green plastic net and some bamboo sticks with which they made a protective fencing along the stretch of land they had worked upon. No footsteps, no risk!

Their boss, a fair and clean-shaven young man with curly hair, around five feet nine inches, was no longer looking so evil. His face glowed in the moonlight, his expressions revealing his gentleness blended with maturity, confidence and determination. He patted them on the backs for their excellent work and leaned against his Honda, gloating over his work. He had a smile of satisfaction on his face. The two-years-old flowering gulmohar plants, freshly purchased from the nursery with a large mass of soil surrounding the roots, all wrapped carefully with plastic, had been quite a weight to carry, handle, place and secure in the soil. The pit had to be deep enough to ensure they did not fall over with the wind. The soil above also had to be firmly pushed in place to make a strong foundation. The plastic they removed ensured that the rich soil and humus in it reached the pit and remained around the roots.

Aditya had been following this routine on a weekly basis for almost eight months. 'Green and clean Varanasi' was one of the objectives his NGO had been passionately chasing.

His driver, who had been with their family for a long time, walked up behind him, paused to gather courage and asked, 'Aditya baba, this is the job of the government, no? Why do we do it?'

'Because I get satisfaction from it! God has blessed me with a lot, I have to give back whatever I can. If the government has not done something, I can't just criticize them in a bar with my friends. So, here I am!'

'But why yourself baba? It is so late, you should be with your family. You could just order the staff.'

Aditya put his hands around the driver's shoulder and answered, 'For the sheer pleasure of it, Shuklaji. The pleasure of standing here...like this...and watching my work.' The sound sleep that followed this session was a bonus.

'You know as a child, whenever I would make a painting for homework, the first thing I used to do when I woke up, even before getting ready for school, was to look at it for a few seconds...feeling happy. If somebody else would have made it for me, would I still get the same pleasure? So, this is something like that...' said Aditya.

◆

Aditya was sitting on a cruise ship on the 9th deck with his wife,

Prachi, and daughter, sipping, *Long island iced tea* and reminiscing about his life. He was wearing a casual round-neck black T-shirt and grey cotton cargos, his favourite holiday attire. Prachi's face was covered with a novel. She was wearing a white gown with a sober floral print that fit well on her shapely and attractive figure. The atmosphere was festive. Lively music was playing and people were sitting in groups and enjoying. A beautiful, tall Caucasian girl with an hourglass figure passed by and Aditya's eyes followed her.

'Caught you Copper Turnings! Checking out chicks, haan?' beamed Prachi, as her novel went down, revealing her beautiful, cheerful face.

'Holy smokes! Can you see through this book?' asked Aditya, wondering if she was actually reading the novel or waiting to play this prank. The indoor pool deck was buzzing with beauties in swimming suits and seductive short dresses. One had to be a saint, to not notice.

'I am bored! I don't really enjoy the crowds...' continued Aditya.

'Yes, of course, do you enjoy anything other than work? You are happy only when you work 14 hours a day.'

'You are right, I feel excited and happy about a vacation for two or three days, but after that I start missing work.'

'Work! Your first love...' Prachi said wistfully.

The mention of first love reminded Aditya of Elena for a split second, a sublime nostalgic memory that had no significance in his present life, but one that could not be erased all the same. 'No wrong! This is my first love,' said Aditya lifting his glass and looking at it lovingly.

'Really? Why not!' Prachi said, sounding slightly annoyed. She didn't mind his occasional drinking as it seemed to relax and open him up, in contrast to his stressful and otherwise disciplined routine.

'I really wonder how these white people can enjoy sitting idle, drinking beer on the beach or pool, day after day. Empty hands, empty mind, what pleasure do they derive in this? Sometimes, I also long for a comfortable life with just three-four hours of quality work every day and rest of the day free for relaxation. But probably that's not my cup of tea. Work is entertainment for people like us,' said Aditya.

'Exactly! It is because of people like you that they can relax. You showed me so many dreams before marriage, what about them? Settling abroad…world tour? We hardly come out for vacation once in a year or two. You barely have time for me,' Prachi complained.

'You know I am not running after money Prachi, money is just a means. I want to do something big, something good for the people. I want to see a stronger, better India,' he explained.

'But aren't you already doing that through your NGOs? There's one in which you adopt government schools and teach the poor children through computer software, like they do in private schools. And then there is another one in which you beautify the city. And a third one in which you rehabilitate beggars. Each has its own share of headaches and commitments. They take up all your time. What else do you want to do?' said Prachi with a hint of sarcasm in her voice. Not that she disapproved of what Aditya did, it was just her style. Deep down she appreciated her husband for being a good man, but on the face she was always critical.

'Apart from that, the factory is ever expanding its operations. You already have a 120-crore turnover! Isn't it sufficient? Who does social service with bank borrowings? Papa is growing old now. You also have to take care of your health. Don't go on spreading work all around... Try to relax a bit and enjoy life,' she added.

'That's true. But if you have a dream in life, you have to work towards it. No matter how unreal and distant it seems,' said Aditya.

This reminded Aditya that Prachi was the source of all joy in his life. Had it not been for her, both Aditya and his father would just keep working endlessly. She was the one who planned the vacations, movies on Sundays and dinner outings. She kept the family happy and bound together.

'I used to think I would earn a lot of money and then do "something big and good". Waited almost 10 years after doing engineering and joining business, but the struggle never seemed to end... It's still on and I don't know when it will end. So, at least I am happy that I am working on my dream to do some good for the country. Even if I do not accomplish what I want to, I will not die thinking that I did not try... Remember what I always tell you, "It is better to at least try your hand at something you fancy rather than just watch and appreciate others do it." *Sirf dekhna nahin...karna hai*,' he said.

Aditya noticed his little daughter who had been trying to climb up to his lap. When she could not, she was lying with her head in Papa's lap, playfully muttering something to herself. He picked her up and hugged her tightly. Prachi stretched out her hand and held Aditya's arm. The vibes of love flowed through them, a dear moment for their family.

They went to the seventh deck where the 'Dance to the Eighties' theme party was to take place. A slow and romantic dance was apt for the moment. The hall was soothingly decorated with two focus lights, one on the seven piece orchestra seated in front of the backdrop and the other on the circular wooden dance floor. There were tables with chairs all around the dance floor, spread across the hall, for guests to relax and enjoy the dance performances by fellow cruisers.

The floor was currently occupied by about a dozen old couples in their seventies or eighties. Some of the men were holding scotch glasses in their hands. The ladies put their hands on their shoulders and tried to sway them to the sound of the music, while the orchestra prepared themselves. The old men were mostly wearing full-sleeved shirts and loose trousers with suspenders. Some of them wore beach shirts and hats. The women wore comfortable but stylish gowns with bead necklaces and colourful accessories, such as scarves and floral headbands. The old people seemed to have come on a group vacation and were having a nice time. They were passing comments at each other in loud voices, changing dance partners and having fun like teenagers at a rave party.

'Look, age does not wear down the soul, they are enjoying like young couples! The wrinkles, the arthritis, the hunched backs, the thin white hair and the walking-with-extra-effort does not seem to dampen their spirits,' said Aditya. Like the others in the hall, Prachi and Aditya took a roundtable, waiting for the elderly couples to vacate the floor as the orchestra would start playing.

The orchestra started with a lively number by The Beatles. Some of the younger couples, who had been waiting all this time, started to approach the floor but had to stop midway. The old men vacated the floor, but only to put their drinks aside and join their partners for a line dance. They organized themselves in four rows and started swaying to the music, performing adeptly the intermittent changing of positions.

The audience was surprised at the sudden change of demeanour and all eyes turned towards them. They could see their restricted yet graceful movements, done with a lot of visible effort. Many of the elderlies could barely move, taking baby steps in their effort to keep their movements synchronized.

'Goodness gracious! What's this?' Prachi exclaimed.

'Seems like they have dance parties quite often, how else could they have practiced this dance?' said Aditya.

The orchestra switched to 'Clap your hands' by Ross Mitchell. And lo! The troop started performing the cha...cha... cha to it. The crowd was getting increasingly curious and fascinated. Hands came together to clap to the beat of the song.

The orchestra then played 'Time of my life' from Dirty Dancing and the troop immediately switched to the apt dance form—Salsa. Now this was getting a bit too exciting! Their frozen joints seemed to be opening up and their movements became less restricted, an occasional drop of sweat beginning to show on their foreheads as they danced frantically, keeping up with every beat.

The crowd was enjoying thoroughly. The band switched to Waltz, then to Disco, Jazz, Ballroom, Jive, Tap and Modern, one after the other, and the elderlies seemed to know each of the dance forms. They were having a blast, changing positions, partners and expressions swiftly. It was a unique experience for the audience. No one had ever seen people in their seventies and eighties dance like this. They were graceful, cute and energetic. The crowd went into frenzy, cheering them and clapping madly to the rhythm.

After almost half hour of continuous dancing they vacated the floor while the crowd cheered. The old couples stayed at the roundtables contrary to the belief of many that they were trained cruise staff and would go backstage. They were actually just like any other group of friends on vacation.

'Wonder who these people are and where they come from? They look Chinese,' Prachi said to Aditya.

'Yeah, the Gensing, I guess! The Chinese drug can do wonders, I have heard,' chuckled Aditya.

While some young couples now took the floor trying to imitate the steps they remembered from the wonderful performance they had just seen, a curious gentleman from Pakistan who was on vacation with his wife and parents had been watching them very intently. His polished looks told that he was either a high-level bureaucrat or a statesman, a connoisseur of life. He went up to the band and borrowed the mike from them.

'Gentlemen, you have made this evening one to remember for all of us. Many of us could see our parents in you, dancing and enjoying like we would wish them to. We are all curious to know that at this age, when people normally cling to a sedentary lifestyle, how come you are able to defy age. Who are you? Where do you come from and what is the secret of your youth and zeal? Please tell us so that we can inspire more of our elders to be like you. And more importantly, to be like you when we grow up. Wouldn't all of you want to be like them?' he asked the audience.

The crowd shouted a deafening 'Yes!'

A short man from the old people's group walked up and took the mike from the Pakistani. He was tired and sweating and his face was all wrinkled with sagging skin, but his glow was eye catching, the glow of a care-free and fully-lived life.

'Thank you my friend. You can't be like us, it's genetic! Maybe when you see me, you are reminded of the rich old man in Macau, who has twenty-four wives and owns most of the casinos there. He just got his twenty-fifth wife at the age of 92 last month. We are from the same family,' he spoke in a typical Cantonese accent with missing terminal consonants.

People looked at each other, listening intently, trying to absorb what this man was saying.

'Sorry, just joking!' he continued after a brief pause. The crowd burst out laughing. He waited for silence to resume, then continued, 'We are from an old-age home in Singapore. Our government promotes such activities amongst us so that we not only keep fit, but adrenalized too. Our government believes that when people become old, they do not become useless, they become an asset to the society. They encourage us to work and use our experience towards the benefit of the society and the country. They want us to live our life to the fullest…till our last breath. I guess, that's why we are here… with lovely people like you.'

The crowd stood up and applauded the spirit of these people. While many would like their parents to lead similar lives, they would probably either forget about it as they would return from this vacation to their mundane lives, or not be able to actually do anything about it.

'What a contrast!' Aditya said, overwhelmed. 'Our aged generally become dependent on their children and are treated like broken furniture and cast aside. Their spirits are squashed. And look at these people here!'

'Have you seen how clean and organized Singapore is? What's the point comparing? Our country is different! We are a different lot!' said Prachi.

'I will bring this philosophy to Indian governance one day,' said Aditya. Prachi shrugged it off, he was probably in high spirits after three rounds of booze.

◆

The cruise was headed for Sanya, a quaint ethnic town on the southern coast of China. Aditya could not get the Singapore old-age-home troop out of his mind. He was lying with his head in Prachi's lap and singing Westlife's

> *I wanna grow old with you,*
> *I wanna die lying in your arms*
> *I wanna be there for you*
> *Sharin' in everything you do*
> *I wanna grow old with you.*

Just then, Aditya's sister came rushing to them and said, 'Bhaiya, Papa is calling you. There was a call from the factory. It seems there is a problem, there.' Aditya's was a joint family comprising his parents, sister, wife and children. They always went on vacations together.

'There is a chlorine leak in the factory, it's 3 am there, all the workers have run away. What do we do now? This Azo chemicals manufacturing work is too risky. I told you to hire some good people in that plant,' his father said, his voice fraught with fear and irritation.

Aditya kept silent for a while, thinking deeply. Chlorine leak is one of the most serious accidents as it can lead to death if exposure to the gas is high. They had the statutory handling license, but in case of any damage, the administration would leave no stones unturned to harass and extort them. And if the press would start taking interest, it could mean factory closure.

He picked up the mobile and called security office, which was located on the other end of the factory, far from the chlorine cylinders storage area. There were hardly any chances of it being affected.

'Where is Shrivastavaji, the night shift manager?' Aditya asked the security guard who picked up the phone.

'Sir, he had informed telephonically that his wife is not well, so he would not come. We tried to contact him, but his mobile is switched off.'

'And both the chlorine section operators?'

'Can't locate them, Sir, and it is difficult to go to that side due to the gas.'

'And our security in-charge who had been trained for chlorine accident handling?'

'Sir, he is in Allahbad. He had taken leave from you one month back for the 23rd and 24th of June.'

'Damn it!' Aditya had tried every option, the situation was really adverse. 'Why do such accidents always have to happen behind my back?' he thought. There was no trained person who could handle the situation there. At least the supervisors who were receiving regular periodic training should have reported to the assembly point at the security gate. Either they had been trapped there, or would have run away in fear of being held accountable. He hoped the latter had happened. A sudden involuntary shiver went down his spine.

'How bad is the smell there?'

'Sir, it's quite uncomfortable, we are finding it difficult to breathe,' said the guard.

'Have the workers from all other sections of the plant been evacuated. How many were there on duty and how many have come to the assembly point?' asked Aditya.

'Sir, 21 out of 24 have reported,' he replied.

'Is Ramesh, the night shift fitter there?'

'Yes, Sir. He is standing nearby, I will just call him,' said the guard.

'Ramesh, now listen to me carefully. You are one of the oldest workers in the factory and I trust your intelligence. You are my only hope right now. Do as I say and we can save the factory and the trapped workers. There is an oxygen mask and full body costume kept in security cupboard. Put it on and go to the cylinder area.'

'I will do as you say Aditya Bhaiya, but I hope this is not life threatening. I haven't done this before. Shall we call the fire brigade?' asked Ramesh.

'We don't have that much time Ramesh. I remember you used to assist the safety squad during mock drills with the mechanical fittings and all. Within half-an-hour, the entire area will be affected and then there will be no hope for the factory to run again. Just do as I say, don't panic!'

'But this costume will cover my face completely, how will I speak to you?' he asked.

'I have seen in the CCTV footage that, the night shift security guard, Ramsingh, uses an earphone to listen to songs. Use that. Plug the earphones into your ears and then wear the costume, putting the mobile in your pocket. I'll just call back.' Aditya disconnected and hurriedly dialed back, the countdown was on…every second.

'Can you hear me, have you put on the costume?' asked Aditya.

'Yes Bhaiya, but I am feeling suffocated,' came the reply.

'There is a valve above the oxygen cylinder. Open that,' said Aditya.

'Ok, now it's better Bhaiya, oxygen is coming, but still it is uncomfortable. It's hitting my face too hard,' said Ramesh.

'There is a red regulator on the line coming from the cylinder to your mask, and there is a pressure gauge hanging on your costume, set the pressure to level 3 with the regulator. Be careful, don't turn it to the wrong side, the pressure should not increase, or you may get hurt,' cautioned Aditya.

'Ok, now it's absolutely comfortable.'

'Fine, did you reach the cylinder area?'

'Yes, I am almost there.'

'Can you see any one lying fainted there?'

'No.'

Aditya let out a sigh of relief. Chlorine is a heavy gas, so it stays down. Probably the trapped workers had climbed up to the upper stories.

'What should I do now Bhaiya?' asked Ramesh.

'Can you see anything? Can you make out the cylinder from which the leakage is there?'

'There is a fine mist all over and I can't make out.'

'See just above the first cylinder, there is a rack on which a plastic bottle is kept, it has ammonia solution. Open it and take it near the connection points on each cylinder, one by one. The one near which dense white smoke is formed will be the one that is leaking,' explained Aditya.

About 50 seconds later, Ramesh shouted, 'Found it Bhaiya! Cylinder number 19 is leaking badly.'

'Use the key on the header near that cylinder to tightly close the valve.'

'The valve is not closing Bhaiya. It's free.'

'Shit. Ok, now listen carefully. Close the valves on the header and remove the connections to cylinder number 19. You have seen the operators using the overhead travelling hoist. We have to use that to lift the cylinder and drop it into the caustic pit, so that the chlorine coming out of it can be neutralized with the alkaline water in the pit. Position the hooks on both sides of the cylinder and lift it with the third green button.'

'Done Bhaiya, the cylinder is in the air.'

'Good. We are almost there. Now press the second green button and move the cylinder towards the gate. There is a pit filled with lime slurry adjacent to the gate, the cylinder is to be placed inside it.'

After a few seconds Ramesh said, 'But the pit is empty and there is some sludge around it, I think it must have been under cleaning.'

Aditya cursed loudly and banged his palm against his forehead. He was so close to avoiding this disaster, but it seemed luck was not on his side today.

'Now, what to do Bhaiya? The oxygen pressure is down to 30 per cent and it will finish in a few minutes. Can we do anything now?'

'No. Go back to the security and call the fire brigade,' Aditya surrendered and looked towards his father. It was the worst feeling in the world to see that fear on his father's face. His father was a strong, self-made man, who had established the business, and he respected him a lot. He also knew his father trusted him like an in-house Superman, sometimes to the extent of taking his efforts for granted. Together they had taken this business from a meagre turnover of five crore to 120 crore in just ten years. It was a very strong, unassailable team. It was the courage and acumen of his father, cocktailed with his engineering and management skills that kept them going. But for now, this was a defeat. Possibly the final and decisive one!

He stared blankly at the empty Pepsi can on the table. And then it struck him. Holy Smokes! 'Stop Ramesh, just try this last thing! Go to the lab just behind the cylinder area. You will find a green metal box, on which 'PEPTOFIX' will be written. It is a two pack adhesive we recently developed for acid pipe joints, a much more effective version of M-seal. It is still under trial, but I think it may work. Mix the two parts properly and apply to the joints of the leaking valve.'

'Got it!' he heard after a while. Then after a few seconds, 'Bhaiya, the adhesive is not holding its place, the gas coming out is pushing it off.'

The adhesive was developed for offline repairs, it would not work for running leakages. Aditya's last hope was also fading. Then, he said instinctively, 'Put the entire adhesive around the valve, even if the valve gets covered in it, and hold it tightly in place with both hands. I think there is some curing time, it will harden after that.' He could hear his heart beat like a drum, his pulse racing.

About two minutes later, he heard a cry of rejoice from the other end, 'It worked, Bhaiya, there is no more leakage now, the mist is also reducing very fast.'

'Well done Ramesh! We are all so proud of you. You will get a special salary increment and your children's education shall be on company account from now. The chlorine section operators must be on the top floor, ask them to run the lime shower so that the mist can be run down before the fire brigade, city administration and press arrive.'

Aditya hugged his father and touched his feet. He was so relaxed to see the expression of despair gone from his father's face. He realized again how his life revolved around his work and family.

As Aditya sat in his room with Prachi, gently playing Eric Clapton's *'You look wonderful tonight'*. He remembered how once an astrologer had said that life would not be a bed of roses for him, and that he would have to struggle hard for everything but would never be defeated in life. He thought about the day's events and how he saw the 'PEPSI' can and remembered 'PEPTOFIX', the peptide-based sealant. The divine forces were with him!

Although he was happy that the immediate emergency had been warded off, this incident as well as what Prachi had said earlier during the day, reinforced his conviction to take the bold initiative he had been contemplating for quite some time.

He was now mentally prepared to drop the bombshell upon their return to Varanasi.

Varun and Radhika
Delhi, 2014

Varun saw the man next to him in the loo spit in the urinal before he unzipped. It amused him and he always used to wonder what kind of a hormonal reaction induced such 'spitting before peeing' urge in people. It was a common sight, not only in India but across countries, specially in public toilets. He had just arrived at the New Delhi airport from New York with new dreams. He was dressed in a formal pinstripe light grey business suit, his staple attire, and seemed excited.

'Hi Radhika! I am here. Will just clear the immigration and be there in an hour or so. What a lucky day for us! Our prayers and patience will finally bear fruit. We have both waited for this for so long.'

He watched the immigration officer behind the Business Class counter scold the tired Economy passengers, who had queued-up in front of his counter too, seeing the long queues in front of the others. Another usual sight at the New Delhi International Airport!

'All is well at home,' he continued. 'Alisha has finally given consent in the US court for divorce. Listen now, I am reaching there straight away, you too make it fast. We can't really trust the government officers, don't know how many formalities we will have to go through. Ask Shyam and Vinti to be there too and ask them to bring a handycam.'

The man behind him in the queue had been watching his excitement for some time now. 'Going for court marriage brother? See, I got you! Enjoying multiple innings! You lucky NRIs! Don't forget to take some flowers.'

'Wow! How did you guess?' Varun mocked a gaping, surprised expression.

◆

Varun took a taxi, the crowded roads of Delhi giving him ample time to talk to Madhav on the way. He always made it a point to meet his loved ones, even on his shortest trips to India. He loved the randomness and energy of Indian cities, compared to the organized and relatively laidback feel one got in the USA. He finally reached the Parliament House.

Radhika, who had been the co-ordinator of his NGO—Kalpvruksha, since its inception, was there with Shyam and Vinti, who worked with them as research analysts. She was dressed in a graceful lemon and white cotton suit. Her perfectly balanced features, fair complexion, glistening straight black hair and large eyes made her look attractive even without makeup.

'You look great Radhika! What's up?' Varun said, a bright smile on his face.

'All well,' said Radhika, 'the three of us are pretty excited. It's our first time in the Parliament! I'll give you a detailed update in the afternoon. The meeting is about to begin. Let's go.'

Their NGO worked on policy research and voiced public opinion to the committees formed by the government. These committees improvised the laws and finally passed them in their best practical and logical version.

Few people in our country would know that our government actually invites its citizens, by way of advertisements in leading newspapers, to express their views and suggest improvements on bills proposed by the Parliament. Today, Varun and Radhika, along with several other organizations and individuals, had been invited for a discussion on the 'Judicial Standards and Accountability Act'. They were supposed to give a presentation too. As the name indicated, the bill was all about setting standards for the judges across the country in the higher courts to live up to, and to bring about more accountability and transparency in their working, appointment and other affairs.

Currently, the selection of new judges to the High Court and Supreme Court was being done by a group called Collegium comprising a few senior-most judges. They selected names, from amongst senior lawyers and lower ranks of judges, and proposed them to the law ministry. The new bill proposed to replace the Collegium with a judicial committee, which would have on board not only senior-most judges, but a few able politicians and eminent persons, representing a wider section of the society. This aimed at making the selection procedure more open and transparent. The senior judges, across the board, were against this as they thought it was an infringement of their autonomy. They also believed that involving politicians would make the judiciary corrupt.

Varun and Radhika were escorted to a large auditorium, with a seating capacity of about 500, elegantly laid out in a semi-circle with an elevated stage that had a large screen in the centre.

Seated in the front row of the central block—reserved for the Members of Parliament—were the six members of the Joint

Parliamentary Committee (JPC). Four of them were from the ruling party and two from the opposition. In the block to their right were IAS officers, including the convener for the JPC and the secretaries of the ministry. The block to the left seated the other guests who had been invited to voice public opinion.

The presentations given by the participating groups made it clear that the bill in its present form had too many flaws.

'You know a very funny thing happened today!' Varun said in a hushed voice to Radhika.

Radhika looked at him questioningly with her large kohl-lined eyes. For a split second he was struck by the hypnotism of those extremely beautiful and honest eyes, but he quickly recovered. He did find her attractive and intelligent. But somehow she was more of a friend and Varun liked it better this way.

She had always aspired to dedicate her life to the country. She had completed an internship with Varun's NGO and on completing her graduation in law, she joined his NGO on a full-time basis. Even though he lived and worked in the US, he was spending a lot of time, money and energy to do something good for India. Radhika was impressed with his patriotism. She was also aware of the trauma he had been through in his married life. She not only admired him for his altruism and patriotism but adored him as a person. However, she never had the courage to express it.

'When I called you from the airport, the man behind me in the immigration queue suggested that I take some flowers for you.'

'Why?' asked Radhika. Her heart stopped beating and she looked intently at Varun. Was something good about to happen? Did he also feel something for her?

'Because he could read my real feelings, as I spoke to you, and could make out that I wanted to marry you.'

Radhika almost stopped breathing. She was motionless. Varun had always been oblivious of her existence as a possible suitress. This must be a dream, she pinched herself discreetly.

'Silly! This is what he assumed. Actually the timing is to be blamed. The way I mentioned my divorce, our long wait for this day, and the role of government officers, topped by the excitement in my voice, made him feel that I was heading for a court marriage. I could have rolled on the floor laughing, had my turn not come,' said Varun.

Radhika sighed. She also cursed herself for being naïve to imagine that Varun could have been saying all this seriously. Sometimes she wondered how she could fall in this one-sided love with a married man. She could never have imagined it as an adolescent. She would feel pity at the stupidity of such women in movies or in discussions when such matters came up. Strange, how love can change your perceptions and convictions! She had always wanted a tall man and Varun was only five feet eight. She liked white, sparkling, linear teeth and he had a partly staggered toothline. She loved watching romantic movies, while he thought it was a waste of time. He would rather sit and chat. The list of mismatches was long. Love can even change your likes and dislikes. One cannot…just cannot understand it, unless one falls in it.

The presentations that were being made pointed out some serious flaws in the bill, for instance, it proposed to form 'Scrutiny Panels' in each court that would investigate complaints against judges from the same court. How could one's colleagues be impartial to them?

Then there were funny provisions for admonishing and

rendering minor punishments to the judges. How could a judge who was accused of unethical conduct be allowed to continue in office or be given a minor punishment? Would the public look upon them with the same respect and consider them fit to deliver justice?

'It is important to bring about transparency and accountability in the judiciary, which is currently lacking, while ensuring its independence. Since this applies to the higher judiciary—High Courts and the Supreme Court, the larger causes like good governance through PILs and judicial activism shall be deeply impacted by any change in this balance between accountability and independence,' concluded a group of retired justices that worked on policy research.

Varun looked at Radhika, shaking his head in disbelief at all the fancy chit-chat that was going on. His looks told her there was something dangerous on his mind. She had heard stories about how he got his nickname, Varun 'Panga' Pandey and it scared her.

Salman Antagonizes Ganesh
Mumbai, 2014

'We welcome our MP Mr Prakash Dubey, our Corporator Mr Bholanath and our very own Mr Ganesh Vidyarthi, who is contesting election for the MLA seat in our constituency, to Ramkrishna Garib Awas Yojna,' announced the President of the chawl. Salman sat on the stage wearing a light blue shirt, black trousers and a black–grey Varsity jacket with a pair of sunglasses that made him outshine the rest of them. As the Secretary of the society, Salman had done a lot for the residents and he felt a sense of belonging to this chawl, where he had grown up.

The President of the society continued, 'Ganeshji has earlier been the Corporator and then MLA from this area, the term before this one. He is known for his dynamism and as a leader who has stood against the administration time and again to protect the interests of the people. He has done a lot for us during his tenure. And since he began his political career from this area, we also have a special connection with him. I can already feel the excitement amongst the people here, so I will request our favourite Mr Ganesh to address the people now.'

'I am not here to deliver some kind of an electoral campaign speech. I have never considered myself any different from any of you. I am one amongst you...your son...your brother. I have always been there with you in times of difficulty, joy and sorrow. When you did not give me an opportunity to serve you in the last elections, I was surprised. But then I thought that this is the verdict of my people and your wish is my command.' Ganesh began his speech adeptly. Dressed in traditional attire—kurta, dhoti and a white cap, the middle-aged man in his forties, instantly connected with the crowd. He wore a thick gold chain, half-a-dozen heavy rings with gemstones studded in them, and an inappropriately thick gold bangle in his left hand, signifying his socio-economic status. He loomed a good six feet two inches with a broad frame that lent a daunting air to his personality. His words, however, were as sweet as honey.

'But your brother has not viled away these last five years,' he continued. 'He has toiled hard to increase his strength to serve you better. Today, whether it is the Party's General Secretary or the State President, no one in the Janhit Party can ignore Ganesh Vidyarthi's words. There are some old memories that are still fresh in my mind. Whether it is facing police lathi charge while opposing the demolition of your shops, or getting our people admitted to the hospital when dengue broke out, or fighting for the development of our park, or being part of your daughter's marriage. I was there with you through the thick and thin. If my opponents think that by siding with a few rich capitalists and promising false dreams they can allure my people, I don't think they have the faintest idea of our bond. *Jai Garib! Jai Hind!*'

The public stood up and started shouting frenzied slogans like, '*Janhit mein hamara sarthi, hamara bhai Ganesh Vidyarthi!*' His supporters were vying to put garlands around his neck. Soon he could hardly hold his neck straight and his face was barely visible. He looked at his MP and then the party workers, all seemingly satisfied that the air seemed to be in their favour. The election seemed already won.

This was followed by short speeches from the MP and some eminent Janhit Party leaders, profusely praising Ganesh for his epic struggles for the chawl.

As the roar settled down, the President of the society announced, 'Now, I invite the Secretary of our Society, our beloved Salman, to say a few words to conclude and offer the vote of thanks.'

Salman felt a sudden upsurge of disgust as Ganesh smiled at him, his usual pretentious smile... *Ise prasaad chahiye...*

'I feel so happy that our Ganesh Bhaiya, who used to play cricket with us in our younger days, has not forgotten us even after reaching great heights. I remember clearly, I was a fast bowler and always used to bowl out Ganesh Bhaiya but the umpire used to be his own, so he would declare it a "no ball". It's great that the strength and leadership which Ganesh Bhaiya used to apply when he was young, when put in the correct direction, has yielded the great leader that he is today I was very young at that time, so I had to remain quiet, but today, I want to ask him just four questions. Four questions, which I want him to answer, to further strengthen our confidence in him.'

There was a buzz as the people talked to each other, mostly not able to understand what their Secretary wanted to convey and why he was talking in an apparently derogatory manner about Ganesh. It was an undeniable fact that Ganesh had been with them through haze and shine.

'What's wrong with this boy?' muttered the Corporator to the President of the society sitting next to him. 'Why is he spoiling the cordial atmosphere with such unpleasant talk?'

Salman was looking straight into the eyes of Ganesh. 'First, you told us that you faced police lathi-charge when the municipal team came to remove the encroachments. Had you got some shops allotted to our poor vegetable-mongers and 'thelewalas' at the time when the newly-built shops were being allotted in the complex, which they rightfully deserved, the problem of encroachment would never have arisen in the first place. When everyone deposited equal amount of security to the Corporation, how come only the rich ones were allotted the shops?'

'Second, you used to look after our people in the hospitals when we were struck with dengue. Why was the DDT fumigation against mosquitoes, which should have been done every month in our locality, not done for over a year? Had this been done timely, the disease would never have spread. The fumigation started one month after we lost some of our dear ones. There was sufficient stock in the Corporation for several months, but it was used for filling pockets rather than mitigating sorrows,' he said.

'It is not like that...' the Corporator started to speak into the mike in front of him.

'Let me finish!' Salman said firmly, signalling Bholanath to sit down.

'Third, you said that you struggled for the development of our park. Now, we don't have to conduct our marriages and functions on the road. Yes, we should be thankful. You got a budget of eighty lakhs allotted for its development, out of which 25 lakhs were spent on a fountain that has been dysfunctional since a month after it was installed. About 15 lakhs were spent on constructing the boundary walls, which were only plastered and that too at a very low cost. The balance was spent on making a community centre that should have had sports facilities and courts, library and theatre, among other facilities for the residents. However, it is an abandoned concrete structure where stray dogs spend their nights. Yes, it is rented for marriage functions, illegally. The next day, the whole park is so dirty that it is not fit for any kind of walk or leisure. The park has lost its purpose and become a marriage ground. Our poor and ignorant people may derive happiness even from the fact that they can get this place on rent, but that is not what they deserve. So much money was spent but nothing changed. The truth is that in 25 lakhs the whole park could have been transformed,' said Salman.

'Where is the party cadre? Why is he being allowed to go on speaking?' MP Dubey whispered to Ganesh.

'I did not ask many of them to come,' he replied.

'Satyaanash! Such over confidence? These are the times we need them the most!' slammed Dubey.

'Fourth and last,' Salman continued. 'You are always there in our social functions, our daughters' marriages, mundans, and almost everywhere...so that with some sweet talk or financial help you can put a lifetime of obligation on a poor man's head, which inhibits his power of logical thinking. The result is here, I think we can all see it. There has been no development in this chawl over the last 10 years. Still we are happy and honouring you for being there for us.'

There was pin-drop silence as people were listening very carefully, the truth probably sinking into many of them. Not that all of them were oblivious to the truth, but it had never been put forth so blatantly.

'It has been our nature since time immemorial to shower accolades and flattery upon our elected representatives and make them feel like kings. Rarely does anyone question them on their work. Even today the maximum that people come out on the streets for and protest against, are things like power cuts and water availability. They have subjected us to such deprivation and limited our needs to the extent that we are happy even if our basic necessities are met. Many a times I have heard politicians complain about how difficult their job is and how they have to put in long hours of hard work to be there amongst the people at all times. Is this what we have appointed you for—to attend our social functions? If you keep yourself busy with these things, who will do your work? It is your phobia of losing your vote bank that keeps you campaigning, even after getting elected? For all we know, all the money from the park, the fogging, the shops allocation, etc., may actually have gone to party fund, as it does... We believe you Ganesh. You are not like that, you are our own. You are only part of "the system" and you did what an elected leader in our country is supposed to do.'

All this while, Ganesh did not speak a word. He just kept sipping the special crimson drink he always used to carry in a sipper and listened intently, partly aghast at the recklessness of this young man and partly alerted. He was a very shrewd politician and a good listener, adept with words and manipulation. He had to form his strategy against this new and unexpected situation.

Salman now turned towards the crowd and continued, 'Friends, it is actually you who have to think. Till the time we keep fighting for benefits for our chawl...our locality...our city... our state, these politicians will keep taking advantage of us. Why do you have to fight to get the roads of your area made or for dissuading power cuts in your locality? All this should happen automatically, for all areas! For everyone! If work is done honestly, then with the huge annual budgets of the Municipality, the Water Corporation, the Electricity Board, etc., every road of the city should remain in perfect shape, there should be no power cuts and no dearth of water. I am not favouring or opposing anybody, absolutely not. Nor am I suggesting that you should not vote for our own Ganesh Bhai. I just want to appeal to you to think seriously and rationally and vote for a person who is honest and passionate about his work. And if you can't find such a person, then we will have to find such a person, together, if not for this election, for the next one maybe... Thank you.'

The whole pandal was filled with an awful din as the people debated, some agreeing with Salman and some cursing him for being so rude and arrogant with Ganesh, who was not only powerful but had served them for a long time.

'Poor homework Ganesh! Didn't you tell me this is your strongest booth?' whispered the MP Dubey. 'The whole atmosphere seems to have turned against us. It is quite likely that the opposition has played their card. Who is this boy Salman? Does he align with some party? Are you on bad terms with him?'

'Oh, he is nothing Prakash ji! No political involvement. I have known him since childhood and he has never shown any bitterness towards us earlier. He is aggressive and rash by nature, but popular here. Don't know why he sounded so poisonous today?' replied Ganesh. 'Just an over-enthusiastic youngster! Anyway, you don't worry, I will set him right,' replied Ganesh.

'Yeah! You better,' grimaced Dubey. 'And what is this drink you keep sipping all the time?'

'Nothing, Sir, just juice! Helps me think better,' grinned Ganesh.

Raghav, the Prince of Sumerpur

Lucknow, 2014

Raghav stared out of the window of his chauffeur-driven Maruti Alto as it sped the highway. He was returning from a surprise visit to the primary schools in the adjoining district of Barabanki. One suspension, two transfers and five verbal warnings. The count was going down, which was a positive sign. 'It is only due to the complete trust Chacha ji has laid in me. He has never interfered with my work,' he thought as he drifted back to his childhood memories.

'Your grandfather was the biggest Zamindar in Sumerpur,' his mother, Sakshi, used to tell him, 'We still hold 1,500 bighas of agricultural land.' The Haveli in which they lived was built like a fortress over 25 acres, on an elevated platform; tall grey stone walls surrounded it from all sides. A broad stone-tiled road with three large carved-stone fountains along its length, spanned the distance from the main gate to the majestic façade of the main building. Between the boundary and the main building was a wall-to-wall lawn with geometrically laid out trees and flowering shrubs.

Inside the main building, there was a large verandah in the centre with at least 35 rooms and halls all around it, in two storeys. The roof was high and if one spoke, the sound echoed from one side of the balcony surrounding the verandah to the other. There were 23 servants including three cooks, three gardeners, eight security guards, two butlers and three drivers.

'My Rajkumar! Crown Prince of Sumerpur!' his mother would shower him with such endearments and pamper him. He would run into her arms, whenever he was upset and she would take his little hand in hers and say, 'Be fearless, little prince! Just hold my hand and I will lead you to safety, to glory!'

Chacha Krishan Singh became the sole owner of all the property after the death of his elder brother, Raghav's father, Virendra Singh. Raghav was only six-years-old when his father was killed by the dacoits, while returning from Jhansi to Sumerpur. Those were the days when the dacoits of central and eastern Uttar Pradesh were most notoriously powerful and ruthless. Flashes of memory, wherein his father's blood-stained body was brought to the Haveli, wrapped in white cloth, amongst heart-rending cries of his mother, family members, relatives, staff and villagers, continued to haunt him frequently during childhood and till date. He innocently laid out meticulous plans along with the servants' children for dacoit Abhay Singh Gurjar's execution, but much to his despair, Gurjar was encountered by the police before he could give shape to his plans.

Soon after his brother's death, Krishan Singh, who had recently joined the Indian National Front, vied for the MP candidature. He perceived that not only would he ride on a sympathy wave due to his elder brother's murder, but it was also a necessity to gain more power and leverage his position against the rampant Robinhoodism against zamindars, prevalent during that time.

His mother died when he was ten years old. They had

gone to the 'Sangam', where the Yamuna and Betwa rivers met. His mother, Chachi ji, cousin Madhur, Raghav and their driver Bhola were part of the picnic. It was exhilarating to see waters of different colours from two different streams mix into one. Raghav was fond of swimming and even used to take training from professional divers (gotakhors), who would be posted there to save people from drowning during the festivals and holy bath days.

While Chachi ji was at the bank helping Madhur build a sand castle, Raghav and his mother were enjoying the water, splashing at each other playfully. Suddenly his mother stepped back and encountered a crater in the riverbed. She lost balance and before Raghav could understand what was happening, she was caught in an eddy that took her down. He went after her, not fearing the threatening swirls of water. Bhola too jumped in though he was not much of a swimmer. He could not gather the courage to get closer to the eddy. Raghav surfaced shortly only to gasp in some air and go down again. Everyone watched in horror as there was no sign of either Raghav or his mother. It seemed both had fallen prey to the vicious currents. There were no divers around and all their cries for help were in vain. After some time, Raghav surfaced, gasping for breath and coughing out the water that had filled his lungs. He had tried his best but could not save his mother, his closest friend.

After this incident, he stopped talking and did not eat properly. He would sit alone on the parapet of the Haveli's roof, and stare at the horizon, unafraid of the perilous height. His mother's words echoed in his mind all the time, 'Just hold my hand and I will lead you to safety, to glory!' And here he was, not having held her hand, when she needed him. He blamed himself for coming out alive, leaving his mother in the water.

No one saw him swim after that.

Krishan's son, Madhur, was just six months younger than Raghav. Chachi ji loved Raghav as much as she loved Madhur. She was the one who brought back life in an emotionally dead Raghav. Uncle Krishan remained busy with his political pursuits. But Chachi ji's affection made up for any vacuum created by his parents' absence. Sometimes he would feel Madhur's jealousy at this, but Madhur was too busy to carry it in his head for a long time. Most of Madhur's time was spent with the servants' and villagers' children, where he was the de facto 'Hi-Kamaan' (High-Command).

The 'High-Command', Mr Jaswant Oberoi, was a popular character amongst the children from erstwhile political families in the Indian National Front, just like Bahubali was amongst the common masses. The title was fancier and sounded more powerful than Bahubali.

Krishan Singh had ensured being in the good books of the High-Command from the beginning. Once, he took both the children to the High Command's palace. Contrary to Raghav's expectation of finding him in an office surrounded by party workers and executives, the High Command was playing golf leisurely. They watched him play for more than a couple of hours, from the spectators gallery, as Krishan Singh stood respectfully with the equipment attendants at one side. After a long wait, they finally got to meet him. He was smart, sophisticated and stylish, like an English Lord. The carefree and royally comfortable lifestyle had shaped his regal personality. As he walked back from the golf field to the residence area, he stopped by and asked Krishan Singh the children's names, gently touched their cheeks, uttered some blessings and walked away. Krishan Singh stood with folded hands all this while with an obliged expression on his face.

'Is he going to come back?' Krishan Singh asked one of the officers.

'Not for next two to three hours. He has gone to the spa section.'

'Why did we come here Babu ji?' asked Madhur in the car, on their way back.

'Why? To show you the High-Command and his house. Didn't you like it?'

'No, I thought you would have wanted to discuss some important matter,' replied Madhur.

'Are you mad, son? I would never discuss work with him directly. There are people occupying important party posts below him to take care of that. My visits to the palace are just to remind him of my loyalty towards him.'

The children were confused. Raghav in his 17th year and Madhur in his 16th were now mature enough, with a sense of propriety. They liked the High-Command for his charisma and genial nature, however, they had expected to see more people-oriented action from him. He rather seemed to be living in a self-made heaven.

The regular visits did pay off and Krishan got the ticket for contesting Member of Parliament election from the Indian National Front, for Sumerpur constituency. Everyone in the Haveli was engrossed in the election campaign. Even Madhur would accompany his father to most of the public meetings. Raghav, however, was oblivious to all that was going on around him, as he was busy taking care of Chachi ji, who had fallen extremely ill. He took her to several doctors in and around the district but she continued to suffer from shortness of breath, fatigue and nausea, accompanied with swelling of legs and feet.

The medicines did not seem to help. The doctors advised Raghav to take her to Delhi.

'Are you sure you can take care of your Chachi alone? Should I send Madhur with you?' asked Krishan Singh.

'But Babu ji, what about the elections? They are just two weeks away?' said Madhur.

'Don't worry Chacha ji. It is important for Madhur to stay here. If I need anything or get stuck anywhere, you people are just a night's journey away,' replied Raghav.

So, Raghav and Chachi ji left for Delhi by car, accompanied by just their trusted driver, Bhola. Chachi ji was admitted to the critical care unit at the best private hospital, Sadafal Trust. Raghav would sit by her side on the hospital bed as some machines remained connected to her body. She would be semi-conscious due to the medicines being administered. He would pray endlessly but nothing seemed to happen. Raghav was emotionally strong but occasionally a tear found its way out as he would remember the love Chachi ji had showered on him and muse with utter frustration why God wanted to take away everyone who was close to him.

One day, Chachi ji became totally unconscious. The machines connected to her body started emitting eerie sounds. The attending doctor and nursing staff rushed to push open her tightening jaw line and shoved the ventilator pipe down her throat.

The senior doctors' team called Raghav for a meeting to apprise him of the actual situation. After fifteen minutes of intense discussions, several forms were put up for his signatures. He barely got any time to inform the people back home.

The operation was successful and he was relieved to hear that Chachi ji was out of danger now. The doctors told him she was really blessed. Had it not been for the recent advancement in the field of specialized surgery, she could not have been saved. And even more, to have a son like Raghav!

'I am fine Chacha ji,' Raghav coughed. 'Guess I caught some infection with this long stay at the hospital. Will bring Chachi ji back by next week. She had to undergo a major emergency operation. Yes, she is absolutely fine, just needs a few days to recover... No, there is no need for you to come, I know the election is just a week away. All is well here.' He cut the line as he could not speak any further. He limped his way back from the doctor's cabin to his bed beside Chachi ji's. She was still unconscious from the sedative effect of the medicines.

After eight days, while they were on their way back to Sumerpur by train, Raghav thanked God for granting his prayers and resolved not to talk about the details of what had happened to anyone. This was the transformation point in his life. He felt grown up and confident to take on the world.

They were welcomed by a cheery crowd back home. The occasion called for twin rejoice as not only had Chachi ji's life been saved, but Krishan had also won the election by a safe margin.

'I am proud of you son,' Krishan Singh hugged him tightly. Madhur also wrapped his arms around the duo. Everyone blessed Raghav on seeing a hale and hearty Chachi ji.

One day, while Raghav was sitting next to Chachi ji on her bed she said, 'What will you do after metric, Raghav?'

'Graduation. And then a good job.' he replied.

'Why don't you join your Chacha ji?'

'But Chachi, you know I am too simple and shy to play this role well,' he objected. 'And besides I have no interest in politics.'

'You want to do something for the people...for the

country...don't you?' asked Chachi ji.

'But I can keep doing this even while I am doing a job,' he said.

'You can, but only in a very small way. If you want to bring about larger good, this is the path son,' she said.

'But I hate the rallies, the crowds, the shouting and the rhetoric filled speeches. They are not for me,' said Raghav.

'You will get used to the rallies and crowds, and you need not do what you think is not right,' she said, comfortingly.

Chachi ji was not one to give in easily. She had an intuition that Raghav was meant to become a great politician and finally convinced him to join the Indian National Front.

♦

He was jerked back to the present as the car came to a halt outside the Chief Minister's office.

Uncle Krishan Singh had called him over for lunch. Raghav entered the office to find him and Madhur waiting for him. Krishan smiled at him and gently ran his hand over Raghav's head, bestowing his blessings, as he bent to touch his feet. Madhur smiled at his brother and hugged him.

'This day harbingers a long period of happiness for our family. Our state's collection for party fund being the highest in the country, the party High-Command has ensured our positions for the next election,' Krishan apprised Raghav.

'This was bound to happen, Babu ji! This state and our people have never before witnessed as dynamic a leadership as yours. It's our state that has contributed the maximum seats to the National Front,' said Madhur.

'That is great news, Chacha ji! I am also trying my best to add to your laurels by continuously improving the work of my department,' Raghav said.

'Yes, I know.' Krishan smiled, pressing the bell button to summon the attendants.

Soon a sumptuous lunch was laid out for them on the dining table in one corner of the spacious Chief Minister's office. Madhur waved the attendants to vacate.

'You said, you wanted to discuss something Chacha ji', said Raghav as he passed the bread basket to Madhur.

'Yes, son. You remember, you asked for permission to fill 70,000 vacancies for primary school teachers?' asked Krishan.

'Of course, Chacha ji! It is the single most critical deterrent that keeps our system from performing well. There is a huge deficit of teachers,' replied Raghav.

'Well, you now have a reason to be delighted. I have obtained the necessary funds allocation from the centre to go ahead with the recruitments,' said Krishan.

'Really?' Raghav could not conceal his excitement and happiness, 'Today is an unusually auspicious day, I have to say.'

'By the way, many higher ups in the party are not too pleased with your style of working,' said Madhur. 'But we know you shall always act in the best interest of our family and the party. That is why Babu ji has given you a free hand. This process is going to contribute another 3,500 crore to the party fund, which will silence all opposition against us within the party.'

'Sorry, I did not get you brother... Where is such a large amount of money going to come from?' Raghav stopped chewing and looked at Madhur and then at Chacha ji.

'Don't talk like a kid dear! Now, if we are going to give 25,000 rupees per month to a teacher, are we not going to take at least a five-lakh capitation from him? Even after deducting say 10 per cent departmental expenses, I am sure we will accrue a minimum of Rupees 3,000 crore. Once we contribute this huge amount to the party fund, our position in the party is going to be similar to Salman Khan's in Bollywood,' said Madhur.

'But there are so many other ministries, brother... You may extract as much as you wish from them. I have sweated and bled for this one and I will not let it be auctioned...' warned Raghav.

'Brother, be wise. In Rome, you have to do what the Romans do. This is not our wish but the High-Command's order. Do you think this news about recruitments will not reach them? We may be the kings of our state, but there are Big Daddies in the centre to whom we are answerable,' replied Madhur.

'I don't care! I will not let this happen till I am in charge. I am amazed, what kind of a person this High-Command is? Such an honest face in public, but behind the curtain, always conspiring to suck in more and more money like a turbine, making the country hollow. Remember, both of us didn't like him in the first place when we met him as children. Then what happened? Why do we have to succumb to his every rotten wish?'

'Try to understand Raghav, they will not only take away the ministry from you but also oust you from the party,' Madhur tried to convince him, with fervor in his voice.

Raghav had seen Madhur slowly transform from the innocent cousin he spent his childhood with, to a shrewd politician...an ambitious one, who would not have to think twice to select between relations and position.

He knew Chacha ji was not so cold and calculative.

'Do what you think is right. I will not run this marketplace in my ministry. Chacha ji, please put some sense into Madhur.'

'Don't worry, son. I will take care of everything,' Chacha ji said comfortingly. Raghav's temper melted, seeing the affectionate smile on Chacha ji's face.

Next day, as Raghav reached his office after his routine school visits, he saw a crowd of people gathered at the entrance. As he stepped out of his car, he was flocked by reporters asking, 'Mr Raghav, why was the education ministry taken away from you? Would you like to tell us about it?'

Aditya Meets the Mayor
Varanasi, 2014

'What? Sabhasad? Are you mad?' shouted Aditya's dad as they were sitting in the drawing room over a family meeting.

'Yes. What's wrong with contesting for Sabhasad? The Corporator of the Municipal Corporation is the lowest step of the ladder and I don't want to take any shortcuts,' replied Aditya.

'But son, I can easily get you ticket for MLA from one of the top four parties. You are not going to contest for this "leader of the sweepers" post. It's below our status. What will people say?'

'Don't worry, Papa. As I have already assured you, I won't let the business suffer. Let me get some experience at the lower level first, then maybe some time in the future, I may be able to do justice to the MLA post.'

'Aditya, you are not able to give us time even now! You will be totally befuddled, don't do it… I am telling you,' jabbered Prachi desperately. Aditya had recently noticed this something very strange about Prachi. There seemed to be a little black dark patch on the front side of her tongue. Whatever she said, used to come true of late. 'Kali zabaan', probably this was what it meant. 'No…don't say that, at least think before you speak!' he screamed in his head.

Aditya turned to his mother for support, being cornered by the other two members in the family. One vote in his favour and they would be even. That was assuming his wish also counted.

'I am worried about your safety son, it's dirty out there.' His hopes came crashing down. The meeting ended without a conclusion and with perturbed minds.

'Radhe Radhe! Why do you want to do this beta?' asked Tau ji, his father's elder brother, who used to come down from their native place, Mathura, whenever there was a deadlock. He was a religious man who wore a rare sixteen-carpelled Rudraksha garland and a chandan tika on his forehead. He was kind and genial by nature, that's why everybody loved him, but firm and uncompromising on fundamental values. He was the final authority and everybody respected his decision.

'Tau ji, you know I am running three NGOs since last four years that focus on primary education, hygiene and beggar rehabilitation. The government machinery almost always makes things difficult for us at every step. I feel that what I am doing through the NGOs is only like setting an example. I want to bring about a bigger and perceivable change,' Aditya explained.

'But for that you can scale up your operations in the NGOs, can't you? What is the need to step into the dirty political arena?' asked Tau ji.

'The Municipal Corporation has immense resources at its disposal. Hundreds of crore of annual budgets! I want to see for myself, where that money goes. Was this money being spent the right way, our city would not be in the despicable condition it is! The roads have been dug up all around, there are stray animals on the streets and garbage is overflowing from the storage sheds.'

'You can discuss that with the existing Corporators, or the Mayor...'

'You know me, Tau ji, I work towards my dreams. I know that without stepping into this so called "dirty arena", there's no way I can make a real difference.'

'So it's like you want to die to know what it feels like... isn't that foolish?' the old man asked.

There was no reply from Aditya. When he stopped arguing, everyone knew there was no point discussing further as he had made up his mind.

After a while he spoke, 'No it's not foolish Tau ji. I will tell you what influenced my decision.

'One day, I reached office a bit early and it was only by chance that I noticed Dinesh, my office peon, crying. He was literally sobbing as he dusted the window pane next to my table. Dinesh is just 20-years-old and a very cheerful boy. He tried to regain normalcy quickly, but could not.

'What happened, Dinesh?' I asked.

'My mother, Bhaiya, I don't think she will make it. The doctors say her head injury is bad. Her backbone is also fractured. She is in coma,' he broke down.

'Then, what are you doing here? You should not have come, you should be with her.'

'I need some advance for her treatment, Bhaiya. I will return every penny, I swear,' said Dinesh.

'Don't worry about it, I am sure you will. Go get the voucher from Gupta ji, I will sign it. Go rush.

'Something struck me and I felt a sudden surge of anger. 'Wait for a moment... What happened? How did she get hurt so badly? Did your father hit her again?

I was almost seething inside at how someone could be so inhuman. I knew Dinesh worked here to support his family while pursuing graduation simultaneously. His alcoholic father was the sorrow of their family. However, I was not prepared for what I was about to hear.

'No, Bhaiya. She was returning from the temple, when two bulls fighting nearby gradually moved towards her, their horns locked. She tried to get out of their path by taking a longer, deviated route. But it was too late. One of them charged at her and threw her up with its horns. Had it not been for the nearby flower vendors, who rushed there with lathis, she would have been trampled to death there itself.' He started sobbing uncontrollably again.

'Go...take good care of her,' I said, and got back to work. It was a very busy day as our most important foreign buyer was going to audit us later that day.

'This thought kept haunting me... What kind of conditions are we living in? This could have happened to me too, or my mother or anybody else in my family. What is the value of human life here? Are stray animals going to decide whether we can walk back home safely or get killed? Why doesn't our administration do something about it? Even the Mohenjo-daro and Harappan people wouldn't have had animals freely loitering around, adorning their streets with dung... But why am I so tensed? It is not the first time I have heard about something like this. Such incidents are frequently there in the newspapers... Someone keeps getting victimized every other day—an infant in the slums torn apart by street dogs, or a motorcyclist facing a fatal accident trying to deflect his path to save a pig merrily walking across the road, or a child jumping off the roof to save himself from a pack of monkeys. Probably, my reason for worry is that, today, it happened to someone I know. Someone whose pain I could feel. What should I do? What can I do? If no one could do anything about it till now, should the insignificant-me even try to make a fuss about it? When people of this country have already accepted it as their destiny to endure this iota of uncertainty as a part of their life, why am I getting all flared up? I slept thinking about it...

'Next morning, as soon as I reached office, I asked our NGO's co-ordinator to take an appointment with the Mayor. He told me it wouldn't be needed as the Mayor had a two-hour "Janta Darbar" every Tuesday. "Wonderful!" I thought because I wanted to meet him as a common man and not as an industrialist.

'The Mayor was sitting behind a table, wearing a serious and authoritative expression. He was a bald and stocky man with a round face and smooth skin. About 20 chairs were placed in front of him, on which some people sat shivering in anticipation of their turn. They shivered not from fear, but from the chilled ambience created by the excessive air-conditioning in the Darbar. The Mayor was however comfortable, thanks to the high-neck shervani suit he wore. One could not help notice the thick gold rings, studded with dice-sized gemstones on four of his fingers. Three people stood on his side handing him files and papers.

'"Namaskar," I said, and folded my hands. He nodded his head in acknowledgement. I handed him my visiting card denoting myself as the President of the NGO "Umeed—hopes, smiles and more".

'Dwivedi ji! I am here to seek your help. Someone is fighting for life as she was attacked by a stray bull,' I said.

'Someone? Who is she?'

'My friend's mother.'

'Help them get the lady admitted in the ICU of the Harris Hospital,' he told one of his assistants and signalled to the next person in the second row to speak about his problem.

'But she is already admitted. This is not what I came for...'

'What is it then?' he interrupted with a hint of unrest in his voice.

'I want to know what is being done by the Municipal Corporation to check this problem.'

'Which problem?' he asked.

'Holy smokes! It did not seem to be in his list of cognizable problems the Municipal Corporation was supposed to deal with.

'The stray animals on the roads! They are responsible for a number of casualties, spread of diseases, and pose sanitation and hygiene issues.'

'Look young man, this is the "Janta Darbar", not a discussion forum. There are others waiting with serious problems. Meet the Health Inspector of your area or the Zonal Health Officer. They will tell you everything.'

'Just two minutes, Sir! I will not take much time. You are the head of the Municipal Corporation, you can answer this best. The inspectors will just blame lack of resources. Your cabinet allocates resources to them. I have not seen any animal-catching squad at work in my locality for a long time. The only sounds of animals being caught, I hear, is the screeching of the pigs early in the morning, who are being mercilessly pinned down and tied for being butchered later by a certain group of people who breed them on the streets. And they are allowed to do so freely! So, is it really a concern? Does your cabinet see it as a major problem? Do you have any strategy or methodology to control it? Do we have a spay and neuter programme to stop them from multiplying?'

The Mayor shook his head in disbelief, a sarcastic smile on his face. He kept silent for a good ten seconds, contemplating whether he really needed to answer this. Finally, he spoke.

'It is easier said than done. The limited number of people we have in the animal-catching squad cannot collect even 10 per cent of the stray animals, even if they work overtime. Besides we have more serious problems to focus on, to run this city.' He looked at me as if he had done me a favour by answering and not having me thrown out instead. It was clear it was the end of discussion from his side and he wanted me to leave.

'But what about the dying lady, Dwivedi ji?'

One of his assistants came and stood near me, signalling they wanted me to leave and not disturb the proceedings of the 'Janta Darbar' any further.

'What about it? What does one say when a man on the road is struck by lightning? It's an accident. It was her misfortune to be there at the wrong time and the wrong place,' he said returning to his work. 'And if you are so concerned, then probably your NGO can establish a shelter home for stray animals. Do something to help us, don't just grumble.'

'I was escorted outside by his assistant, who assured me that Dwivedi ji was the finest Mayor the city had had since Independence and if I wrote to him, he would certainly take care of this petty problem, given sufficient time to think and plan at ease.

'It has been eight months since I wrote to them. I also met the health officers and several Corporators. There was a team of just nine employees in the animal-catching squad. They caught a few animals once in a while and would take them to the outskirts of the city and leave them there, since there was no shelter home or any spay and neuter programme to stop them from reproducing. How could money be spent to make animals sterile when there were not even enough antibiotics for humans in the hospitals?

'Dinesh's mother died recently, leaving him under massive debt incurred during her treatment.

'I keep wondering what they do with all the money. How much of it really reaches the ground? The more I thought about it, the better I understood it. It is the quality of people constituting the governance, their intention and capability that are responsible for the state our country is in. Everything is possible, just the will is lacking. At least I could make a start, play my part rather than depending on others and pushing them from outside to do it.

'Now tell me Tau ji, do you really think it is stupid of me? If I can manage the business, my NGOs and pursue my hobbies, I can also manage the ward no. 29 of my city,' said Aditya.

His Uncle loved him very much. He knew Aditya's capabilities and the high emotional quotient that made him an achiever in whatever he did. He was not the most successful businessman in his trade, but he was doing fairly well. God destines glory and failure to people in different ways.

'What are your chances of winning?' asked the old man.

'Should be decent, considering that my stiffest competition will come from the current Corporator Pappu Shukla. He is a graduation dropout, has four criminal cases, lives on rental income from the three buildings he inherited and has hardly done anything for the ward in his last two terms.'

'Then why did he win the last election again?' asked Tau ji.

'Because he spends a lot of time amongst the people, he knows their weaknesses and how to please them. Also, he is an Indian National Front candidate. Pappu Shukla is a true Khalifa of the locality—omniscient, omnipresent and omnivorous. Omnivorous as he can eat everything, from the Halal at Imran Bhai's Iftaar party to the road repair funds...from the bhaang discreetly sold around the nukkad, to the money the roadside food hawkers give him as bribe for immunity from municipal and health checks. This pan masala chewing creature is a street-smart nose-poker, whom you would find at all occasions, whether it is some scandal, theft, fight or cremation. He is always there. Always smiling and genial, but equally capable of delivering ear-rending abuses, he knows where and how to change his stance. He knows how to take credit from situations and how to cleverly detach himself, deriving the best for himself, his image and his vote bank. He is so fake, I can't stand him for a minute! His presence makes me sick and angry. How can we have such people as our representatives?'

'So what's your strategy then? I am sure you would not have met even a tenth of those families, let alone knowing them inside out,' said Tau ji.

'Not thought much about it yet. But if knowing every family was all that mattered, then the postmen would have been the most potent candidates!' he chuckled.

'Radhe Radhe!' said Tau ji, smiling.

Once Tau ji bestowed his blessings, the family had no option but to accept Aditya as their official Corporator candidate with unconditional support. It was only a coincidence that Mallika Sherawat danced to the latest superhit number '...ke Razia gundon mein phans gayi' on the television screen right behind them in the living room.

Varun and the JPC
New Delhi, 2014

Now, it was Kalpvruksh's turn to share their observations and suggestions on the Judicial Standards and Accountability Bill. 'Best of luck!' said Radhika, as she smiled at Varun. He trotted up to the podium, cleared his throat and smiled at the audience as he greeted them, his neck rotating a quick 150-degree span that covered the audience from one corner to the other.

'Three million pending cases which will take 466 years to be heard; a ratio of 15 judges per million against a minimum international requirement of 50; countless poor, innocent people rotting in jails as their families cannot afford to pay for their files to be brought up; an equal number of guilty out in the open as justice can be indefinitely kept in abeyance with minor tips; innumerable construction and development sites lying dead due to unresolved legal disputes; and the list of sufferings is endless.... This is the state of justice in our country. If justice delayed is justice denied, then I am sorry to say that we have denied justice to crores of our citizens. When a judge comes to his desk he has the burden of thousands of cases lying unattended. With an average time of five minutes per hearing, how can we expect quality judgements?' Varun's presentation started on a totally different note.

'Please keep it to the point,' intervened the convener. 'We are here to discuss the Judicial Accountability Bill.'

'That's my point, Sir! Why are we adding another department to an already sick system? When our courts are not able to handle only a quarter of our work, should we not first make sure that this overburden gets reduced, so that the quality of justice can be restored? If this bill becomes a law, there will be so many complaints against the judges, both true and frivolous. A number of ad hoc committees will have to be constituted to resolve them. With this, we will only be adding another unmanageable task to our already ailing system. Kalpvruksh has been running from pillar to post to find out what stops the Law Ministry from creating new posts against the shortfall of judges in our system and from ensuring that none of the existing posts remain vacant. At least 45,000 judges should be appointed immediately. Today, our Union Law Minister Mr Brijmohan Gupta and senior IAS members are here. I want to ask you, Sir, why during the last so many years of your governance, have you not taken any steps towards this?'

The audience was stunned. No one expected a young man to directly confront the Union Minister with such a straight question.

The convener interrupted again, 'You are spoiling the decorum, young man. Kindly step down, others are waiting to share their views. We can't have this off-the-topic discussion now.'

'No, I will answer that,' Minister Gupta retorted. 'Running the government is not like writing an enthusiastic article for a campus magazine, young man, or giving a humanities presentation, or having a heated drawing room discussion on how to make things better. It is a very complicated set of calculated decisions based on a lot of internal and external considerations. Moreover, appointing three times the existing count of judges is not something one can do overnight.'

'But, Sir, who asked for overnight results? Your government has been in power for years,' said Varun.

'We have appointed around 2,500 new judges in our tenure so far. Appointing a judge is not just about adding the burden of his salary to the exchequer. Each judge has to be provided facilities, including a cabin, back-office staff, front-office attendants and security. If each building accommodates, say 30 judges, from where would we get 1,500 buildings for 45,000 new judges at once? And what kind of expenditure would that involve, do you have any idea? Every ministry has a budget to adhere to,' said Gupta.

'Sir, it is not necessary to run courts in the kind of aristocratic set-ups we have. It could be done in a simple cabin with decent infrastructure. Besides, once the load on each court is reduced and they are run in an organized way with proper appointments and time slots, they won't be crowded like a fish market, as they are now. We could use rented properties too.'

'There you go, talking like an over-enthusiastic teenager. We are planning to increase the count by 1,000 every year, which itself is a very ambitious plan. None of the earlier governments have done that,' said the Minister.

'With that speed it is quite improbable that the poor people of our country will get justice even in the next hundred years. Because while it would take 35 years for you to reach the international average, the population too would have increased and this figure will again fall short, grossly,' Varun said.

'That will be all, young man. Do you have any suggestions

about the bill at hand?' asked the convener.

'Sir, but my question is still unanswered. You can choose to snub my question but you can't say no to these people waiting outside the Parliament house to listen to your answer?' Varun pressed a button on the laptop and a picture of six villagers in the waiting area with Vinti and Shyam appeared on the large screen for presentations. They had wrinkled and sunken faces, shadowed with utter hopelessness. They held up and waved the small boards they were carrying, facing the camera that Shyam pointed towards them. The boards said: '**Give us death or justice**,' and '**Six murders—thirteen years: No justice**'.

'This is outrageous! The proceedings of this meeting are confidential and not allowed to be covered,' cried one of the Ministers sitting next to Brijmohan.

'I am not covering the proceedings. I am merely trying to connect you to a few victims, who would never make it to this place. These people come from Bisramau village in Bihar. When they refused to sell their land to the Pradhan's son-in-law, their entire family including their two sons, daughter-in-laws and their grandchildren were forcefully filled in a tractor and carried to some unknown place. Six days later their bodies were found, brutally molested and hacked to pieces without any clothes on them, just a few meters from the Pradhan's son-in-law's house. After that, almost all villagers whose lands fell on the land bank being assembled by the Pradhan's son-in-law, migrated, selling their lands at throw away prices. The Pradhan's son-in-law was arrested but got bail the next day. He is now one of the biggest developers in Patna. The file still lays buried deep in the Darbhanga courts, while these people await justice,' said Varun.

'This is sheer waste of our time. First of all, this is not

the platform for such a discussion, which you don't seem to understand. Secondly, how would having more judges have helped this situation?' said Raju Gowda, a member of the Bhartiya Janhit Party from the opposition and a member of the JPC.

'If there were not tens of thousands of files in the court, under which their files are buried, justice could not have been denied to them even after thirteen years. Maybe it is the politicians' way to spend more time out of jail too? Maybe you intentionally keep the judicial system crippled, just like the education system. If the judiciary becomes effective, maybe most of the current breed of politicians will find themselves behind bars,' screamed Varun.

Radhika's mouth was wide open in disbelief and fear. This was not planned! No one spoke to an auditorium full of Ministers and IAS officers like that. No one, except of course, the legendary Varun 'Panga' Pandey!

By now, the marshals signalled by Gupta were already dragging Varun off-stage.

'I did not expect this kind of a hollow reply from the people at the apex. This is probably the biggest problem our country is facing. Everything else will fall into place if speedy justice comes within the reach of the common man,' Varun's voice faded as the marshals pulled him out of the auditorium.

Radhika rushed behind him, but only to see Varun being made to sit in a white Ambassador, sandwiched between the two marshals, which drove off promptly.

She was joined by Shyam and Vinti in the waiting area. They called friends and relatives frantically but no one had any idea what to do in this situation or where he could have been taken. They tried to get back into the Parliament House but they were denied entry. They visited the police stations in the vicinity, but he was not there. It was an unprecedented situation. It was not usual for a person to be arrested for disrupting the proceedings, insulting and throwing accusations at the JPC in a public forum. Finally, they decided to go back to the Kalpvruksh office to plan their strategy ahead.

They were surprised to find Varun waiting for them there. 'How did you get here, at least you should have called us!' Radhika cried. She was both relieved and angry at the same time.

'They just dropped me here. They interrogated me for a long time, trying to squeeze out any hints of a political or anti-government connection. When they found out that I was merely an activist and could do nothing more than scream in vain, they let me go,' Varun sounded depressed and shaken. 'I don't know whether there is any point in continuing to do what I do.'

Radhika sat beside him and placed her hand comfortingly over Varun's. It was an involuntary reaction to his dreary state. She had never seen him so dejected. But it was not the only thing that had happened for the first time. She had touched Varun for the first time and it did feel special. She did not know if he felt anything at her touch, but she was electrified for a few microseconds, something she had not experienced before. 'Why did you get so aggressive?' she asked softly.

'I could not stand their indifference.'

'Forget it! It was only a bad day. You have a long day ahead tomorrow and also have to fly back in the evening,' said Shyam.

'No. I will not go back to the USA now…not until we have a better set of people to listen to us,' Varun replied with an expression of deadly determination.

Salman Quits his Job
Mumbai, 2014

As Salman was on his way to Mahi's home next afternoon, he was trying to figure out why he had erupted so brashly against the MLA candidate, Ganesh Vidyarthi, the previous day. The reaction had been almost impulsive. He had considered not being so straightforward but couldn't hold back his pent-up anger against the system. The miserable state of things around him had been making him more and more restless. He looked at his watch. It was 5 pm. Mahi would have reached back home. She had not called him since yesterday and by this time she must be really mad at him.

He decided to scrap these thoughts as he barely had any time left to rehearse how he would present himself in front of Mahi's family. He stopped at a Haldiram's outlet on the way to pick up a box of jalebis, her father's favourite. His father-in-law-to-be was a retired Colonel, which was one of the reasons he was prompted to be more cautious. Not that he was scared, but he had seen in a number of movies how army men reacted to their daughter's love. He also took a bunch of flowers for her mother and the latest album by Nickelback for her little brother.

He was glad he had put his fears and apprehensions behind

to take things ahead in his relationship with Mahi. He could barely conceal the smile on his face as he thought how happy she would be to find him at her door. Yes, it would be a bit of a shock and probably she could have prepared her family better for this occasion, had he informed her in advance. Watching the expression on her face was any day a worthy trade-off against the comfort of a pre-informed introduction, he thought.

He pulled up at the row house next to Chintel's play school. He had never had the chance to drop her home. It would be too risky, both of them had thought. However, she had explained the location clearly and it was easy to find, being just around the circle at a prominent spot. There seemed to be quite a few cars parked outside her house. 'Shit!' he thought to himself, 'Seems like there is some kind of a get-together. I can't possibly bang into an unknown family surrounded by their friends and relatives and say, "Namaste! I am your daughter's suitor. Allow me a seat and I will explain..."' As he sat there in his car thinking, another car pulled up and a man and his wife rushed inside the house. There was something unusual in their manner, which made him curious. He got down from his car and walked to the main gate, which had a small door that was open. He mustered his courage and stepped in.

He saw around 30–40 people gathered in the portico. Some of the elderly ones were sitting on chairs, some were standing and talking amongst themselves in a hushed voice. The mourning sounds coming from inside the house signified there had possibly been a death in the house. He could not wait to reach inside and comfort Mahi. He knew just the sight of him would give her the much-needed strength.

As he rushed inside the house, he saw a body placed on the floor, wrapped in white cloth. He approached closer and saw the face. The world seemed to spin around him. It was Mahi! He felt his legs give way. He heaved himself, his back to the wall. He could not believe god had been so merciless, taking away the only person he could call his own. She was everything to him. She was the one person he loved more than himself. His existence did not seem to make sense any more. He could not remember crying ever, after he lost his father. Every cell in his body sobbed. Yet, his eyes were dry. The moments spent with Mahi started passing before his eyes in a kaleidoscope of memories.

A gentle touch on his shoulder brought him back. 'Who are you son?' asked a firmly built man in his fifties, with upturned moustaches, probably Mahi's father or her Uncle.

'Salman, Mahi's friend.'

He cursed god at the circumstances and the manner of his introduction. This was not how it was meant to be. It was all wrong.

'How did this happen Uncle?' he asked in a trembling voice.

'Her scooty was hit from behind by a mini truck on the highway. They didn't even stop. Had she been brought to the hospital in time, she could have been saved,' the old man replied.

Salman wanted to hug her and tell her there and then, in front of everyone, how much he loved her. He would rather accompany her to the other world. He would have given anything to just touch her face once, to sit next to her body right now and let his tears flow. But he couldn't do anything like that. God did not find him deserving enough to be given this opportunity. To her family, he was a stranger. He could not bear staying there any longer. He came out and started driving back.

He did not even get a chance to tell her he would have talked to her parents today. She had gone from this world thinking that the man she had loved did not have the guts to own up his love for her. And he would have to live with this guilt forever.

His eyes welled up. As tears trickled down his cheeks and moistened them, his mind took him back to that day when Mahi came to his room and he had felt her wet cheeks pressing softly against his. He had made her cry so many times thereafter, possibly every time he asked her not to be 'emotionally dependent' on him. And now it was his turn to cry…ever after.

He did not remember when he reached home and slept. He was in a daze.

The next morning he woke up late. He saw the clock on the wall and it was well past his time for office. But he was in no hurry. After losing Mahi he had lost interest in materialistic pursuits. He wanted to give back in a bigger and better way, be the change he wanted to see. He had decided to quit his job and become the man he had asked the people of his chawl to find…

Raghav Quits Indian National Front
Lucknow, 2014

Raghav had not expected Chacha ji to do this…to side with Madhur in throwing him out of the Education Ministry. 'He had assured to take care of everything! Just like he took care of my thing with Neha,' he reminisced sourly. Neha, the only name in the world that reminded him that he had other things in his life, he cared about, apart from his work. The only one he would do anything for and yet could do nothing for. His thoughts took him down memory lane to his college days.

'Can I borrow your notes for a day please?'

Raghav turned around to find a girl, with sharply chiselled features, standing behind his desk. She was wearing a blue and white, georgette salwar-suit with a high neck. She wore no make-up. Her straight, silky black hair dropped way below her shoulders. She was tall, around five feet nine inches, and looked elegant despite her simplicity. She seemed to be quite shy and was blushing, making it quite obvious that she had mustered a lot of courage to approach a stranger for notes.

He smiled back at her and asked, 'Are you sure? I am not the best person to copy notes from.'

'Maybe! But you are the only one I felt I could speak to. I

have missed a fortnight of lectures as I have joined the college today only,' she said, genuinely worried.

'Well, I don't know you, but still I will give you my notes. It is not so easy to trust a stranger.'

'You can count on me,' she said softly.

'Thanks. They were really good!' she said, as she returned his notes the next day. She was dusky, her glowing skin and her expressions emanating juvenile innocence made her look extremely beautiful and attractive. She had the most perfect features amongst the girls in the college. She wore a nose-ring that made her look like Goddess Parvati. Raghav's eyes followed her as she walked back a few rows to take a seat with some other girls. He wondered why he had failed to notice this yesterday. Love grows on you...

It struck him that he was attracted to this girl. For the first time, a girl had induced these feelings inside an otherwise focused Raghav. After joining the Indian National Front, he had made it his life's aim to become an MLA and bring about some good to the ailing masses. He would drive from the University to the party office at Hamirpur, after college every day and go for public contact along with his team.

He did not want to get distracted, but every time he saw this girl, his heart skipped a beat. It had been a week since she had returned his notes and they would only exchange a casual smile or greeting in college. He was infatuated with her. He could not sleep the way he used to. A strange restlessness made him toss and turn in his bed all night.

'Excuse me. Can I have a word in private with Neha?' he requested her friend, Drishti, as he joined them at a table in the college canteen. Drishti gave Neha a confused look before obliging the stranger and walked away.

'Do you have a boyfriend?' he asked.

'No,' she blushed.

'I am a shy person, just like you Neha, so it has taken me a lot of courage to come up to you and say this. I would like to take that unoccupied place in your life and I assure you, I will be good,' said Raghav.

'We don't have boyfriends in our culture. Besides, I have been able to come to college after convincing my family a lot. So, thanks, but no!' she said politely yet firmly.

After that day, Raghav felt Neha had started avoiding him. She would try not to make eye contact and if they seldom did, her greeting was more perfunctory than ever. It was clear his love was unilateral.

One day Chachi ji saw him lost in deep thought and asked him if something was bothering him. Chachi ji listened to the entire story and insisted on meeting Neha. After a lot of deliberation, she assured Raghav that she would only watch the girl from a distance and return silently to Hamirpur. When she had accompanied him to the college, he did not even have to tell her who the girl was and she had charged straight at Neha as soon as they had entered the canteen—typical zamindarni style. 'What is the problem with my son, young girl? He is tall, handsome, intelligent, rich and above all, has a golden heart! Complete husband material! Let me assure you, you will never find a better person. If I were in your place, I would have married him without wasting any time.'

Raghav cursed himself for having confided in Chachi ji, and then succumbing to her insistence of having a look at the girl.

'Please, Chachi ji! From where did this marriage thing come in between? I should never have told you about this!' Raghav was embarrassed beyond imagination. Not only would Neha hate him, but he would also become the laughing stock of the college. He could see Neha's bewildered expression at the sudden assault by Chachi ji.

'Promise me, you will bring my son out of the blues. I am advising you as a woman... He will be a big man one day and you will be proud to be a part of his life...' Chachi ji kept snarling as Raghav pulled her out of the canteen, holding her hand. The damage had been done, thanks to the 'motherly love' Chachi ji had just showered upon him, publicly.

'I have to end this respectfully and with dignity,' he promised himself as he went to sleep that night.

The next day, he walked up to the table where she was sitting with Drishti. Drishti got up to leave. 'Don't bother!' he told her. 'Everyone knows about it anyway...'

'I am sorry, Neha. Honestly, I did not know she would do this.... I did not want any of this to happen. I promise, I will never bother you again,' he said and began to walk away.

'Wait!' He heard a feeble voice and turned back. 'Now that you are sure you have dropped the idea of being my boyfriend, never bothering me again as you just said, I think it's safe to be friends with you. But just that! Nothing more.' Raghav couldn't understand if it was merely a display of sympathy or to return the favour of borrowing his notes, but he was more than happy to accept the offer.

Neha and Raghav were similar personalities. They were both introverts to a certain extent, sober and righteous. They made good friends. Some say opposites attract, while some say that like-minded people get along better. There is no universal rule. God decides who is meant to be with whom and people adjust, even in the most adverse situations. After all, he did not make any two beings entirely identical.

One day, as they shared their family details, they discovered that their families—the Chandels and the Yadavs—were foes, with swords drawn towards each other. Not only was the rivalry political but there was a personal animosity between Krishan Singh and Vishesh Yadav, Neha's father, who would happily behead each other, given the opportunity.

The bond of friendship, however, proved stronger and they decided not to continue the tradition of rivalry and hatred through their generation. Another thing which this revelation did was that it reinforced their belief that there would be no scope for anything other than friendship between them, as it would lead to outright bloodshed between the two families. Love always finds a reason…to hold on…

'What happened? Why do you look so worried? Is everything all right?' Neha asked Raghav as he disconnected the mobile call.

'Chachi ji… I have to rush!' He hurried towards his SUV as Neha followed him.

'She will be all right. Can I come with you? I kind of feel attached to her.' They had talked a lot about Chachi ji as she was the only person Raghav was really attached to. He had told her so many incidents about his life in the haveli with Chachi ji and how she had been his friend and guardian all along. Neha, despite the only one dramatic encounter with her, felt like she knew her for years. Her character seemed to emit vibes of affection and care.

'But what if anybody finds out that you are from the Yadavs? It would not be safe.' He jumped into the driving seat.

'How would they find out?' asked Neha as she quickly took the other front seat. Raghav had no time to argue. He was lost and reticent during the drive and did not speak a word. They reached the haveli. The crowd outside told Raghav that his worst fears had probably come true.

'You told us she was completely well and would have a long life. It has been only six years!' Madhur was shouting at Dr Hemang Juneja, the endocrinologist, who had been summoned from Sadafal Trust Hospital, Delhi.

Chachi ji was lying on the bed, completely covered with a white sheet. Krishan Singh was sitting next to her, serenely. Slabs of ice were being arranged on the floor nearby to place her body. Raghav felt dizzy and collapsed into a chair beside her bed. He uncovered her face and looked at her as his tears flowed freely. He had lost the only person he truly loved, his only true kin, and also the only person who truly loved him. He was on his own in this world now...

Madhur charged towards Raghav as soon as he saw him. 'Bhai, didn't you assure us that mother was completely well. We sent her to the best hospital, did everything you told us to do, spent eight lakhs on her treatment. For what? Can't you do anything properly?'

Raghav was in a shock and in no mental frame to respond to Madhur's accusation. 'I am sorry, Bhai. I did my best,' was all he could manage to say.

Their driver, Bhola, who had accompanied them to the hospital, had been watching this and was seething with anger at Madhur's sudden display of love for his mother and at the humiliation he was subjecting Raghav to.

He walked up to Raghav and said with folded hands, 'I can't keep quiet anymore, son. I have to tell them the truth.'

'No, Bhola Dada! You cannot. You are under oath,' said Raghav.

'What is this drama?' shouted Madhur. 'What are you hiding from us? Had you told us, we would have taken care of it. I'm her son, damn it! I could have done anything for her. We trusted you completely and you played with her life.'

'If you are such a good son, Mr Madhur, you should have accompanied your mother to Delhi for treatment, or at least visited her once,' said Dr Juneja. He walked up to Raghav and put a hand on his shoulder. 'He was alone. What he did for his aunt, not even one in a thousand would do for their real parents.'

Without warning, Dr Juneja pulled up Raghav's kurta, exposing a six inch operation scar on his stomach. Before Raghav could respond, he pointed towards it and said, 'This young man donated his kidney so that Mrs Singh could live through these six years. She would not have lived a week but for his kidney. Tell me who amongst you would have had the courage to give their kidney to your aunt at the age of nineteen? It is because of people like him that there is love and humanity in this world today!' He patted Raghav on the back and before leaving whispered in his ears, 'Have courage, Raghav. No one can live forever. She lived a happy life and will always bless you from the heavens above.'

Neha felt a lump in her throat and could not control her tears. She knew Raghav was a good human being, but she had never expected anyone to be so brave and loving. She stayed with the family as the funeral rites and ceremonies were performed over the next three days. Luckily, no one recognized her. Her excuse to her family was that she was off to a friend's sister's wedding.

'I have changed my mind Raghav,' she said as they drove back to college the next day.

'About what?' he asked.

'Us!' she said.

'What happened?' Raghav asked in disbelief.

'As Chachi ji had said, you are going to become a big man one day and I don't want to regret that I missed the chance to be a part of your life.' She put her hand tenderly over his hand on the gear. Once again, Raghav was no longer alone in this world.

'But what about our families, Neha? It's too risky, I love you too much to put you through this risk.'

'If a man can love the woman to whom he gave his kidney so much, tell me how much he would love the woman to whom he gives his heart! I have no fears now,' Neha chuckled. Love makes you fearless, daring and maybe foolhardy too. It's true!

'What? That good-for-nothing boy Raghav? Not only is he worthless, you should have at least thought about our family esteem.' Neha's father scolded her. She respected her father too much to argue with him. 'Mark my words, he is a loser and will never make a successful politician.'

Her father, Vishesh Yadav was a prominent leader of the Bhartiya Janhit Party, the party in opposition. He was a staunch opponent of inter-caste marriages. He had committed Neha's marriage to his friend Arunesh Yadav's son, Vishal. One day he telephoned Krishan Singh and blamed him for secretly supporting what was going on between their children. Krishan Singh reprimanded him with furious rage, shocked at the allegation.

'So, this is why you refused to marry Brijesh Singh's daughter? We could have doubled our strength with this alliance. You told me you wanted to finish college first... You lied to me?' Krishan said in a firm voice to Raghav as he stood near the sofa in the drawing room. He never raised his voice or shouted in anger. His voice just became stern and it was extremely intimidating.

Don't you care about our family's reputation, brother?

Yadavs—our eternal enemies? Couldn't you find any other girl in the world?' shouted Madhur, standing next to him. Sometimes Raghav wondered why Chacha ji allowed him to be the brat that he was, shouting and behaving rashly in front of his father.

'I can wait, Chacha ji. But I can't part with Neha now,' Raghav said with his head bowed down.

'Vishesh will never allow his daughter to come to this house. And I too would rather see you a bachelor all your life than allow you to marry her.'

'Don't worry. Both of us have decided not to go against our families. We will wait till you reconcile. We are sure your love for us will prove stronger than your hatred for each other.'

Raghav had grown up without his parents, not expecting much from anyone. But Uncle Krishan had taken care of his needs, been there for him always, never letting him feel deprived of any need or comfort. True they did not share that intimate bond like Chachi ji and he did, but he had been a good guardian. Something told him that Chacha ji would understand gradually.

'I am proud of you!' Krishan Singh said, relieved at Raghav's assurance, running his hand over his head.

'You have been more than a father to me. I could never go against your wishes. Besides, if I can't take care of my old relations, I don't think I can do justice to the new ones.'

'Don't worry. I will take care of everything,' Krishan said, patting his back reassuringly.

Raghav was attacked at college by Vishesh's goons and in turn Krishan Singh's supporters set fire to Vishesh's factory one night. The tussle between the two political families grew intense day by day. Raghav and Neha tried to pacify their families but could hardly do anything to contain the malevolence.

Neha's father had a heart attack. In the hospital ICU, he

emotionally blackmailed Neha into marrying Vishal, Arunesh Yadav's son, who had just returned from the USA after completing his graduation. Raghav's world fell apart. He had never imagined fate would make them drift apart like this. His Neha was going to be somebody else's now. Listening to their families further would probably be a bad idea. It would be better to elope for the time being.

'Please don't call me again, we were not meant to be. If you have truly loved me, this is all I ask of you,' were her parting words as he called her the day her father was discharged from the hospital. She has probably traded our relation for her father's life with god. I was right. I should not have trusted a stranger. He remembered his first instinctive reaction the day she had approached him in college for notes. 'But you told me I can count on you?' He spoke to the beeping instrument as the line was disconnected.

Vishal turned out to be a drug addict and died in a car accident two months after their marriage.

Meanwhile, Raghav picked up his life's broken pieces, put himself together and delved deep into work, so deep that no memories of Neha could reach him there.

Raghav met Neha a few months later at the marriage reception party of Mr Rupani, a local influential businessman. She was sitting a few tables away in the lawn with her mother-in-law and sister-in-law. Dressed in a light pink saree, without any bangles, necklace or other jewellery, she still looked divinely beautiful. Their eyes met for a couple of seconds and in that moment they knew what Neha had said was probably correct. They were not meant to be! They could not be together even now as Neha's father was still in a delicate position and her in-laws had accepted her as their daughter. She was a part of this family now. Besides, Raghav's family would not be willing to accept her, especially Krishan Singh. How could he allow a Yadav, that too a widow to become his daughter-in-law?

'You really took good care of everything Chacha ji!' thought Raghav as he looked with moist eyes at Neha, walking away from him, accompanied by her in-laws. He would continue to live a half-alive man. It hurt him that despite his promise, Chacha ji did not take any initiative, or show the slightest care for his feelings. Would he have done the same with Madhur?

The buzzing reporters brought Raghav back from his drift. 'It is being said that you are being given charge of Ministry of Renewable Energy to rev it up, just like you did with the Education Ministry? What is your vision for this Ministry?'

'No comments!' he said politely as he walked back to his car, got into it and asked the driver to take the road to Dehradun.

He called Krishan Singh. 'I shall not be coming home Chacha ji. I shall also not be working for the Indian National Front anymore.'

'What happened, son?' asked a dazed Krishan Singh. He had not expected this. 'Where will you go? I don't take party decisions single handedly. Try to understand.'

'Charansparsh!' he said as he disconnected the phone and lay back. He was feeling relaxed and light. He had just discarded the baggage he had been carrying for a long time. At least he would be in control of his life from now on. The debt of 'taking care' of him had been more than paid off.

Kali Zabaan Works in Aditya's Favour

Varanasi, 2015

The election was a much more complicated affair than Aditya had imagined. His efforts at micro-management and reaching out to the people seemed to bear no fruit. He spent three hours in the morning and three hours in the evening meeting people in his ward, sharing his plans and vision to make it a model ward for the city. The ward had a population of about 50,000, which meant about 15,000 families had to be contacted. The rest of the time he spent working with augmented speed in his office and factory, taking rapid-fire decisions, and delegating less important work with periodic scrutiny of the same. He enjoyed the thrill of multi-tasking.

He was contesting as an independent candidate—not supported by any political party. To reach out to the maximum number of people, his election team and activist friends would organize meetings with groups of people living in flats, colonies and slums.

Although some people appreciated his spirit, the bulk of them, specially from the slums, looked at him the way a housewife would look at a salesgirl with a heavy canvas bag, stuffed with detergent powder packs, knocking at her door.

'Bauva, you already have everything—big house, car, money. Then, why do you want to intrude in this field?' It was as if they had sole right over the Corporator, as if the Corporator's post had been created to give them reassurance that someone within their reach, was in power. It pained him to see how the mirage worked to bring solace to these poor souls.

'Oh! You must be eyeing our garbage… You will set up a plant to utilize it and churn money out of it.' It was now dawning on him, why his father wanted him to refrain.

'Go live proudly and eternally atop your stinky hillock of garbage, you filthy, mindless creature,' was what he wanted to scream back, but he had learnt to chew his words, especially when in anger. At least, contesting this elections had given him a chance to put to use the deep-breathing techniques, he had learnt in the two basic courses of Sri Sri Ravi Shankar. He still wondered what the multiple Sris before the name meant!

It also bewildered Aditya how steep the ravine between the rich and poor had become. There was so much mistrust and insecurity on either side. It was commonplace to find the upper class look upon the lower ones with suspicion and disdain, but he had never imagined that even these people were equally insecure and believed that the rich wanted to take away whatever little was left with them, even the garbage!

'You are not a man rooted to the ground. Our current Corporator is always there in our social ceremonies, even in the birthday parties! Will you be able to match his hard work?' Aditya used to face some of the most incredible questions on daily basis. 'Will you be able to rescue our children from the police station? You don't have political support like Pappu. He is on hotline with the MLA, being from the same party.'

He already felt like a new bahu from a rich family, whom the mother-in-law would humiliate every day by comparing her with the old bahu, who is adept at all household tasks. He remembered how Prachi, with her kali zabaan, had told him he would be befuddled, and here he was...having no clue what to do to make these poor people realize how they were being used by the evil Khalifa. Prachi too, probably had no idea, that she had this extra sensory perception, otherwise she would be less impulsive with what she uttered.

Many a times he would cross paths with Pappu. Once, as Aditya walked into a multi-storey housing complex, Pappu, who was coming out with his supporters, saw him and said sarcastically, 'Oh ho! Look at you, chote Garg sahab! Sweating all over! Didn't you always think Sabhasadi was a piece of cake?'

Pappu called his father Garg sahab and him Aditya Bhai, but after Aditya's candidature, the 'chote Garg sahab' was his cunning and cheap contrivance to make him feel small, to make fun of him. Aditya felt a ghost escape from within at his sight. He was filled with disgust and anger as usual. Inside, he was seething and wanted to castrate Pappu with the same betel nut knife with which Pappu used to cut the betel nuts he chewed.

'Namaste, Bhaiya,' he said, smiling at him as he always did and walked by.

During his public contact, Aditya used to focus on the poor sanitation, lighting, roads and water supply, trying to convey that the job of the Corporator was not just PR. A lot of intelligent- and hard work was required to design and get schemes and projects sanctioned for the ward. He shared his thoughts about getting financial support for his model project from the ruling MPs' funds, from CSR budgets, and even foreign grants—something his rivals could not even imagine. He also emphasized on reviving the interaction between residents of the ward, something that had vanished over the last few decades. Nowadays, people hardly know their next-door neighbours. He gave PowerPoint presentations outlining how he would revive the community auditorium which was in shackles and lying locked since years. It would also serve as a bridge between the rich and the poor. He also emphasized on his plans to renovate the park in the ward, which had become a garbage dump yard, and start a sports club there for the children. This would give the children the much needed physical activity and interaction that was disappearing due to their fascination with the internet, mobile and television.

'It isn't working,' said his campaign co-ordinator Jaspreet. The elite class may believe us but it seems we have not been able to strike the right chord amongst the lower strata.

The final blow came on the last day of the nomination.

'What happened Jaspreet? Why are you looking so tensed?'

'Pappu Shukla is not filing the nomination.'

'So?'

'His wife Baby Shukla is!'

Baby Shukla was a sober lady with a religious image and was quite popular amongst the female residents. She accompanied Pappu to most of the social ceremonies and gatherings—almost certain to be found in the front row at mata ki chowkis and jagrans. She would definitely be the first choice of many of them. It would also mitigate the anti-incumbency factor that would have worked against Pappu. However, she would only be a puppet in the hands of Mr Shukla. Checkmate!

◆

It was a hot and sunny day. The booths of the various political parties and independent candidates, set up outside the polling stations at the Sriddha Devi Ladies College and Bharat Vikas Sewa Samiti Inter College, were buzzing with supporters and party workers. Not only were the maximum number of voters turning up at the Indian National Front camps of Pappu Shukla, for getting their voting slips, there was also remarkable activity on the booths of Hamid Mirza, from the Indian Kaumi League and Kallu Sonkar from the Dalit Panthers Party.

Aditya felt sad and hurt to realize that after all, the voters were still divided on class, caste, religion and community. Development still took the backseat. Voting was more of a festivity amongst these people, where they vent out their pain of being oppressed. They were driven by 'us against them' waves created by parties and voted in unison, rather than using their individual discretion.

The so-called educated and elite on the other hand, who understood the game and could not be misled, mostly abandoned the ballot. There had been a mixed crowd in the morning hours, but after that the upper- and middle-class voters' strength had dwindled.

'Where did we go wrong Jaspreet?' Aditya said.

'The turnout is dismal, Sir. The voting till now is estimated to be barely 40 per cent and seems will close at a maximum of 50 per cent. It seems we have not been able to mobilize our voters. They are more interested in the World Cup cricket match.'

It was 3.25 pm and the voting would end in about an hour-and-a-half. Aditya decided to go home and get a quick power nap, which he hoped would take away his negative thoughts. The local channels' unofficial surveys almost declared clear verdict in favour of Mrs Shukla, so there was nothing much left to do anyway.

Aditya dozed off as soon as his head touched the pillow. He dreamt of Pappu walking towards him, his face barely visible from amongst the scores of flower garlands hanging around his neck, followed by his gang of crooks shouting '*Pappu Bhaiya ki jai*'. Pappu tilted his head with massive effort to one side, bent a little and ejected a stream of betel juice on the road. 'Well tried, chote Garg sahab... *Magar zamanat to zabt ho hi gayi*,' he said, shaking his head wickedly and walked away. He also dreamt of the Mayor making a disgusted face and throwing his application on his face. '*Dafa ho jaiye! Chale aate hain, kutton ka parivar niyojan karana hai... Yahan insaan to sambhal nahin rahe.*' Meanwhile, he reached home and gloomily narrated his defeat to Prachi, who said, 'Go back and check. There must be some mistake. You cannot lose!'

'Is this a joke, Prachi? Stop nagging me... Jaspreet and my representatives were present during the counting. We have lost. Had this not been true, why was Pappu wearing so many garlands and why were his supporters chanting victory slogans? Just leave me alone...' he said, still dreaming...

He woke up with a start and looked at the wall clock. It was 4.35 pm and he had slept a good 10 minutes extra. He turned to get up and saw Prachi sitting next to the bed on a chair, staring at him.

'What?' she asked, looking at his weird expression.

'Nothing!' he said as he remembered his dream and shook his head.

He splashed his face with cold water and rushed outside. On the way, he passed the patch of greenery that his NGO had been maintaining. He couldn't believe what he saw. It was loaded with construction debris from the adjacent road, which was being made under the JNNURM scheme. The beautiful flowering bougainvilleas, roses and orchids he had lovingly nurtured had been mercilessly crushed beneath tons of mud and concrete piled over them. He felt his heart sink. Another omen of defeat! Another indication of how he was a helpless nobody in front of the caucus of professional politicians he was faced with. They could crush him and his aspirations just like this plundered patch of greenery...anytime.

There was a massive crowd at the Shraddha Devi Ladies Inter College voting booth, so he turned his car and took the other road to reach the Bharat Vikas Sewa Samiti College, where Jaspreet was waiting for him. The crowd was even denser here.

The queues seemed to be endless. The boys and girls seemed to be enjoying their time in the queue, as if waiting for a reality show audition. They took selfies, passed comments at each other and some just chatted away on their mobiles. Many of them waved at Aditya to say, 'Hi' as they saw him approaching from a distance. It was a mixed crowd. These were middle-class and upper middle-class people, who were usually known to abandon the ballot. The queues moved fast but never seemed to end. It was like a grasshopper invasion. Such a crowd was normally noticed during the Holi hud-dang or at the Durga Pooja celebration pandals in Varanasi.

'What is happening?' Aditya asked Jaspreet.

'The one day Indo-Pak cricket match, Sir...we did not fail so miserably after all.'

'What? Who did not fail? We or India?' said Aditya as he constantly tried to keep smiling back and waving at people, acknowledging their greetings.

'Both, Sir. India played their best innings so far against Pakistan, today, at the Quarter Finals of the World Cup in Melbourne. Not only did they bowl out the Pakistani team, who chose to bat first, within 30 overs, but also hit the target in a record 22 overs, another world record for the fastest run-rate till date. The match was over a good two hours ahead of schedule. As soon as the match was over, they came out to vote. Specially the youngsters and the educated crowd, who are more into this kind of stuff.'

Aditya was stupefied. Every class has their own way of relieving stress and feeling festive. He did not know whether to curse this cricket-mania or consider it a blessing. He hadn't watched a cricket match for years. He thought it was a national waste. And here it was, turning around his destiny by driving people into a voting frenzy to express their joy.

'How many of them do you think are voting for us?'

'Most of them came to us for the voting slips. Since we had fewer volunteers and the rush was tsumanic, we could not attend them all. Many of them then took their slips from other booths, but I think they will still vote for us.'

Aditya thanked Bajrang Bali for this unexpected gift. His mind had already started racing, preparing a mental list of the things-to-do to fulfill the promises he had made, to make this an imitable ward for the city and the country. It was 4:50 pm and the voting would close soon. At least 5,000 people would be left standing outside, most of them his supporters.

'What is the current trend as per the survey reports?'

'We could be leading by around 2,000 votes.'

'Great work Jaspreet, Benny, Nikunj, thanks to all of you. I have to make a move, take care.' He turned around and rushed straight back. There was so little time and so much had to be done. The *'Dekhna nahin, karna hai'* philosophy always kept him on his heels.

On his way to the dilapidated community centre, which he

wanted to survey, the feel-good chemical reactions kept looping inside him. This was one of the happiest moments of his life, only next to when his father had agreed to Prachi's parents' proposal. That reminded him of Prachi, how she had appeared in his dream and told him to go back and check...and that he could not lose.

'Holy smokes! So now the kali zabaan works even in the virtual world of my thoughts and dreams? This time for good! Thanks Prachi!' he said to himself.

BOOK 2

Naya Bharat Comes to Power
New Delhi, July 2018

It was the summer session of the Parliament—the first one after the recently concluded Lok Sabha elections. It had been a historic election. For the first time in Indian history none of the two major political parties had come to power, nor had the third front gathered any substantial seats, and the average voting had reached up to 85 per cent on pan-India basis. People had come out to vote the way they would queue-up in the 80s and 90s outside the stadiums to buy tickets for India–Pakistan cricket matches.

It was people's anger against corruption, mis-governance, rising prices and the sheer apathy and mistreatment of the masses that led to a clean sweep by the newly-formed Naya Bharat Dal. It was a new-age modern political party that practised principles of democracy and transparency, both outside and within the party. There was less of conventional political wisdom that characterized the existing parties and more of raw emotions that had surfaced on numerous occasions, including the anti-corruption movement and the protest of youth against lack of security for women. No one had imagined that the public would really break the barriers of caste and religion to vote for good candidates and support the agenda of development, irrespective of the party.

Naya Bharat's founder and kingpin, Dr Sabbarwal, reminded one of the famous saying, 'Cometh the hour, cometh the man!' He had been a crusader since childhood. He worked as domestic help to support his studies and later, became a doctor. He then quit his government job to fight corruption and thus, formed the Naya Bharat Dal. His interpersonal and organizational skills were beyond comparison. He emerged as the face of the anti-corruption movement that led his party to a thumping victory.

It was a bright sunny morning and the Parliament House was abuzz with energy, the newly elected MPs congregating from all corners of the country.

'You really missed something dude, the weekend party on my cruise was out of this world! We had 42-years-old exquisite single malt whisky, specially brought in from Scotland, the best entertainment crew from Argentina and on-board service staff from Uzbekistan,' said Jatin Oberoi, as his car drove past the Parliament House entrance gate. Jatin was the young General Secretary of the oldest political party, Indian National Front and the son of the High-Command. Smartly dressed security guards saluted and stood in attention. 'All right, I am there. Will tell you the details after the Parliament session, let's worry about Naya Bharat at the moment.' He was talking to Krish Nimani, the young son of brewery business tycoon, Harsh Nimani.

He stepped out of the car, a fair and handsome man, just a couple of inches short of six feet. With his crew cut and stubble, this bachelor was the heartthrob of innumerable females across the country. He walked up to the flock of MPs, dressed in sparkling white kurta-pajamas standing in the lawns outside the Parliament building, engrossed in chatting and fellowship.

'Can't see a single Naya Bharat MP, Gupta ji,' said Jatin. He had been seen as the strongest contender for the Prime Minister's post till National Front's defeat. 'Don't know what our new inexperienced hero, Dr Sabbarwal is up to?'

'Just wait and watch. I have a strong feeling these people will not be able to run the country even for three months. Very soon we will be faced with a mid-term election,' agreed Brijmohan Gupta, the ex-Law Minister, a loyalist of the Oberoi family for the last 35 years. There were rumours that he had gifted a private mini cruise with seven star facilities to the 'prince' of the party on his birthday.

'Have activists ever run countries?' added Ranjit Shastri, the young son of five times MP and ex-Finance Minister Vinod Shastri and heir to the legacy of the royal Shastri family of Udaipur. 'Only Indian National Front has the experience and smartness to run this country.' It was said that the Shastris owned one-fourth of the real estate in and around Udaipur, besides a 4,000-crore business empire of mining, mills and construction. Ranjit, the young MBA from Oxford, had won the election from Nandangarh, which was the seat from where his now-retired father had been winning. Ranjit was the closest friend and ally of Jatin.

'These people are only fit for candle marches, fasts and protests. If we give the country in their hands, the whole country will be fasting five days a week,' said Raju Gowda, a prominent MP and ex-Defense Minister from the Bhartiya Janhit Party, the other major political party...and they all burst out in laughter. He had been part of several committees during the earlier regime along with Brijmohan, hence was quite pally with him.

Krishan Singh and Madhur Singh, who had been waiting for the right moment, quickly walked up to Jatin and bowed into the same sub-servient trade-mark 'Namaste' that had signified their loyalty to Jaswant Oberoi. Jatin acknowledged with a smile. Madhur hadn't seen much of him during his visits to the palace of the High Command, as Jatin's childhood was mostly spent in London.

Jatin continued to mingle in a very courteous and simplistic fashion with the MPs, both from his own party as well as the others. He was a really powerful debonair, whom everyone wanted to be on good terms with. His party had ruled the country for most of the post-Independence period. He had inherited the number one position in the party last year when his father had a paralytic attack, which immobilized him. It had been six years after his coming back from London, where he had completed his graduation in political science. Jatin's expressions and body language never gave away the shrewd, unrelenting schemer within him, or the superiority complex he inherited since birth.

'Sir, meet our new dynamic MP from Navi Mumbai,' Brijmohan introduced a man dressed in traditional attire of kurta, dhoti and a white cap to Jatin. He wore a thick gold chain and half a dozen heavy rings with gemstones studded onto them, and an inappropriately thick gold bangle in his left hand.

Jatin stepped back, startled, as the six feet two inch burly man suddenly stepped forward and bent down to touch his feet.

'Gosh. You scared me!'

'His seat had been a Janhit Party stronghold till now,' Brijmohan Gupta added.

'My name is Ganesh Vidhyarthi. Consider me your humble sevak in that region, Sir. For anything from funds to rallies, police to the underworld, builders to celebrities, you just have to wink an eye. The whole area is under your command, now.'

'He has a massive following in Navi Mumbai area,' Brijmohan continued. 'His networking and resources are unmatchable. The Janhit Party did not value his capability. He will initiate our attack today.'

'Come to Mumbai some time, Jatin ji. I guarantee you an unforgettable experience. Mine is the area of glamour, luxury and indulgence.'

'Of course, I can see that!' said Jatin. 'Welcome to National Front.'

Ganesh Vidyarthi folded his hands in a courteous namaste and stepped back, thanking Brijmohan profusely for the favour.

'Is he a gold smuggler or something?' Jatin asked Brijmohan and they burst into a suppressed laughter. 'Just three minutes left, don't know what these bastards are up to! Is the plan clear to all?' he asked Brijmohan in a hushed voice.

All heads turned suddenly as they heard the sound of bus horns from a distance. They saw a procession of six buses come to a halt in the portico of the Parliament. Dr Satish Sabbarwal, leader of Naya Bharat, stepped out, followed by his 280 MPs. They paused for a moment to salute the national flag and the temple of democracy—the Parliament House. Then, without even casting a look around, they headed straight into the building to occupy the seats allocated for the ruling party.

Not a single Naya Bharat MP was missing. They had gathered three days earlier for a symposium and training session to face their first day at the Parliament. The experienced ones in the party knew the perils of a group of mostly fresh MPs facing a hostile and badly defeated opposition.

'See, the drama has already started,' Mr Soumik Dey Mistry from the Left Front, commented sarcastically to his friends.

The fellowship session in the lawns came to a sudden halt

as all the MPs rushed behind them into the Parliament hall. Many of them had served several terms of five years and they were curious as well as stunned to see this kind of a dramatic entry. This kind of group arrival could normally be seen in India when the relatives and friends of the spouse arrived from another town to attend the wedding functions hosted by the other side.

The first day of the session began with a few minutes of observation of silence by the members standing in their places, followed by the reading out of the long list of newly-elected members by the last speaker, Smt Reema Kumar. Finally, she invited the leader of the majority party, Dr Satish Sabbarwal, to read a few lines about the two deceased members, who would not be able to take the oath.

Dr Satish Sabbarwal was a sober man in his fifties, with grey hair and a french-cut beard. Behind his calm and serene face was hidden an ocean of knowledge, wisdom and determination.

Dr Satish was barely halfway through reading the notes about the deceased members, when the tall, profusely moustached overweight Indian National Front MP from Navi Mumbai, stood up and started shouting at the top of his voice, 'Shame on you, Sabbarwal, shame! You have no right to read out these names. You are a fraud, a killer. You were yourself thrown out of the medical community.'

Another one popped up and raising his hands, started screaming in collusion. Owning an aisle seat, he utilized his privilege to walk down a few steps towards the podium and shouting slogans hysterically, he threw up both hands in sheer revolt, as if ready to launch himself upon Dr Sabbarwal.

Two more walked down the other aisle, shouting their own versions of why Dr Sabbarwal was a disgrace to mankind and immediately needed to resign.

The speaker pulled herself closer to the mike, strictly ordering the hooligans to silence.

The mayhem, instead of subsiding, grew out of control and her voice drowned. No one in the house could hear anybody else now.

The rebellious MPs were now surrounding Dr Sabbarwal from all sides, shouting and pointing fingers at him.

Raghav, second-in-command at Naya Bharat, sitting in the front row, got up from his seat, turned back to his MPs and raised his hand with three fingers up and the thumb and the first finger touching in sukhasana. Ten Naya Bharat members got up and walked towards the podium and covered each of the excited opposition MPs, telling them to keep their fingers down and to return to their seats.

None of them budged. In fact, they started bickering with renewed aggression. Raghav could see that Dr Sabbarwal was no longer enjoying this. He stood up a second time and raised two fingers to his team, the first and the little finger, in the 'yo-man' gesture. Now all Naya Bharat MPs started shouting in unison *'Bharat Mata ki Jai…Vande Maatram'*. Dr Sabbarwal was accompanied back to his seat by the ten Naya Bharat MPs who had gone to fight the invaders, who obviously took it as their first victory in their objective to disrupt the proceedings and marched toward the homeland of the enemy, the Naya Bharat block. The regiment swelled to around twenty as they stood in front of the Naya Bharat Pavilion asking them all to resign and go back. The speaker shouted helplessly on her mike. Jatin Oberoi, the leader of their party, stood at his place muttering something that probably would indicate he was trying to make his MPs come back. Actually he was happy that everything was going as per the plan. It would be a demoralizing blow to these over-confident novices.

Raghav now stood up again and raised his middle finger, in the 'up-yours' position. Somewhere from within the backbenches, three young MPs emerged, wearing black T-shirts and blue denims. They were Varun, Salman and Aditya. They reached the invaders and looked at each one carefully, as if trying to recognize them. Then they asked them their names, shuffled through the bunch of yellow envelopes each one was carrying, and handed them the one with their name. They had neatly typed 'to' and 'from' white labels freshly stuck on them by the Naya Bharat team of about 20 volunteers, who had identified each one of the invaders. The ferocious Turks would look at the envelope, turn it front and back, peep inside and quietly retreat to their seats.

Dr Sabbarwal trusted the quadro—Raghav, Aditya, Varun and Salman a lot and saw them as a bundle of energy and intelligence, overloaded with the passion to create a 'Buland Bharat'.

'Finally on a level playing field, Ganesh Bhai! Let's see how well you can bat now,' Salman said, looking Ganesh in the eye, handing him over a yellow envelope.

'I spared you that day junior, but you've already had your day. Do you have the faintest idea of my powers? I can crush you like a dry leaf. One more time you act insolent with me, you will regret it for the rest of your life!' Ganesh replied snatching the envelope from him and about to fling it aside.

'No...wait, wait... *Prasaad hai, Phenkte nahin! Ek nigah dekh to lijiye,*' said Salman.

Ganesh peeped inside, then quickly shut back the envelope. He stared hard at Salman, gritting his teeth in exasperation.

'Beware! One spark and dry leaves like us can turn into a hellfire,' Salman stared him back in the eyes, his aggressive posture revealing his bellicosity.

'Once again, I will make you pay through your nose for this,' Ganesh said and turned back, putting the envelope in his pocket.

'Wait, there's one more,' said another defender, handing him another envelope. Ganesh stared harshly at him, then turned back and headed to his seat.

'Once again?' Salman couldn't get Ganesh's contorted face out of his mind.

'What's the cheque amount?' an annoyed Brijmohan Gupta asked Ganesh, the tall, moustached Maratha senapati of the invaders, who had re-occupied his seat in a state of stupor. He held the envelope between his legs and pulled a picture halfway out from it.

'The bastards, they kidnapped your wife?' snarled Gupta.

'No. She's my mistress in Ulhasnagar.'

'So? What's the big deal? It's your personal matter,' said Gupta, as he wondered at the repulsiveness of the so-called mistress of this fat guy. The picture had 'Ulhasnagar' written over it.

The Air India mascot from Navi Mumbai pulled up another photo hiding behind the first one, with 'Thane' written on top... and yet another one that said 'Alibag'. He now looked at Gupta innocently as if asking 'What would you have done?'

'Are you a Mughal emperor or something? I didn't know you guys keep multiple mistresses? How did they come to know?' mumbled Gupta in disbelief.

'No, everybody can't have my kind of mojo. Some people got investigation reports of murder cases against them, some got their pictures with the underworld or details of their underground properties, and so on...'

'Bloody crooks! They have been spying our bold and aggressive frontliners.'

'Brijmohan ji,' said the Air India mascot with his head still down.

'What?'

'That guy there sent this for you,' he said as he pulled out another yellow envelope from his kurta pocket, pointing towards the guy standing next to Salman.

Varun waved at Brijmohan zealously, smiling ear to ear. Brijmohan had a sharp memory but for a moment he was perplexed at the friendly smile from this stranger. Then it hit him! 'Is this for real!' he wondered. This was the young boy he had ordered to be thrown out eight years back during the public feedback session on 'Judicial Reforms and Accountability Bill'.

From a corner of his eye, Gupta could see Ranjit too peeping into an envelope. Their best laid plans had failed. These young guys were not naïve.

Dr Sabbarwal's party not only had young and dynamic MPs as the quadro, but also many seasoned and thick-skinned old timers. It was like an emulsion and his job was to keep it stable, without letting the water and the oil separate. He was very well aware that now that the elections were over, his greatest challenge would be to strike a balance of power within the party and keep everybody moving ahead in the best interest of the country.

The ones with flourishing personal interests that had accompanied their long political careers, would slowly try to take charge of things and dominate. However, the younger rebels, who were all geared-up to live and die for the country, would not allow that to happen. He had to make sure the adjustment process was gradual and would not turn self-destructive at any point of time. It would require a lot of weight and strength.

◆

'*Hamara bhai, Hatimtai!*' they said in unison, as they raised a toast to Varun, the mastermind behind the ward-off. The proceedings had gone smoothly after the envelopes were handed over. It was Varun's brainchild to hire a team of detectives, something he specialized and believed in, since Pinktouch Software days. 'Homework, homework and homework!' was his success mantra.

'Spy on them? No! It is immoral and over the top,' Dr Sabbarwal had retorted when Varun had introduced the concept to him.

'Not so immoral when used for self-defence and in the country's best interest,' the quadro had convinced him.

Raghav had called Aditya, Varun and Salman over to his place for dinner and to celebrate their first strategic victory. The four had developed a special bond during the training session.

'What a joker!' said Salman. 'What were Jatin and his team trying to do? Everybody knows Dr Sabbarwal was impeached from the CMO post ten years back for going against the pharma companies-doctors nexus.'

'It was so shameful for some of the Indian National Front senior members as well. I could see the helplessness on their faces,' added Varun.

'I wouldn't underestimate him by thinking of him as a joker or something. That's the way a belligerent opposition in our country has always tried to pull down a majority government,' said Aditya.

'But I am wondering why the National Front stalwarts did

not advise him against doing this on the first day itself?' said Varun.

'Actually, Jatin is surrounded by sycophants. He has sidelined the senior members—another dangerous sign!' said Raghav. 'It is good that we had planned our defence in advance. I agree with Aditya. This man worries me. After all he is the progeny of Jaswant Oberoi, the man who literally ruled over this country for decades. Such egoists have a superiority complex and will go to any extent to prove it. We have to be very cautious.'

The Planning Commission—
The Quadro vs Oldies
New Delhi, May 2019

'I deserve this job because I have suffered from the ill effects of our system. I have a Masters in law with two years practice in civil courts. I have completed an internship project under ex-CAG team member, Mr Pradeep Jain. I am a columnist for the Hindustan Times, writing a series on poor condition of our civil amenities, for which I do regular research into the working of the government departments. I have worked for six years on adult education…'

'Of course! I can see all that on your résumé.' An officer from the interview panel interrupted the passionate discourse of this young lady sitting in front of them. They were here to select young officers for the CSAT (City Social Audit Team). The new government had embarked on this aggressive plan to form a team of six to ten officers in each of the 500 cities across India that would have enormous power to spur performance of various government departments in their city. They would be working directly under the central government's Home Ministry. Once this model was successfully implemented, another 8,000 towns would follow suit with smaller teams.

After qualifying two rounds of written tests, she was finally appearing for a personal interview, for which about 50 candidates had been shortlisted from the city of Jaipur. 'If you don't mind, can you tell us a bit more about how you suffered due to the system.'

'My father died of septicemia in a government hospital. They could not provide him proper care, nor arrange the antibiotics and anti-fungals in time. He was a bank clerk. After his death, my mother kept striving hard to get his pension released. She was a simple housewife. She had never earned money. I was just 12-years-old, then. The pension never came. She did odd jobs, worked as domestic help and barely got rest or time for herself. One day, she went missing. I could not find her! No one could find her! No one seemed to care! I was just a child. I could not do anything... I was sent to live with my cousin maternal Uncle in another city. They used to beat me for the smallest mistakes. For all practical purposes, I was a bonded servant to the family. I was scared and lived an intimidated life. I had nowhere to go and no one to complain to. So I lived in this hell for eight long years, till I completed my 10+2 and found a job. I often wonder what kind of governance our country has, which does not provide any security to its people in sickness, its widows, and to its children?'

'What about your immediate family?'

'None! I am single.'

'Can you give us some instances of real life moments when you have displayed courage and strength in the face of adverse situations?'

Radhika, who was sitting on the corner-most chair of the panel, did not listen to her reply. Her eyes were glued to the file of this extremely good-looking and assertive lady. She carefully went through each detail. Out of the thousands of candidates they had interviewed in the past few months, she stood apart as one of the most beautiful and focused. However, there was overconfidence, almost amounting to arrogance, about her, which she did not like at all. Radhika realized that she was comparing herself with this lady and a sense of envy filled her.

The candidate left with a graceful namaste to the panel. The form was in front of Radhika. She just had to strike the checkbox in front of 'Rejected' and she would probably never see her again. She, however, did just the contrary.

Radhika was a part of Varun's core team ever since he became a part of Dr Sabbarwal's cabinet. Within three years, from a patriotic NRI activist, he became an MP with a portfolio in the cabinet. Radhika had been his CEO at Kalpvruksh. Now, she was the CEO of his nation-wide audit team. All this, however, was only a cover-up to keep herself busy. If only Varun would make her the CEO of his home, his heart, she would rather sit at home and nurture their children.

Her thoughts took her back to old times.

It had been a few weeks since Varun had decided not to go back to the USA. He did not go back to Indore either, as his NGO Kalpvruksh, required him to be in Delhi. He tried hard to convince his parents to shift with him, advising them to rent out the house they had built for post-retirement days, but didn't succeed. He took up a work-from-home job in Prism Softwares, Noida, that gave him ample time to expand the NGOs work. There were, however, stringent deadlines for projects involving strenuous long hours of work. Radhika would come over to his place often, after office hours and make coffee or some snacks for him to go along with their discussions about the NGO-related work.

For Radhika it was like living her dream. Getting to meet the self-appointed beau of her dreams, every other day, was bliss for her. Knowing well that Varun did not look at her that way, she was happy to just be with the man she idolized, to spend some solitary time with him. Even though it was just work for Varun, she would feel the same intoxication in the air, that lovers feel...when he would look in her eyes to explain his point of view on an important by-law, or when their arms would touch accidentally as they walked together discussing something in his balcony, or when making coffee for him after a long brainstorming session.

Little did she know that even Varun used to find her attractive, but never let it show in his behavior. Being a lecherous boss was a 'NO'! Besides, he was no longer interested in love. But finding someone attractive is not something you can instruct yourself not to do, it is involuntary. With each passing day, he admired her more and more for her simplicity and dedication to the cause they were pitching for.

'How come an attractive girl like you is single till date?' Varun asked Radhika one day as they were having dinner at Gulati's at Pandara Road.

Radhika blushed for an instant at the sudden question. 'I guess my Prince Charming is still looking for me!' she laughed. It struck her that she had not been able to let Varun know her feelings for him in all these years.

She had to go to Jaipur the next day; her mother was not well. When she came back a week later, she was not her usual self. She was distracted and irritable. The volunteers at the office wondered what was wrong. They guessed some big problem must have happened back home with her. She refused to discuss it with anyone.

'Don't be reticent with me, Radhika. I am not only your boss, you are like family to me,' said Varun. He too had observed Radhika's melancholy. She was at his house to discuss about the presentation to be delivered before the parliamentary committee on Right to Education that was due next week.

'Nothing, just feeling depressed!' She said, as a tear rolled down her cheek.

'Why? Radhika! It hurts me to see you like this.' He put his hand comfortingly over hers, as they sat across the table. She was turning pages with one hand and the other was placed on the file cover.

This non-accidental, intentional touch sent an electric wave through her whole body. He had touched her for the first time in all these years. Even though it was a platonic one, it felt magical. The tears started flowing profusely and her face became red as she struggled to keep herself from sobbing.

'Is everything all right at home? Are Uncle and Aunty ok?' Varun stood beside her, putting a hand comfortingly on her shoulder.

'They are fine,' she said.

'Then why are you crying like this? Come let us take a walk,' he held her palm and pulled her up.

Radhika was now standing face to face with him. Her face glowed from the wall light behind him, bearing an expression that would make even the most callous heart feel for her.

He held her face in his hands, 'I am there, Radhika. You are not alone. Tell me, what is the problem?'

'You!' She broke down and clung to him. She cried hysterically as her tears permeated his kurta and wet his shoulder. Suddenly she pulled back, coming to her senses. 'Sorry!' she said, futilely trying to wipe the incessant stream of tears.

Varun was taken aback. The pieces started falling in place. He was the cause of her agony. She loved him but had not let it show all these years, the shy little girl! He remembered how unendurable the fortnight that he spent at the institute was... not able to show his feelings to Alisha. Radhika had been living with this agony for years. He felt a piercing sense of guilt. Right now, all he wanted to do was to comfort her.

'You stupid girl! Why did you keep it to yourself? At least you could have told me.' He hugged her and lowered his head to kiss her on the forehead. She lifted her face at that very moment and their lips brushed. She let herself go, opening up. Their lips were locked in a gentle warm kiss, a kiss that felt like divine healing to her ailing soul. She felt his embrace tighten as the passionate kiss became the epi-centre of their existence in the universe, at this moment. Years of restraint melted into a sparkling, untainted stream of emotion.

She felt his grip loosen. He gently held her by the shoulders and separated them. She felt love in the air and the vibes salvaged Radhika's soul. She felt like she had just been set free.

'You are a very adorable and attractive girl, Radhika. I can easily count you as my best friend after Madhav, but I can't be with you...'

'Why? Do you love someone else?'

'No. I don't. In fact, I can't love anyone.'

'Still not over Alisha?'

'It's not like that. Time is a healer and I have moved on. Had there been anything left between us, it would not have been difficult for either of us to find each other.'

'The way you kissed me, it seemed you felt something for me.'

'It was only a weak moment. I want you to be happy and

I would do anything for you. But I can't ever fall in love or marry again.'

'Neither can I...what an irony! I would give anything to be with you and you would give anything for me, but can't be with me,' she chuckled.

Varun felt relaxed on seeing her come out of her grief and wondered at the unique situation their destiny had put them in, which was aptly described by Radhika.

He realized how light she would be feeling after confessing her feelings. He had been through the same phase with Alisha and had even walked out on her after blurting his heart out. A love confessed and lost is half as burdensome as a love one could never show.

'Now, will you tell me what was making you so grumpy ever since you returned from Jaipur?'

'My parents are after my life to get me married. I could neither give them a proper reason, nor to myself. I felt like a failure, as a daughter and as a person. But now, I feel all right. I can face anything.'

'Are you a modern Meerabai or something? Get married, you stupid girl,' Varun patted her sportingly on the shoulder. 'Come, let us go for dinner.'

'Yep, you owe me a gala dinner. For me, it is by far the happiest day of my life. The first and last kiss of my life,' she teased.

'Well, in all probability my last too!' said Varun. 'By the way, I forgot to tell you, I met one Dr Satish Sabbarwal yesterday, at the Habitat Centre. What a man! He is a doctor-turned-politician, who has been crusading for the last 20 years for clean governance. Has been MP twice from Nasik constituency and recently formed a new-age political party, Naya Bharat. He almost convinced me that I needed to become an insider in the system, rather than just giving suggestions from outside.'

'So, what have you thought?' she asked.

'Let us see. I am meeting him again, tomorrow.'

◆

Time flew by and Varun joined Naya Bharat, worked as a party member, won the election and became a member of Dr Sabbarwal's core team and cabinet. Radhika always stood behind him like a sergeant-at-arms, whether it was his election campaign or his booth management. It was difficult for one to understand the pious bond that tied them together. Krishna–Meera would probably have been an apt example. How else would one describe their decade-long relationship, in which Radhika had devoted her life to him and his cause expecting nothing in return?

'Why do you look so worried?' asked Radhika. They were sitting in the meeting room along with Madhav, where they often brainstormed about the numerous decisions he had to take as the Defence and the Home Minister. While Madhav was his CEO for the Defence, Radhika was the CEO for Home Ministry operations.

'I just got you into a big soup, Radhika.'

'What is it this time, Mr Varun "Panga" Pandey, can you be more clear? You are scaring me?'

'It's June 2018 and you and your team have to appoint about 4,000 people across the country, as Social Audit Officers, by March 2020. We barely have two years.'

'Phew! Sounds Herculean! Don't worry, we will figure it out,' said Radhika, her usual reassuring self. 'But what happened?'

'Let me tell you in more detail, so that you know the background,' said Varun as his mind drifted back to the meeting held two days back...

♦

Dr Satish Sabbarwal was addressing the members of the Planning Commission, to share his vision, invite suggestions, and form a consensus, based on which the Five Year Plan would be formulated.

Aditya, who had been appointed as the Vice-Chairman of the Planning Commission, was also the Minister for Industry, HRD and Social Empowerment, and was seated next to him.

Dr Sabbarwal's knowledge of political history told him that every successful leader needed a capable core team of deputies and trusted allies, in just the right number. Neither too big to be difficult to closely co-ordinate, nor too small to be vulnerable. Nobleness alone would not survive. He needed a street-smart, shrewd and calculative, yet honest team, which he found in the quadro. So, he consitituted the planning commission such that it comprised 15 members—Dr Sabbarwal, the quadro and 10 other members—three Chief Ministers, three other cabinet Ministers, three eminent economists from public domain and one senior secretary.

'We have to do away with both MGNREGA and Food Subsidy. Although they are very popular among the masses, they are leading to a culture of free benefits. Rather than providing an opportunity to work hard and thrive, they tend to take away the very reason to work at all,' said Dr Sabbarwal.

'But we must remember that these were the schemes due to which the last ruling party enjoyed three consecutive terms? It would be a big risk to abolish these schemes altogether,' opined Ujjwal Shinde, the new Chief Minister of Maharashtra, who was from their party. He had been a strong player in the state politics for the last thirty years and had served as the Deputy

Chief Minister ten years ago from Bhartiya Janhit Party. His elder son was also an MP and his younger son looked after their family businesses. He had resigned from the Bhartiya Janhit Party around two years back to support the anti-corruption movement being led by the Naya Bharat Party.

'Dear Mother India, we promise you that we will work only for you and our countrymen's wellbeing, and not for any selfish interests, appeasement of party leaders or vote bank... Isn't this a part of the oath that each one of us has taken?' reminded Salman, who was the Minister for Finance, Urban Poverty Alleviation and Roads and Highways.

'My dear Salman Babu, you are too young to understand the implications. We don't want to see the same people who supported us, throwing rotten eggs and shouting abuses at us when we go back to our state after this session,' said Jitendra Sachan, Cabinet Minister for Rural Development.

'We have been amidst the masses and we will have to remain so, not like you young people who may serve a single term like guest artists. I respect Dr Sabbarwal very much, but I still wonder whether he has taken the right decision by taking so many young, first time MPs in the cabinet,' added Prashant Rajawat, the new Coal Minister. He had almost the same background as Shinde, the difference being that he had only a daughter, who was the MP from Sikar, while her husband looked after their business interests. He had switched from the Indian National Front.

'Let us not talk about both the schemes as a bundle, they are very different in their nature,' said Aditya. 'Although the MGNREGA scheme provides opportunity for work through which rural development plans can be furthered, this scheme proved to be disastrous due to improper implementation and corruption. If we can make some changes to correct its implementation, I don't think we will need to take away this scheme.'

'Correct! If the rural population does not get the free remuneration, without having to work, sitting at home, not only will the rural development take off rapidly, but the shortage of manpower faced by industry will also be solved as many of them would rather work for industry to get higher earnings,' added Varun.

'That makes sense,' said Dr Sabbarwal. 'But we will have to figure out how to make that happen, I mean how to curb corruption in the rural employment guarantee scheme. It is spread down to the lowest level, in the 6,50,000 villages across the country. The other thing is that it is not so easy to withdraw the food subsidy. What will happen to the thousands of crores of investment the last government has made in the cold storages, vehicles and other infrastructure? Not only this, about 80,000 employees have been recruited under this scheme nation-wide, what will we do with them?'

'Sir, are you aware the food grain prices in the USA do not change for years together, unlike in our country where every year the prices go up by 20–30 per cent,' said Varun. 'I feel it is a very wrong policy to charge ₹20 per kg to the common man whereas it is distributed at ₹2 per kg to some select, so-called BPL population. The common man pays the bill for this free gift distribution through taxes and raised prices of other commodities. While the rich hardly mind, the sufferer is the huge middle-class population,' said Varun, who was the Minister for Defence and Home Affairs.

'So, what do you suggest?' asked Dr Sabbarwal.

'I suggest that we bring down the price of wheat and rice, the two essential food grain to ₹8 and ₹12 per kg, so that it becomes affordable for one and all,' said Varun.

'Yes, why not? Now, we have two puzzles to solve, "How to remove corruption from MGNREGA?" and "How to bring down prices of food grains to less than one-third of their current prices?" Seems like a topic for group discussion in an MBA class,' said Bhuwan Purohit sarcastically. He was the Cabinet Minister of Foreign Affairs and Ujjwal's close ally.

There was a sudden roar of laughter in the conference room. Most eyes were on the young quadro, who had been assigned these seemingly over-demanding responsibilities as Cabinet Ministers, that too handling multiple ministries. They apparently had no acumen in these matters. After all, running the country is not a trivial job. Still there were many, mostly the young lot, who believed in the aggressive, 'change bringing' modus operandi. Dr Sabbarwal, although not so young, was one amongst them.

'I have an idea!' The buzz was silenced as all heads turned towards Aditya in curiosity. 'Why don't we combine the two schemes? We can give food grains as compensation for work under the MGNREGA scheme, that way the cash which is the source of corruption shall be removed from the circuit. The benefits of the work guarantee scheme shall be carried forward and the godowns and infrastructure already developed for nationwide stocking and distribution of food grains shall also be utilized.'

'What an idea!' Varun tapped the table in excitement, applauding the brilliance of the idea. It took a great amount of self-control to hold back the hidden Anil Kapoor inside him from coming out with '*Jhakaas!*' in place of 'What an idea!'

'And one more thing,' Varun continued, 'I assure you that there shall be no corruption, down to the lowest level, across the 6.5 lakh villages, neither in the employment nor the food security or any other government function for that matter, only if we ourselves remain totally honest. How is it that some of the public sector units run so well, take for instance GAIL, BHEL and the IOCL? The government enterprises can run better than private ones, all we need is the will power to develop that culture amongst our workforce.'

'Not only public sector companies, but our hospitals, schools, railways, Municipal Corporations and numerous other government bodies...once they start working honestly and efficiently, the whole country will be transformed,' added Salman. 'The agony index of the common man must go down.'

'I am sure having an honest and committed top cadre will solve half the problem, but what about the people at the execution level, the bottom rung, who have to deliver the services?' asked Surjeet Sengupta, an economist of international repute. 'It is hard to imagine a group of municipal gardeners working hard during the summer days to keep every patch along the roadside green and flowery, like we see them doing in China or Singapore. Or that a policeman would stop by and ask a common man in distress on the roadside, "Can I help you, Sir?" The general approach of the government employees is negligent. It is almost impossible to fire an officer-level government employee. Even the World Bank has commented that our labour laws are amongst the most restrictive for enterprises.'

'The law provides protection against firing of government employees, to avoid discrimination and exploitation. In the current scenario this law is doing more harm than good. We will make the hire and fire procedure simpler. Not only in government jobs but also in the industry. At the same time, we will have to ensure that the minimum wages are revised to respectable levels and strictly enforced,' said Dr Satish. 'The minimum wages in China are ₹25,000 to ₹30,000 per month, we need to ensure that we pay at least ₹15,000–20,000 per month in the first phase.'

Ujjwal Shinde stood up. 'With all due respect, Dr Sabbarwal, I have longer experience than most of the people present here. And I can challenge you that all these discussions are only like groping in the dark. They are just amateur, over-enthusiastic, impractical suggestions that cannot be implemented.'

'Why do you feel so?' asked Dr Sabbarwal.

'Look at how our young Home Minister, Mr Varun, is talking! He is vouching to make each and every department in the country honest in no time. How? By being honest himself? I feel like I am sitting amongst a bunch of college students. We have to take some solid practical decisions here to run the country.'

'Then what do you suggest Mr Shinde?' Dr Sabbarwal asked patiently.

'Let us assume that a certain level of corruption will remain, and cannot be completely removed and move forward with the planning and resource allocation.'

'So, you mean that we should allow half or more of our resources to go waste and turn a blind eye to that?' Varun said in an unbelieving tone.

'Yes, that's how governments have been running this country till now, but if you young boys are so foolhardy, I throw an open challenge before you. If you can control corruption by even a third in the next five years, that is our term, I will not contest the next elections,' said Rajawat.

'We will not contest elections,' said Shinde, raising his hand, followed by Jitendra Sachan and Bhuwan Purohit.

'*Jhakaas*! Sorry, accepted,' Varun blurted out and looked towards Dr Sabbarwal to get his consent, as everyone broke into laughter, lightening the tense atmosphere the heated discussions had created.

'Ok,' Dr Sabbarwal shook his head. He could see that the Planning Commission had already split into two groups in the very first meeting. Not a very healthy sign, but inevitable all the same. 'You will have my full support on this Varun, including resources. But don't take it as a competition. Mr Shinde and Mr Rajawat, jokes apart, we will need your inputs and suggestions to make this successful.' He knew they would not help, but he had to try keeping the emulsion stable for the time being.

'And how would the level of corruption be monitored?' asked Shinde.

'Through international ratings by independent agencies and the same internal statistical surveys have told us in the past that less than 25 paisa out of a rupee spent by the government, actually reaches ground,' said Surjeet Sengupta.

'Fair enough!' said Dr Sabbarwal.

The meeting ended. Varun knew he had opened up a Pandora's box. Uprooting corruption and ensuring performance of government departments, down to the lowest level? Easier said than done! Trial time, Hatimtai!

Varun's Operation Colonoscope
New Delhi, August 2018

Varun was rushing his way up the stairs, to his office in the Ministry of Defence, catching glimpses of well-dressed policemen saluting him along the way. His mind, however, was glued to the problem due to which he did not sleep the entire night. How could such a lapse have occurred on part of the Intelligence Department. He had never felt such a heavy responsibility on his shoulders. The whole country was looking at him for the decision.

He was wearing a smart fitting light grey cotton suit with a white shirt and dark grey tie. He looked dashing as his soft bouncy centre-parted hair swayed with his gait. He still dressed like he used to, during the Pinktouch days, something his high post had not been able to change. His crazy zeal, attitude and spontaneity…nothing much had changed within him.

He entered the conference room where the highest police and defence officers including his childhood friend and now head of defence wing—Madhav Singhal and his team member from Kalpvruksha, now DGP Shyam Mehta, were waiting for him with the updates. Only his old friends could read the turbulence he was going through, from his expressions.

'Sir, they will kill one out of the 28 hostages in the next thirty minutes. What should we communicate to them?' asked one of the officers.

'What about the NSA commandos who specially flew in from Mumbai? Could they formulate a safe plan?' asked Varun.

'No Sir. The terrorists are equipped with the latest weapons and the hostages are mostly staff of the company, who were working overtime. They have planted bombs at various points in the building which they demonstrated by blowing off the east wing of the building a few minutes back,' said Shyam.

'Sir, these people have demanded the safe release of six most dreaded Lashkar terrorists, in lieu of our 28 common men. These terrorists, if released, will kill thousands more. The 28 hostages do not include any high-profile persons. I think we will have to sacrifice them for the nation,' said Madhav. 'We have worked out the complete plan, we will not let any of the terrorists go alive. We just need your approval.'

Varun looked Madhav in the eye. He was reminded of the day when they were sitting in the library at the Institute, discussing how each human life is precious. Fate had now made him flip positions. He was on the other side of the frame now. He realized how different it is to talk about such things, than be actually confronted with a situation that requires you to take a decision. He finally spoke, 'Officer, each life will have to be saved. We can't let these innocent people die. It's not an option. We have to give the terrorists what they want.'

Everyone in the conference hall was staring aghast at Varun. How could the Defence Minister behave so weakly and jeopardize the nation's security in a fit of emotion!

'Sir, are you sure...?' Shyam began to ask, but was interrupted halfway by Varun. 'Yes Shyam, you have to talk directly to those men in there and tell them we will release their friends by tomorrow.' He then turned to the entire team and added, 'We have to ensure that the building is kept under strict vigil. However, we also have to make sure that we don't make any such move that they hurt any of the hostages. Also the decision to release their men should not go outside this room till my next instruction. I don't want to create national panic.'

'What are you saying Varun? Won't everyone come to know when we actually set them free?' asked Madhav, now almost sure that Varun was probably too boggled to think about the problem logically.

'We will let them escape clandestinely,' said Varun. 'That way we won't upset the public.'

'What?' Madhav almost thought out aloud, now wondering whether time had really changed his friend so much. Changed Varun 'Panga' Pandey into a candy-ass hypocrite? On one hand he was talking of even a single human life being above all, and on other hand he was going to jeopardize thousands of lives, not having the courage to reveal his stand in fear of losing political ground. Was he not worried about the long-term consequences?

'But Sir, these six terrorists are being held in two different jails, if they escape at the same time, that too during this hostage episode, who will believe us?' asked Shyam.

'I will manage all that,' said Varun. 'You people get down to work urgently and keep me apprised of each detail.'

Now, only Varun, Madhav and Shyam were in the hall. Varun said, 'Shyam, organize some of our commandos to act as Lashkar terrorists and help these people escape by attacking the jail. Organize everything discreetly taking only our selected people in confidence. I know, I can trust on you to pull this off. We have some eight hours to go.'

Madhav could not hold himself further and burst out, 'Do you even know what you are doing?' But before he could complete, Varun put his hand on his shoulder, looked him in the eyes and asked gravely, 'Do we have an option? As the country's Defence Minister and Naya Bharat Party's core member, trust me, I am doing best justice to both responsibilities.'

'I don't know, Varun, but this does not seem right. I wouldn't be thinking of Naya Bharat or any other political benefit or loss at this juncture,' said Madhav.

◆

At a terrorist camp near Rawalpindi, some senior PAK Army officers and some turbaned hardliner terrorists were having a victory party.

'General Gazni, did you expect the India to give in so easily? Bloody cowards! Within two hours our brothers will be back in our arms.'

'Yes, Mr Murtza, the Indian aircrafts shall leave them near Wagha LOC and from there our choppers will pick them up and bring them here. The clowns even planned attacks on their own jails, by their own people, to make it look like our people escaped. As long as India has such Ministers, we are not very far from our dream of a free Kashmir and a weak and unstable India.'

'Cheers, Ghazni sahab, for this great day. Even our boys who were holding the hostages will be back to the Pak-occupied Kashmir camp in Indian choppers soon.'

◆

Back in India, a morning newspaper's headline read: 'Six most dreaded Lashkar terrorists escape amidst demands from fellow terrorists holding 28 hostages at Hinduja building'. The whole nation seemed to be talking about it. The leader of the opposition, and General Secretary of the Indian National Front, Jatin Oberoi, was addressing the press, saying that the escape of the terrorists, at this time, cannot be a coincidence and the Defence Minister was a traitor. Another opposition party leader, Raju Gowda, from the Bhartiya Janhit Party was saying that it was a big mistake by the ruling party to give such an important portfolio to a young and inexperienced person. The terrorists should have been shot dead instead of conspiring to let them escape in such a shameful way. Everyone was demanding Varun's immediate resignation.

Varun was feeling sad and disappointed. What was he supposed to do? He could not have ordered 28 innocent Indians to die, not while the decision was in his hands. However, he had not expected things to become so heated up. He was also having a tough time handling the media and party seniors.

'Mr Defence Minister, we can all read between the lines. The whole nation is feeling let down and it cannot digest this coincidence. Such a shameful fiasco has probably been witnessed for the first time in the history of Indian defence. Every single terrorist from Hinduja Building, who were holding people hostage, as well as six dangerous Lashkar commanders have escaped safely. How is that possible? Opposition is even blaming you of coalition with anti-Indian forces,' a reporter said at the press conference Varun had called to explain his situation.

'I am more than happy that I could save 28 lives. I agree there was a security and intelligence lapse and in this process we had to release six dangerous terrorists from our custody. They knew our entire focus was on the hostages and they took advantage of that,' said Varun, wiping sweat off his forehead.

'Do you take responsibility of what has happened? We have news from our sources that you ordered to provide the terrorists in Hinduja building a safe passage in Indian choppers with unarmed Indian pilots at gunpoint, just after these six terrorists escaped from jail? It's such a shame! Are our defence forces capable of nothing? What about the lives of those two pilots?' the reporter fired a few questions at Varun.

'No! That is not true. These terrorists attacked one of our small air-force camps near Panipat and took these pilots hostage. The pilots, however, have returned back safely. Also, not a single hostage from Hinduja Building was killed. The last six persons that they were holding hostage were also released at the airbase a short while back. Not a single Indian life has been lost. That was my priority! No more questions please, we'll take a short break here,' replied Varun, got up and made a beeline to his office on the floor above.

◆

The six deadly Lashkar terrorists who had been released were now sitting in a PAK chopper flying them back to the camp. The party had already started and they were sipping Black Label and munching on delicacies... Welcome dishes were laid out for the heroes in the chopper.

Mazhar, the topmost Lashkar assassin said to Imran, 'Brother, why are you not having the meat? I know the scotch is a Lone Wolf but have some mercy on the lamb too.'

'Just not feeling like eating anything! Probably the joy of being back is so fulfilling that my stomach is already full,' said Imran, shifting uneasily, trying to ignore the mild lingering pain in his lower abdomen.

Farhan said, 'Me too, I was feeling the same, but I quickly

gulped down three pegs, so now my stomach can't tell me anything... After all, the tongue also has some rights.'

Babar, the dreaded right hand of Mazhar pointed out to the archipelago of lights below.

'I can't wait to meet Aslam and his company,' said Shahid, the man behind the explosions in the Kolkata subway, which had killed half-a-dozen innocent people two years ago. 'They must have reached the camp half an hour back. I trained the boy personally in one of our camps just six years back and look... Today, he saved our lives by leading the Hinduja Building Operation. It all comes back to you in this life itself! Allah is great.'

The six of them stepped out of the helicopter and proudly started walking towards the camp, their turbans flowing in the wind, their postures emanating confidence and a sense of victory.

BOOM! A loud explosion suddenly tore apart Imran who was on the chopper steps and the chopper went flying into the air with flames engulfing it.

They turned in disbelief, 'Those cowards planted a bomb in our chopper? Imran! they will pay for it. Brother,' shouted Farhan.

'I smell danger,' said Mazhar. 'Let us move to the camp,' a he said and took hold of Babar's hand and they doubled up towards the camp, followed by Shahid.

Farhan and Bashir were still glued in terror and sorrow. They recovered and started to follow. When **BOOM!** Another explosion. Mazhar turned back and he could see pieces of Farhan and Bashir flying in the air.

The three, still quite far from the camp, started running in terror. They were puzzled where the second bomb, that killed

Farhan and Bashir, came from? Had the bastards hidden it in their turbans? Mazhar pulled off his turban and threw it like shot-put with all his strength signaling the other two to follow suit. Panting, they reached the camp which was engulfed in festivity—terrorists firing guns, grenades and rocket launchers amongst deafening sound of Arabic music.

With expressions of heavenly relief on their faces, they entered the passage to the camp lined with militants holding machine guns. Before they could tell what had just happened, they were greeted by the entire team of friends in the camp standing in their honour as they started to sing the oath song. Senior militants and strategists of Lashkar and allied organizations were here to celebrate the occasion. And then again **BOOM**! The camp was on fire. **BOOM**!! No one was able to understand what was going on. **BOOM**!!! The entire crew went down as the whole camp turned into an inferno.

◆

Back at the press conference, Varun was holding a microphone to the mike, which was live telecasting the sounds, right from the time the terrorists were talking in the chopper.

He turned to the press who were dumbfounded at what was happening. 'Shahid was right. It all comes back to you in this life itself. Allah is great! These demons did not deserve anything less for the sufferings they inflicted on innocent people… And yes, for all those present here who may have felt let down, cursing me for my actions… I knew what I was doing all along. Those were micro-bombs we planted in the bodies of the terrorists.'

'But how did you do it, Sir? Did they not realize it from the surgery stitches and pain?' asked a reporter.

'There was no surgery! We told them we had to do a little

health check-up and put them on local anesthesia. Since they had no clue about what was happening outside, they had no reason to suspect or retaliate. We used a colonoscope to insert these micro-bombs recently developed by our scientists, which cling on to the epithelial tissue lining inside the intestinal tract. There were eight synchronized bombs inside each one. So, now you know why they were feeling heavy and did not feel like eating anything!' He laughed the last laugh as the whispers in the hall grew to roars.

Back at the Rawalpindi camp there was no one left to laugh.

'Colonoscope?' asked a reporter, adding, 'What is that?'

'A medical device that uses the right path to the insides, that these people deserve!' Varun said with a grin. The crowd burst into laughter.

'By the way, a message for the country's enemies and traitors… This is my country, don't you dare! There will be no dialogue, just colonoscopies! So, run for it! Jai Naya Bharat!' He saluted smartly before walking out of the conference hall.

♦

Salman, Raghav and Aditya were waiting at Varun's house for the cocktail party to celebrate this success. He had not forgotten to invite Madhav and Shyam, who would be feeling so relieved after all the trauma he had put them through. Their friend Varun 'Panga' Pandey had not changed after all.

Not a single terrorist, who had dared to underestimate India, had survived. This had also been the single biggest blow ever to terrorism being nurtured on Pak soil. Their entire think-tank and senior team had been destroyed. The best part was that Pak could not take it to any international forum, as it would only prove they were fostering terrorism.

'*Hamara bhai Hatimtai!*' they all said in unison, as they raised a toast once again for Varun and a new India...one that knew how to answer back its enemies in their own language; one that would go to any extent to sustain its self-respect; one that terrorists would dread to mess with.

Jatin and Gang at Macau

Macau, October 2018

Jatin woke up and it took him almost a minute to recollect where he was and how he had reached there. He recollected the long dream he had been having…of his life in London—a stark contrast to his current state. The mobile lying on the side of his king-size bed at the Hotel Lisboa kept buzzing incessantly, augmenting his misery. His head throbbed from the extra bouts of cocaine he had at the Uno Karaoke-Bar last night.

'What is it Mom? Why do you keep calling me at odd times?'

'It's 9:30 am there… Odd time?' he heard the confused voice of his mother. She would obviously be thinking he was in Delhi. He looked at the wall clock, the arms were aligned upwards. Macau was two-and-a-half hours ahead of New Delhi. It would be 5 am in London.

'I mean, for you. Why don't you get proper sleep?' His body ached and his left shoulder and arm felt numb. 'I was busy with some work. Can I call you later?'

'You won't! I know. You have not come to London for the last sixteen months. Don't you feel any pity for your mother? Just come here once. Let me see your face and touch you. You're all I have…,' she said, helplessly.

'I will, mom. After dad passed away, all the responsibility has fallen upon my shoulders. I can't even sleep properly.'

'Yeah, I know. You are not like your father. I raised you like that…to be responsible and hard working,' she said.

'Sorry mom, I have to rush. There's a press conference in five minutes,' he lied. 'Will call you later.… Love you.' He disconnected, letting out a deep breath, his mother's dialogue made him feel uneasy.

She had raised him like that… 'Like what? To be a moron, a disciplined, lifeless nobody?' he thought. He took out a small bidi, hashish wrapped in tobacco leaf, squat on the floor like a villager and started throwing spirals of smoke. This was the only way he could soothe his body after high nights in clubs.

All through the school and college, he had watched his friends enjoy their childhood and adolescence, while he remained slave to the schedule designed by his mother to make him an achiever. From academics to piano classes, from horse-riding to model UN debates at college, he was an all-round and a brilliant performer. He felt her pain and plunged into the fire to be moulded the way his mother wanted him to be.

She had suffered a lot. She was a religious and disciplined lady, extremely beautiful and intelligent, and the sole heir to Maharaja Group of Hotels after her father's death. Mr Jaswant Oberoi had fallen for her at a charity event in Paris. She too was drawn to him. His gentle, kind and calm personality made one feel Jaswant must have been a prince since many births.

Only after few years of marriage did she realize that he was a compulsive womanizer, promiscuous and detached to anyone and everyone. He didn't care for anyone except himself. On the exterior he was soft and benevolent. And that's how India knew him. That's what the long queues of party workers, who waited for him inside his royal palace while he played golf, adored him for...his princely charms! Inside, however, he was a grass addict and a reckless schemer, who knew the nerve of politics in an evil kind of way that people would take a lifetime to decipher.

But it was too late for divorce! She already had a son and knew that it would shatter the child. She could not bear to live with him, or to imagine that her son would become like his father one day. They decided by mutual consent that she would shift back to London, where her hotels were, and they would not have a formal divorce. It would save both of them a lot of embarrassment and inconvenience.

She sold off her hotels and dedicated every single moment of her life to make her son a virtuous man, keeping him away from every vice and trying to instill in him the values that the Oberois lacked. His statutory trips to India were designed to be short and he was apprised well in advance about every possible trap and pitfall that he might encounter during his royal stay at the palace. His brain was conditioned to look through the camouflage at the villain that his father really was. Although Jaswant kept telling him that he loved Jatin very much and that he was the one who would have to look after everything in the future, he didn't really develop any bond with him...not till he was 21-years-old.

He happened to be on a trip to the palace following the completion of senior high school. A lavish party had been thrown to celebrate the occasion. Left with no option, he was meeting his father's friends from the National Front nonchalantly. That's when he met Shreya, daughter of the then Foreign Minister, who was visiting India from the USA. She rescued him from the misery of throwing fake smiles at people and offered to accompany him on a walk across the sprawling lawns of the palace. At first, Jatin was nervous and clumsy, as the code of conduct designed by his mother had kept him at a safe distance from girls, but he soon became comfortable. He had never felt like this. It was a strange feeling of freedom. He tasted Pina Colada and Blue Lagoon with her from the bar, for the first time, as they returned to the party. They shared happy moments, laughed and hugged. Later, they also made out in his room.

It was not a big deal for the open-minded girl from the USA, but it changed Jatin's life. He had tasted blood. London suddenly appeared like a prison cell. He extended his stay by days and then months. He started taking interest in party work and would rarely visit his mother. She was heartbroken. Was it his father's genes starting to manifest? How else could years of moulding and instilling values be undone so quickly? She made herself believe that her son had not changed, it was only work that kept him busy.

The truth was just the opposite. Jatin utilized every moment of his new found freedom to make up for the years of deprivation. As fate would have it, he became exactly like his father. Even the squatting bidi position he used to sit in, to ease up his body, had been picked up from him.

It was a deadly combination. The skills of an all-round champion coupled with the diabolical Oberoi genes. His mother had unknowingly created a Frankenstein's monster.

With his oratory, planning and execution skills, he was quickly accepted within the party as the unopposed successor to Jaswant. One of his first acquaintances, who later became his closest friend, was Ranjit Shastri. He was educated abroad, had access to all luxuries being the only son of Cabinet Minister and industrialist Vinod Shastri, and nurtured the ambition of becoming more powerful than his father.

Of course, there were many other National Front members close to Jatin, but Brijmohan Gupta, though much older, enjoyed special respect as the 'Chanakya' of his core team. Not only did he have the acumen and insight into the ground realities of Indian politics, his cross-party networking was unbeatable.

The sound of the intercom phone ringing brought Jatin back from his thoughts.

'Good morning! What's the programme?' he heard Gupta say.

'Let's meet in twenty minutes at the Waterside Coffee Lounge,' replied Jatin.

'Okay, I already called Ranjit. He too had too much sniff last night. It's not good for you people,' said Gupta.

'Don't worry about us, Chacha Chaudhary. We know how to handle it. How is your Saboo?'

'Ganesh? He is perfect! Couldn't be better! Where else could he feast on a foursome, that too white skinned?'

'Foursome? What a beast! You told me he has three mistresses back in India too. The yellow envelopes, remember? You have adjacent rooms with a common door in between? *Apna khayal rakhiyega Gupta ji,*' Jatin laughed.

◆

'Friends! Enough of fun and frolic! Six months have passed and we have not made a single dent. A new government is entitled to the "honeymoon period" but not a defeated opposition like us,' Jatin said to Brijmohan and Ranjit, as they sat at the outdoor pool restaurant at The Lisboa, sipping Cappuccino.

'Defeated! No way! Defeat as you say, is when one stops striking. They have only been unduly lucky,' Ranjit said.

'Yeah! Not only lucky, they are smart at defence. But they

have follied in estimating their adversary. They will have to face a volley of attacks and there's no way they can escape it,' said Jatin.

'True. We have to nip them in the bud. Our core team is working overtime to execute the master plan we have designed for their destruction. It's only a matter of time,' agreed Gupta.

'Ranjit, is everything in order for the series of rallies and public meetings that I have in Andhra Pradesh and Telangana for the Lok Sabha elections?' Jatin asked.

'Yes, of course, 47 rallies in 22 days. It'll be hectic, but I know you will pull it off,' Ranjit replied. 'Party hard. Work harder… That's what you say, no? Now that the party is over, we will all slough our asses.'

'That reminds me the party fund will also need replenishment. What say Gupta ji?' said Jatin.

'Leave that to me. I have a series of meetings starting next week. Our ruling chief ministers, corporate alliances, overseas contacts, religious and communal outfits, all will be tapped in a systematic way,' replied Gupta.

'How do you put up with this weirdo?' Ranjit said, looking at Ganesh, who was walking around the pool towards them.

'Oh, he is sweet,' said Brijmohan. 'He will prove to be an asset for us in the times to come.'

'Sweet? Crass!' Ranjit looked at Brijmohan, shaking his head in disbelief as Ganesh came and stood there, looking sombre and distraught.

'Come, take a seat. I heard you had quite a blast last night. Then why are you looking so depressed Ganesh?' Jatin asked, biting deep into his eggplant pizza.

'Just received a call from Vashi. The Municipality bulldozers are at my new construction site. They are going to demolish sixty row houses almost on the verge of completion.'

'What, sixty row houses? That's quite a project. I did not know you have such large businesses running. Didn't you get the plan approved?' asked Ranjit.

'No, not exactly. There are some papers but you wouldn't call it an approval. Actually I had good connections within the Bharatiya Janhit Party when I initiated this project. I was directly in touch with the Chief Minister. No one could dare raise a finger on my work. But when I left them and joined you, I had thought that once the project would be completed and possession given to the buyers, the best the administration could do would be to ask for penalty. I could even go to the court and get a stay. But the project got delayed. Now with the Naya Bharat in power, there is hardly any hope for relief,' Ganesh said dismally.

'What about Ujjwal Shinde, the Naya Bharat CM? Don't you have good liaison with him, like you have with everybody else?' asked Ranjit.

'No. Actually he is not from Mumbai. Unfortunately, I haven't yet been able to approach him. I wish I had been a little more pragmatic,' said Ganesh.

'Don't worry, they can't take away your land, can they? When we get back, this time you can get proper permissions and restart,' Brijmohan teased him.

Ganesh stared at him angrily. It was a poor joke and mistimed.

Brijmohan looked slyly at Jatin and Ranjit and they all burst out laughing. Ganesh looked at them, flustered.

'Don't worry,' Ranjit said finally. 'Talk to Ujjwal, Gupta ji, before our friend has a heart attack.'

'Actually Ujjwal is very close to Gupta ji,' Jatin explained.

'We helped him save his face in the highway construction scam a few years back.'

'I don't know how to thank you!' Ganesh exclaimed, looking at Jatin adoringly, as Gupta ji strolled away calling someone on his mobile to comply with Jatin's instructions. Ganesh sat down on the floor next to Jatin's chair and started massaging his legs.

'Oh, stop it! People are watching,' Jatin said, looking at Ranjit as he turned his face away, giggling at Ganesh's gaucherie.

'Can't we stay here for a few more days?' Ganesh asked, re-occupying his chair. He sounded like a child on vacation.

'Seems you really like it here? Foursome and all?' Jatin teased him, Ganesh's raw spontaneity having made the atmosphere quite informal.

'*Langoor ke haath mein angoor,*' Ranjit whispered to Jatin in a hushed voice, still giggling.

'Stop making fun of me Ranjit ji, if you consider me your friend,' he said and then turning to Jatin replied, 'Of course! I love it here. Don't you? It's heaven here, the beauty is beyond words.'

'Let me confide something in you Ganesh. I am fed up of all this. I have had enough. I really crave for some desi stuff now,' said Jatin.

'What? That's like owning an orchard and saying you crave for fruit jam.'

'It's not so simple. Put yourself in my shoes to understand this. Here nobody knows me, so it's okay, I can do what I want. Back home, I am a national figure. One word against me from a girl and it would make headlines. We would be finished.'

'Oh! Right! You are too high profile to even risk a mistress,' said Ganesh.

'Of course! That's an even bigger hassle. The expectations,

tantrums and all,' said Ranjit, turning to Brijmohan Gupta who had just joined them after pulling the strings for Ganesh. 'Ask Gupta ji! No one knows the misery better than him. Every time our 120-kilo Mrs Gupta gets the faintest hint of his affairs, she becomes proactive, sexually! Whenever Gupta ji comes to the party office hunch-backed, it's a sure sign he has borne the brunt. She likes to be on top.'

Brijmohan laughed with them to conceal his embarrassment.

'Jokes apart, I have a ready-made solution for this,' said Ganesh. 'I have done it only once, for a film-star. Jatin ji, didn't I request you in our first meeting itself to give me an opportunity to extend my hospitality.'

'I trust you, Ganesh. But how?'

'Don't ask me that! You may choose from the most mind-blowing girls. Sometimes they will be under the influence of drugs, sometimes not. You can enjoy any kinky flavors you want…' he said.

'Oh yeah! Bondage, fetish, BDSM…?' Ranjit exclaimed, lost in fantasyland already. He was a voracious consumer of adult content on virtual space.

'But how can you be sure that the girl will not puke?' asked Jatin.

'Your honour is mine, my lord!' Ganesh said, 'I may look uncouth, but don't doubt my intellect. Half of the business community and politicians in Mumbai invest their black money with me. My designs are invincible.'

'Don't get me wrong. Even when we have to get some puny activist removed from our way, we do it in such a way that there are 10 links in between and nothing can lead back to us. Here you are talking about having a live witness. It could be suicidal!' said Ranjit.

'Who said your witness has to live?' Ganesh retorted, a bit angry at being taken as an under-wit. 'So many girls disappear every day in this country. One more gone is not a big deal. I'll make sure there is no clue or trace.' He looked alternatively at Jatin and Ranjit, unable to make out whether they were convinced.

'Hmmm…no clue or trace. How?' they asked.

'The body goes straight to my meat factory, even the bones are digested in the acid tanks,' he added with a pause, exuding self-admiration at his ingenuity.

'Eww…grotesque! I don't think I would like to use that helpline,' said Jatin.

'Sweet?' Ranjit smirked at Gupta, then added quickly, 'Sending Dr Sabbarwal's quadro to the meat factory would be a better choice.'

'Sure, you just have to order…,' Ganesh replied, sipping the drink he had carried down from his room. 'I would love to personally maul each one of them.'

'No!' Jatin said. 'No blood-stains on our hands. Those who rise will also fall. These over-enthusiastic scouts of Dr Sabbarwal will fall victim into our trap sooner or later. Just be patient and watch.'

'Hey! What is this drink you keep sipping all the time? You seem to really enjoy it, carried it all the way from your room! It looks darker than the usual Bloody Mary,' said Ranjit.

'The real piquant Bloody Mary,' replied Ganesh.

'And what's so real about it?' asked Gupta.

'Tomato juice, vodka and goat blood! Wanna taste?' Ganesh extended his hand as Gupta turned his head to the side and threw up.

Gold Strikes Salman
New Delhi, January 2019

'They say that the poverty line in India should be called 'starvation line'. If a person can earn just enough for two meals, he is no longer poor! The World Bank estimated that a massive 65 per cent of our population still earns less than $2 or ₹150 per day. Can anyone of us imagine surviving a month with that kind of an income? One of our earlier governments once declared that ₹36 per day was sufficient for a family to obtain two meals. Those who could not afford even that were the real poor people. This scared the shit out of the beggars, who thought, 'We earn ₹200 per day, five times the minimum limit, is the government going to put us in the creamy layer?'

The crowd burst out into laughter. The Minister for Finance, Urban Poverty Alleviation, and Roads and Highways, Salman was addressing the youth at Delhi University on their convocation day.

'It is a really selfish view of politicians and bureaucrats, who want to achieve minimum statistical standards, at the expense of their own people. If they live a poor man's life even for a single day, they would realize their agonies. I have seen what poverty really means. I have felt it...lived it. When the morning newspaper declares that the price of petrol has increased and one's heart skips a beat, wondering what to strike off from the monthly necessities to keep one's children's school bus fee going, that's poverty! When the grocer says that wheat-flour increased from ₹20 to ₹23 and one realizes now that he cannot afford sugar in his tea, that's poverty! Even a family earning ₹20,000 per month is faced with such blows every other day. The inflation is making the richer rich and the poorer poor. Have we all not come to terms with the fact that prices can only increase?' Salman was speaking his heart out. That's what connected him with the listeners.

He carried on, 'I too, cannot promise that prices will remain stable. But what I can do, or rather will do, is to make sure that they go down every month, till the commodities reach a fair price. I know it is difficult to believe. As the Finance and Poverty Alleviation Minister, I promise that I am going to change things and change them very fast. *Jai Naya Bharat!*'

The crowd gave a standing applause as Salman walked out waving towards them in acknowledgement. Although some thought he was too dramatic and raw, most people liked his bold and impulsive style. However, what everyone knew would finally matter, were the results, which were yet to be seen.

'He hails from a chawl in Mumbai. They say he has a bad temper. He does not have sufficient political or financial experience, nor a degree in economics,' analyzed a young reporter on Zee News, standing beneath a lamp post, trying to put in as much energy and punch in his words as he could. 'Today's speech by Mr Salman Mirza at the Delhi University has been labelled as a sheer hyperbole of a misfit Minister by Mr Ranjit Shastri, son of ex-Finance Minister Vinod Shastri, who is an MBA in Finance from Oxford University. Even the pundits of Indian economy feel that the promises made by the Minister were over-enthusiastic and unrealistic. Mr Rajan Iyer, retired senior advisor to the Ministry of Finance, said that such unrhythmic remarks can take the economy off track and advised the young Minister to be more cautious.'

Salman switched off the television, after watching a 15-minute brief video of the relevant news his staff prepared for him every day. He cursed himself for being so magnanimous with his promises at the university, yesterday. He knew that the economists, reporters and opposition were right. He really had no idea about how he was going to deliver what he had promised, irrespective of how truly he wanted it to happen.

He was in the conference room with his Secretariat, his 25th meeting since he had assumed office, eight months ago. The Secretaries, Additional Secretaries and the retired advisors and corporate consultants had all been asked to come up with brief PowerPoint presentations on 'How to achieve what your in-experienced Minister chose to blabber in an emotional frenzy at a public gathering'.

Salman was all ears. He was a science graduate. Whatever little knowledge of finance he had stemmed from his experience as the CEO of Coffee Moment. This knowledge had been grossly insufficient to help him cope with the responsibility for the first few months, but gradually he developed an acumen for it. His reasoning ability had always been top class. Although he did not understand many economic graphs and jargon, he more or less understood the path suggested by each presenter.

'Do you think the old man with the white dhoti only knew satyagrah? He was a learned economist as well. If we really respect the Mahatma, the father of our nation, we must tread the path promulgated by him. Swadeshi is the key. We must throw out the foreign companies sucking our blood,' opined Mr Mohit Trivedi, who was a Finance Secretary during one of the earlier governments.

'Make India a duty-free, open trade country,' suggested Dr Nitin Vij, Additional Secretary, as he continued to give logic in support of his theory: 'How tax havens like Dubai and Switzerland had become such beautiful countries with high per capita income?' Everyone present understood and sympathized with his condition. 'What better do you expect with a day's preparation that included choosing the correct slide design, font sizes and colours? How can an overburdened officer at the secretariat answer in a few hours, the question that remains unanswered in seven decades, that too with the compartmentalized exposure you give him in his specialized job? thought the presenters.

Salman was totally confused by the time all the fifteen presentations were over. Many of them gave contradictory suggestions, although the logic seemed in place by common sense. 'Tomorrow morning, same time!' he announced and walked out.

'Don't get a brain hemorrhage,' joked Aditya. 'Take some time to understand things, it has barely been eight months.' An emergency meeting of the quadro had been called by Salman.

Salman wore a grave expression. 'We can't keep borrowing from the World Bank to make our roads and to construct homes for our poor!'

'Why not! When it is time for repayment, you can simply handover the list of Indian Swiss bank account holders to the World Bank. You can tell them to go and recover the Euros from those accounts,' chuckled Varun, 'That way we can kill two birds with the same stone.'

'I know somebody who can be of help,' said Raghav. 'Murli Iyengar, retired IAS, an authority of sorts on Indian economy. The previous governments turned to him for advice whenever they were in trouble—the stock-market crash of 2010, growth rate decline to 4 per cent in 2013, rising inflation in 2015—he was always there and showed the way to pull through. He's your panacea, get him!'

The meeting with Murli went well, but Salman went to bed with the same predicament. The angry young man was in a hurry to turn things around as fast as he could, to make the best of his tenure.

As Salman was on his way to the ministry next morning, his mobile rang. It was Raghav. 'So, what was Murli's theory?'

'Foreign currency earned is the country's actual income. So keep dollar rate high to encourage exports, which will keep trade deficit in control. And much more…will tell you later. My meeting starts in another two minutes. His advice was so deep, it kept me up and thinking all night.'

'All the best, just follow Murli's advise to the word, he's the best and keep in touch,' said Raghav.

'Actually, I plan to do just the opposite, the result of his doctrine is what we can all see. We are in deep shit. I will take his advice at every step and do just the opposite…Will call you in the evening,' Salman confided in Raghav before hanging up.

'To bring down prices of foodstuff and essential commodities, the first thing we need to do is strengthen the Rupee, which is currently standing at ₹75 per USD, it should be no more than ₹45,' announced Salman at the meeting with the Secretariat and the Advisory Board.

'But Sir, if we do that, our exports will go down as our products will no longer remain competitive in the international market. That will deplete our Forex reserves and trade deficit will increase,' Ravi Shankar, the Finance Secretary, pointed out.

'I don't think so Mr Shankar. For a start, it will make petrol, diesel and petroleum products cheaper instantly, reducing the cost of transportation and a lot of other inputs. In fact, the basic raw materials for industry will become cheaper, leading to a fall in prices in the domestic market and competitive prices in the export market. This will boost exports and keep the import–export balanced,' said Salman, his mind crystal clear.

'But Sir, if Dollar is cheaper, won't it open the flood gates of import?' asked the Joint Secretary, Navendru Chandra.

'If import becomes cheaper, the domestic trade will also become cheaper. Let me explain. Due to higher dollar price, the imports are restricted and large-scale domestic industries earn profits by lobbying and by following monopolistic practices or playing with the elasticity of demand. As the basic raw materials produced by these industries like polymers, basic chemicals, cement, iron and steel, etc., become costly, everything else becomes costlier in a cascading effect. We all know how the large industrial houses in our country have been aligning with the government to mould policies in their favour. We have an abundance of natural resources and manpower. I strongly feel that we need to create a sense of plenty and change the mood of the manufacturing sector from being margin-driven to volume-driven,' said Salman.

'Sir, technically you are correct but...'

'Yes, I know what you mean. Didn't we immediately slash the petrol and diesel prices in line with international prices as soon as we came to power? We will do that again as dollar would become cheaper. Any reduction is to be immediately passed on. We will not keep the prices high to fill the treasury in the name of development. What's the use of such a development? Naya Bharat does not have any compulsions or obligations towards any of the conglomerates. This ministry will not work for meeting statistical figures, or keeping the share market vibrant. From today, you will all work with only one objective, that is, to bring down the cost of living. Is that clear?' concluded Salman as he got up to leave. There was an arrogance in his voice, which not everyone would have liked.

It is our country's tragedy that we want to be led by white-haired, elderly looking politicians and leaders. It is very difficult for us to accept young blood as our leaders or bosses. They are generally snubbed aside as over-ambitious fools.

'Yes, Sir,' resounded the choir of Secretaries and Advisors, many of whom liked his righteousness so much that the authority in his voice only motivated them further.

'Sir, the 50,000 compact homes, for which we granted funds to the UP Government, have not been occupied so far. When we called the State Secretary, today, he said that the people in the slums are not willing to shift,' said Mahendra Pratap, Secretary Urban Poverty, walking with Salman as he headed from the conference hall towards his car.

'Amazing! Unbelievable! How can anyone turn down free shelter, that too well equipped? What reason do they give?'

'They say it's too far from their place of livelihood. Also, they don't want to pay the electricity and water charges.'

'So, what do you suggest Pratap, how do we deal with this?'

'Sir, I am myself in a fix. On one hand, we can't have a running budget for paying the consumables bills. On the other hand, I sympathize with the poor people's reservation about paying monthly bills, who can't even afford two meals for their families.'

'Talk to the Chief Minister. We have Naya Bharat Government there. Have the slums demolished,' said Salman, 'Then, they will have no option but to shift.'

'But Sir,' Pratap looked up at him in disbelief. This did not go well with his image and nature of favouring the poor.

'You build a temple in the middle of the road and it hampers the traffic for decades. The hawkers occupy and block the footpaths and it becomes their rightful place. Why? Because they are poor? No! Because they from a formidable part of the vote bank. We have to bring some order to this country, yaar. People laugh at us when they travel to India, they wonder how we even exist like this. It may seem cruel now, but it will be good for them in the long run. Let them understand that they cannot have their way always. They have to follow the law! Open an employment office in the new colony built for them and depute our best employment counselor, Vinay Bhatia, to handle it. Let him contact all nearby factories and NAREGA office. Ask him to give me a weekly update.' Salman signaled the driver to move.

'Yes, Sir!' Mahendra Pratap said as the Minister's car sped away. The smile on his face gave away the pride he felt within, on being part of this reform process. This decision reminded him of how Naya Bharat government had recently handled the reservation movement of a particular community from Haryana. It had become a fashion over the last few years for communities to launch aggressive and violent movements to get the government to succumb to their demands, specially for reservations, flouting the law of the land. The government had adopted a 'No-non-sense' approach to crush the movement. The violent protestors were warned, beaten up by the police and military, and many of them were put behind the bars. Tear gas, rubber bullets, water cannons and even lathi charge was done. Some people suffered fatal injuries too, but the message went out loud and clear—no one was above the law of the land. Appeasement politics was not the flavor of the season.

Salman had just laid back to rest for a while, when his mobile rang. 'Sir, we have some really messy evidence on money laundering against the Bijlani Group. I need your urgent permission to raid their factories and offices all over India.' It was Arindam Chaudhary on the other end, head of the Central Economic Intelligence Bureau (CEIB).

'Why are you asking me Arindam? Follow the procedure.'

'I am sorry, Sir, but the last Finance Minister had given us clear instructions to seek permission before any large operation against a listed blue-chip company or a politician. And we hardly had time to seek your written permission as per the procedure. We may be losing valuable evidence each minute,' he explained.

'Arindam, never ask me again. And do mention every detail in the daily progress report that you send me.'

Naya Bharat core team had instructed all department heads to send an email report at the closing of the day. They personally read and replied to these mails every day. The newfound answerability amongst the entire bureaucracy was the effect, the cause being the healthy ownership exercised by the Naya Bharat team.

Salman had a clear plan. A plan because of which he had taken up the formidable task of managing the three ministries of Finance, Housing and Urban Poverty Alleviation, and Road Transport and Highways. It had taken a lot of convincing with Dr Sabbarwal, who finally conceded, seeing his plan, passion and spirit. He planned to tap a resource that was enough to bring India to the league of developed countries in just a few years.

It was so abundant, you just had to pierce a hole and the black gold would gush out from the channels that ran like arteries in every corner of the country. No, this resource was not natural gas or coal. It was the underground economy, with a rippling flow of black money. It was an irony that a sizeable chunk of population lived a life of deprivation, while this resource continued to flow right below the very ground they inhabited.

Departments including the Investigation Division of Central Board of Direct Taxation, Director General of Income Tax, Enforcement Directorate, Financial Intelligence Unit, Central Board of Excise and Customs, Directorate of Revenue Intelligence, Customs Overseas Investigation Network, and the CBI had been given a free hand to attack the underground economy and bring the black money to the government exchequer. This money was used for infrastructure improvement—construction of roads and highways, bridges and dams, and houses for the poor etc. The highways lined with moulded aluminum railings and the roads neatly divided by greenery and multi-coloured flowers, were beginning to resemble those that an Indian would see and envy in Guangzhou.

'Are you sure all the money actually reaches the government treasury, Sir? Who knows, in many cases the officers may be striking a deal with the business houses?' asked Rehman, the famous columnist who wrote for The Times of India, at the Lead India conclave, where Salman was the chief guest.

'Who told you we raid only the business houses? Our departments raid bureaucrats, professionals, state government officers, judges and even Ministers. Just a sniff of black money and we are there. I know my officers are working honestly.'

'How can you be so sure? These are the same people in the same departments which had become corrupt and almost defunct earlier? They used to be puppets in the hands of the ruling party. What have you done to change them?' asked Vimal Thapar, another activist and writer, who wrote for the Midday.

'They are still puppets in the hands of the ruling party as you can see. The difference is in the intentions of the puppeteer. The only special thing that I have done is to establish answerability. I will not take any favours and my team knows I won't allow them to do so either. I don't spend my time in inaugurations, public gatherings and useless political meetings to enhance my vote base. Instead, I do the work for which this office was created and for which this country pays me,' replied Salman with an infectious passion. Standing at the podium under the yellow spotlight, dressed in a high-neck black suit, his hair neatly combed, he looked more like a rockstar than a politician.

'I hope you won't stop me from doing what the country pays me for!' said a tall, dark-complexioned, lean officer with a thin authoritative moustache and resolute expression, who was standing in the aisle in the middle of the auditorium facing the stage, just a few steps away. He was wearing a grey safari suit. He was flanked on either side by about ten sturdy, well-built officers.

'What is the matter?' asked Salman.

'Vinod Saxena, CBI. You have to come with us, Sir,' he said, holding his badge.

Salman climbed down the stage, his security persons following him closely.

'Yes, officer?'

'You are under arrest, Sir.'

Salman tried hard to think what he could have done. He had done so many insane things before joining politics, he would not have been surprised had he been arrested then. For instance, the incident at the ESI hospital when Amit's father was fighting for his life and he had beaten up the clerk. But he could not recall having done anything recently that could have him arrested, that too by the CBI.

And then it struck him! It must be one of the cases lodged against him by various temple management committees. Three months back he had passed a government order, attaching the wealth amassed by temples and other religious establishments to a special fund created to facilitate provision of courtroom buildings for the 20,000 judges that were to be appointed. The Naya Bharat core team, after intense deliberations had concluded that it would be more apt, because the crippled judicial system forced people to turn to God for justice and this could be a way of answering their prayers. Many of the temple trusts moved to court and not only sought relief but also blamed him for hurting the religious sentiments of the people. But why would the CBI get involved? Maybe some court had ordered a probe by CBI, but in that case the legal department of the Finance Ministry should have informed him!

'What are the charges against me?'

'There are many, Sir, including money laundering, amassing disproportionate wealth, cheating the country and misappropriation of national funds, to name a few. We have orders from the High Court and the Speaker of the Lok Sabha has been intimated about the same too,' said the officer.

Oggy and the Cockroaches
New Delhi, January 2019

'That's the difference between God and human beings,' said Sumant Srivatsan, Deputy Director, Central Economic Intelligence Bureau.

'But Sumant, he was really playing God so well! Fearless, fair, all powerful! Like Mahadev! Why did he have to do this and shatter our faith? I respected him. It is hard to believe he did this,' replied Arindam Chaudhary.

'I remember few days back he told you not to seek his permission for doing what's your job, no matter who is involved. I saluted his boldness and righteousness then. I feel like a fool now,' Srivatsan said sadly. 'Thotti!' he muttered under his breath.

A team of about 50 officers had been busy since morning, taking stock of the jewellery and gold biscuits filled in trunks spread across the 100 square meter underground basement, situated at the rear end of the Finance Minister's bungalow.

The bungalow was surrounded by CRPF jawans. Vehicles with red lights on top swarmed all around. They were greatly outnumbered by the profusely branded media vehicles with satellite dishes on their roofs, parked on the other side of the road.

'Naya Bharat has faced a big setback as their heroic quadro minister fell from grace today. The house that you see here is where the Finance Minister spends most of his time. Located in the posh Friends Colony area, this three-storey building is located in a densely populated neighbourhood. This morning several investigation agencies including the CBI raided the house against information that the Minister has siphoned a large treasure for himself from the "Temple jewels for justice" operation launched by him three months back. This operation was being closely controlled by the Minister himself, and now we know for what reason!' the ABCD news reporter Jagat Bindra, shouted vehemently at the cameraman standing just four feet away from him. For Bindra, it had been an eventful journey from being an obscure regional reporter at Sahara Uttar Pradesh to the most notorious one on this national channel. He had mastered the art of negative reporting, reaping rich dividends. He was five feet four, a thin and sly reporter who could spice up and extract juice from a banana. As he spoke, his hands swayed like an orchestra director in a strange mannerism that the audience loved. He felt a sense of deep satisfaction and pride in bringing out such unexpected and dramatic truths, as if he himself had nabbed the culprit. 'Mr Salman is a traitor, no less than Kasab. Kasab had shot a few innocent people, but the Minister has stabbed 140 crore citizens in their back.' Both his hands stabbed an imaginary human as he spoke. 'People are anxious to know what Raghav Chandel, Aditya Garg and Varun Pandey have to say about this. Were they aware of this scam? Were they part of it? Or has Minister Salman Mirza been manipulating them? Don't go anywhere, we will be with them shortly, after the break.'

'The value of the treasure found in Mr Salman's basement

must be way over 5,000 crore, which once verified may become the largest scam of its kind, by an individual in the history of the country. There have been scams like the Coal Allocation Scam and 2G Spectrum Scam, much larger in value, but in both these cases the value of the scam was the notional value of loss suffered by the country. Never has cash or gold been found stowed away so shamelessly by a person in such high position. The people are feeling let down, more than ever before,' analyzed Sumit Bakshi from Indian TV. The race for TRP was in full swing. Sumit was a bald, dusky, tall man with a thin moustache and a serious expression. 'With me I have here Mr Vimal Raizada who lives just four houses away in this lane. Mr Raizada, did you ever see any suspicious movement around the house, such as that of trucks or something of that sort?'

'Well, it's the Finance Minister's house as well as his camp office and there is a regular movement of vehicles, both small and large, to and from this building. The point is that from whatever we know about Mr Salman, it is hard to believe he could have done this,' replied Mr Raizada.

'So you mean this may be a conspiracy? You mean someone discreetly sneaked the trunks full of gold and silver into his basement, worth over ₹5,000 crore? Well, let me and our audience chew on that!' said Sumit, as the camera closed up on his face, to capture every twitch of his eyebrows and lips, his trademark favourite with the audience.

♦

'The entire country is enjoying the gossip, our national pastime. They are relishing the downfall of their own hero, deriving excitement from it in their otherwise mundane lives. Why is it that a country of 140 crore cannot take any issue seriously?

They can come out on the streets, shout slogans and support a cause for days and weeks, and then totally forget about it! Some say we are a media-controlled emotional lot. Media wields the power to control our emotions and manipulates it to their benefit. Maybe it is God's way to keep the people of this nation happy in such adverse and regressive conditions, which would otherwise make them insane or cannibals. My Lord, I would like to remind the honourable court that Mr Salman is one person who has burnt his blood to change all that,' Advocate Rohit Singla said, addressing the bench of two retired Supreme Court judges now serving the fast-track special court established in the Naya Bharat regime for trial of elected public representatives.

'Objection, My Lord! Today is the third day and my friend seems to be doing nothing but taking us into flashback. We have objective evidence against the accused. There is no end to the questions the defence can keep putting up. Can we find the vehicles that carried the treasure? Can we locate the people whose fingerprints are there on the treasure chests? I mean, what kind of questions are these? We are not talking about a packet of brown sugar, we are talking of 30 tonnes of precious metal and diamonds, stuffed away in the basement of one of the most powerful political figures in the country. And for the last three days the defense has not been able to give any convincing explanation,' Joyesh Bhangar, the state counsel submitted.

Raghav, Varun and Aditya were sitting in the front row. They had hardly slept for 24 hours in the whole week. They had tried to think of all their political and non-political enemies who could have conspired against them, had all kinds of investigations done, but could not arrive at any conclusion. What was mind-boggling was the kind of money involved. Salman also did not have any clue how this had happened, right under his nose.

'I would like to call upon my final witness, Mr Sumant Srivatsan, Deputy Director, Central Economic Intelligence Bureau,' announced the State Counsel.

'Mr Srivatsan, your colleagues including Mr Arindam Chaudhary have investigated every atom of detail in this case. Mr Salman says that his basement had not been opened for many months. He had never personally been to this basement, which is at the rear end of his house, in the past one-and-a-half years, after he shifted to this house. Your report says it had signs of regular frequenting by humans, footprints, fingerprints, etc. Tell me is there any way by which someone could sneak in 30 tonnes of treasure into his basement?'

Srivatsan kept silent for a while, thinking really hard. He had pondered over this question a thousand times already during his investigation.

'We tried to match the fingerprints of all the workers and servants in the house with those on the chests, but there was no match. There are only six fingerprints on the entire lot. It would take several days for six people to sneak in that kind of quantity into the basement, past all the security. I would say it is kind of impossible,' Srivatsan replied. 'Thotti!' he muttered to himself. He hated being fooled. He prided himself for having an invincible power to look through people's character, which had failed him here.

The defence could not hold ground. The treasure had been found in Salman's basement and there was no way his entire team could prove his innocence. He was sentenced to imprisonment for five years and the treasure was made government property.

'Jisne bhi ye kiya hai, use prasaad to milega,' Salman smiled, as he stopped to have a word with his friends on his way to the

police vehicle parked outside the court. He did not want them to feel weak. 'It won't be long,' he added, jerking his head to throw back strands of hair from his forehead because his hands were held by police officers standing on either side of him. His fearless expression and confidence in his friends moved them to tears. They helplessly watched him being taken away from amongst the dense crowd of supporters, journalists, bystanders and advocates.

'What is this bugger doing here?' Varun whispered to Raghav. He spotted Ranjit Shastri standing with his gang a few yards away, talking to somebody gleefully over his mobile.

'Come, let us find out,' Raghav charged towards Ranjit, closely followed by Varun and Aditya.

'I am so sorry for Salman,' Ranjit said, extending his hand towards Raghav. He tried to show concern but could not conceal his buoyancy. He quickly took back his hand realizing his mistake, since there was no reciprocation from the other side.

'I knew it all along. You guys are behind this...,' Varun burst out, not able to control his anger.

'Arrre... Hold on! Is something wrong with your friend, here?' Ranjit retorted, looking at Raghav, trying to sound indignant. 'Has Salman's betrayal affected your mental balance or something?'

'I know what Jatin and company is good for. Cheap plots are what you people excel at,' said Aditya.

'F*** off. I came here only out of curiosity,' Ranjit snapped back. 'And let us say, we did it...Go prove it. What did you think? You think you are running the country? We have been in control, all through. We can throw you out of power like this,' he said, rubbing his thumb and middle-finger. 'What a pathetic bunch of losers!' he muttered audibly as he walked away.

The trio seethed in anger. They could see him walking

away with Joyesh Bhangar, the State Counsel, who was waiting for him near a tea-stall.

◆

It had been two weeks since Minister Salman was convicted. Sumant Srivatsan was watching Oggy and the Cockroaches with his five-year-old son and seven-year-old daughter. This was his ultimate stress buster and also helped him spend some quality time with his children, giving them an opportunity to laugh together. By default, he supported Oggy and the children cheered for the cockroaches. Our children are the only ones we happily lose against.

'Thotti!' he mumbled as Oggy faced another humiliating defeat from the cockroaches. The cockroaches were taking away the birthday cake Oggy had locked away in his cupboard and was guarding, sitting with his back resting on the cupboard door. The cockroaches stole the cake by entering the cupboard by drilling its base through a sewer line below the house. The children laughed in sheer delight when Oggy opened the cupboard and found a big round hole at its bottom. The cockroaches were shown feasting on the cake in the adjacent house.

'Come to the dinner table sooner than the cockroaches in our house!' Rukmani, Sumant's dominating and eternally irritated wife peeped through the half-opened door and shrieked at them. She loathed the 'hee-hee haw-haw.' It reminded her of children gone wild and out of control in her class. As a teacher she was dreaded far and wide, in her own school as well as by the children from other schools, who joined the tuition batches she took at home. But her being a strict teacher was not the reason behind her irritable behavior at home. The true reason was that she suspected Sumant was having an affair.

Rukmani was a good-looking woman with a dark complexion. She had been brought up in a conservative south-Indian Hindu family—religious, disciplined and in control of their lives. Sumant and Rukmani had been married for fourteen years now. For the past few months, there was a cold war between them. First, Sumant tried to reconcile, but later gave up thinking that maybe it was some hormonal change that happens to women in their mid-age and makes them irritable. It would auto-correct with time.

Rukmani sat at the table and watched Sumant sip the sambhar, spoon after spoon. She found the slurping sound highly irritating. Even more irritating was the fact that he was lost in his own world. He had all the time in the world to watch cartoons, but none for her. She was about to say something when suddenly he raised his head and said, 'I will have to go, I just remembered some urgent work.' He got up, put on his long coat, sprayed some perfume from the adjacent shelf and walked out of the door, not looking at her even once.

'Keep some condoms from the drawer too,' she shouted at him in her mind.

Rukmani wearily removed the dishes. She was holding back her tears. How could he be so shameless? A few tears rolled down her cheeks, as she went to bed. 'I have to divorce him, tomorrow,' she decided that she would not take it any longer.

Srivastan brought his car to a halt outside a house and honked several times. Arindam scuttled down the road in the middle of the lawn sprawled outside his bungalow, as the guard held the door open.

'I want the engineering team and about 20 workmen at 24/2, Friends Colony within half-an-hour,' commanded Sumant to someone over his mobile, as Arindam gave him a puzzled look.

Arindam trusted his deputy's IQ and had given him a free hand, deputing most of the investigation and execution work to him.

They were standing in the now empty basement of Salman's house. 'Arindam, I know what I am about to do may prove to be a stupid whim. But if I am right, you must start watching Oggy and the Cockroaches. Promise me!'

The engineering team arrived. He got the linoleum flooring cut and removed. 'Break the cement cover,' he told the chief engineer. The electric hammers promptly broke away the inch-thick plaster. Below it was RCC.

'What now, Sir?'

'Start cutting,' he said.

It was rock solid RCC, strong enough to break several hammer tools but by the dawn the four-inch RCC was broken to small pieces and swept away into a corner, leaving them standing on the soil below.

'What now Srivatsan?' Arindam yawned at him. 'What are you trying to do? Is there more treasure here?'

A man with a gadget in his hand walked down the stairs. 'Sir, here is the ultrasonic density tester you asked for from the Jabalpur Geology office.'

Sumant scanned the entire floor inch-by-inch looking at the digital display and marking the area of interest with a white powder-releasing marker. He ended up marking a circle, about five feet in diameter, at the back side of the basement.

'Dig!' he said, and six men with spades started digging inside the circle. After some time they encountered fairly soft soil and the heap above started growing rapidly as they sunk below ground. The soft soil was telling them where to dig.

It was slightly past noon, when Sumant's mobile rang. His

head spun from what he heard. 'Where are you?' he asked.

He and Arindam reached the court premises. Rukmani was sitting in advocate Nair's room and had the divorce papers ready.

'Rukku. What's the matter?'

'₹1 lakh per month, the house in Tiruchirappalli and both the children! Nothing less! Give it peacefully and you can have your way,' Rukmani said firmly, though her sore, swollen eyes that gave away her vulnerability.

'Are you out of your mind? Are you having an affair? Why would you want to do that?' asked Sumant.

Rukmani slapped him on the face. 'How dare you? Aren't you ashamed?'

'Of what? You want to divorce me for watching Oggy and the Cockroaches?'

'It really does not matter to you, does it? You think you can keep cheating on me and be so cool about the whole thing?' she yelled.

Sumant was silent for a while, thinking how she might have got that ridiculous idea. 'Look Rukku, I know I have been preoccupied with work for the last few months. I enjoy my work, it's true. I have been out many nights, but I was in the headquarters working on some really important projects. I'm not having an affair.' He turned to Arindam for support.

'Yes, Bhabhi. I would have been the first one to tell you if he did anything like that,' said Arindam.

'Look at me, Rukku, who would put up with me for a single day other than you?' Sumant said, comfortingly.

His mobile rang and he listened for a while. 'We will be there in half-an-hour.'

A kiss on Rukmani's cheek took her by surprise. She couldn't remember when was the last time he had kissed her so tenderly.

It's intriguing 'how little' women need in terms of reconciliation. A tender kiss can weigh more than a lakh a month, a house in Tiruchirappalli and a hassle free (husband-free) life.

'Duty calls! I have to rush but I'll be home early and I promise to make it up,' said Sumant as he walked out of Advocate Nair's office hurriedly.

They could hardly walk erect in the tunnel as they entered and started walking along it. The density monitor had shown the team which way to dig. They were re-excavating a tunnel that had already been dug some time before, the mud was still soft in that passage. They had hardly walked 30 meters, when they saw the other end of the tunnel open above them. They climbed up into a damp and dingy room.

'Sir, this is the basement of 32/3, Friends Colony. This house is owned by some Ajay Bhargava, who lives in Singapore currently,' informed an officer.

'So, this is how the treasure was planted in Mr Salman's house. Quite an ingenious scheme!' said Arindam as they drove to the headquarters where the press would be waiting for their comments. 'The conspirators must have done a lot of meticulous planning and hard work to put the soil back in place, match the RCC and plaster finish etc., after the job was done. Had it not been for the density meter, we would never have been able to find out. Who would think of breaking the RCC to discover some hidden tunnel underneath. I am sure this basement must have been locked for months, as Mr Salman had said. How did you think about it Srivatsan?'

'I must thank the cockroaches for that, I saw them stealing the cake from Oggy through an underground tunnel and it struck me how easy it could be.'

'Who are our cockroaches? Any idea?'

'We'll soon find out,' said Sumant. 'Whoever he is, he has to be a Nizam of sorts to pump in that kind of wealth to knock out the Minister.'

'Yes, someone for whom defaming him is worth much more than 5,000 crore.'

The phone rang and Sumant listened to it carefully.

'The fingerprint experts have confirmed that the fingerprints in the basement of 32/3 match with those found on the trunks. Yes, this was a conspiracy! The owner of the house has been taken in custody at Singapore and is being deported to Delhi. Very soon, we will have the real culprit under the scanner. For now, that's all friends,' Arindam stated at the press conference.

Outside, the celebrity reporters were busy giving bytes. 'Today, Salman Mirza has been reborn. Like a Phoenix he has risen from the ashes and so has Naya Bharat. The last two years have seen more growth and development than the last two decades, thanks to Naya Bharat. There are many who would like India to sink...China, Pakistan, ISIS, the underworld...the list is long. We shall keep you updated with each bit of detail as this mystery unfolds. For now, it is time to celebrate! This is Sumit Bakshi live from Indian TV.'

Raghav at Tokyo
New Delhi, July 2020

Raghav got up early today; he did not feel fresh like he would every morning, but he couldn't stay in bed. He walked to the balcony, switched on his mobile and called someone. 'What is the news, Major?'

'Not good, boss. Our plans seem to be failing,' said Ramdas, waking up from shallow slumber, in his hotel room. 'I feel so guilty... This mission is so important for our national pride, we have spent 10 times the budget of Pakistan this time and still, yesterday, we could hardly reach the target.'

Raghav's voice was reflecting the turbulence within. 'What is the problem? I have personally been involved in the final training of these boys for the harshest conditions and to face the toughest international studs. I know they will snatch our rights from the USA and China. These people have been dominating for too long. Get what you have gone there for and call me back with some good news, today.'

'Yes boss, once this mission is successful, the world will give us the respect that we deserve. I will call you back by evening with some better news,' said Ramdas, his voice fraught with determination.

Raghav's mind was racing. He was turning all figures and information upside down in his memory. It was 7 am, he observed in his wristwatch as he walked down the stairs to the portico, where a chauffeured Ambassador was ready to take him to his office.

He was hastily taking out one file after another in his office and flipping the pages quickly, looking for something. He did not have the time to wait till 9 am for the staff to arrive. He was actually looking for details of Avinash Rathaur, the shooter who could hit the bull's eye five times in a row, who was leading a retired life in a small town in Himachal Pradesh. He vividly remembered his encounter with Avinash, who had called him about a year ago and sought appointment. His simple clothing—a loose fitting trouser and untucked shirt, and the cloth bag hanging from his shoulder made him look more like a village teacher. He had expressed his desire to be part of any such mission. Avinash had told him very confidently that it is not so easy to go outside the country and achieve the target even under adverse conditions and tremendous mental pressure. As Avinash had spent his entire life on this and been on four such missions earlier, only he had the master plan to get the best results and to keep the motivation the spirit of killing high.

At that time Raghav was not too impressed and eventually forgot about it. He had been working on this mission ever since he had been given this office. He had proved himself to be an excellent Education Minister in his state, but holding a Union Minister's post was much more demanding than he had thought. As the Education Minister, his decisions had implications inside the country, but now this portfolio had the whole world looking at him.

He could not understand why only Avinash came to his mind, out of so many people who wanted to dedicate their life to the nation. He remembered that he had had this strange dream and his men were losing one after another, when Avinash had stepped in and guided them to victory. 'Oh!' he thought to himself, feeling stupid. 'How can I act so strangely, probably I am under some kind of subconscious influence due to this tension!' He sank into his chair, depressed and tired. His mind drifted again to that day when Avinash had come to his office. As the scene played in his mind, he could see the serene expression on Avinash's face as he talked. And the phenomenon dawned on him now. This expression of saintly serenity, engulfed in ocean-deep confidence had struck his subconscious mind then only, even though the meeting ended like countless others. This impression had surfaced in the form of his dream last night. So, his search for the 'navigator' was not just a wild dream, it had a logical connection.

Raghav's helicopter landed in a farm in Dharamgarh, where Avinash was waiting for him, practicing shooting. Varun caught a glimpse of the target board, all shattered around the centre. They walked to his small two-room house and after ordering some tea for the guests, Avinash said, 'I have a feeling like today could be the day I have lived my life for. Tell me, how I can help you?' Raghav explained the situation and asked for his advice. 'I am a soldier, Sir, not a consultant. I have to be there...on the scene...to make any difference,' said Avinash, picking up a thick briefcase intricately decorated with inlay work.

They had a brief discussion on Avinash's techniques and methodology to facilitate the success of the mission. Though Raghav could only partially understand them, he followed his gut feeling about Avinash.

'Ok, it is 9 am and if we fly now by a chartered plane from Delhi, we will reach Tokyo by 4 pm,' said Raghav.

As the plane landed, Avinash could feel the itching in his stomach that accompanied the thrill of going on such missions—the feeling one has while taking a roller coaster ride. Tokyo is the land of the 'Yazuka'—the dreaded tattooed mafia, hi-tech criminals, internationally feared drug syndicate and what not. Had he been chosen for a similar mission by the previous government, maybe he could have been in a better place like Rio de Janeiro.

They quickly stepped into the SUV from the Indian Embassy that drove them to the site of action—a large stadium. The Indian crew at Olympics was waiting for them at their pavilion. They were thrilled to see the Sports Minister at the battleground. Mission 'Golden Bird' that was initiated two years ago, when Raghav assumed office, had culminated in an Indian crew of about 200 people contesting the Olympics. They had targeted a total of 75 medals including thirty golds, of which 10 medals were to be bagged on the opening day, including two golds. However, Ramdas had called Raghav this morning and informed him that they could win only one gold, two silvers and two bronzes on the opening day.

Most of the crew seemed to know Raghav as a result of his personal interaction with them over the last two years in training camps and sports academies that he had specially set up across the country. 'I feel pleasure to introduce to you our Dronacharya, Mr Avinash, who will be with you for the rest of the mission and help you at every step to achieve your targets.'

'Yes, at least with all sports related to violence,' said Avinash in a lighter mood, 'like shooting, archery, boxing, wrestling, judo, fencing etc.'

'You are with the right team, Sir,' said Aakash, India's ace boxer. 'That's the especiality of our country! While we may be known world over for non-violence, our troop has the largest contenders for these sports.'

'Yes, 82 gold medals can be won in these sports alone, my friends,' said Avinash. 'So our target of thirty golds is not hard to get. Those of you who have their events today, please come with me for a few minutes.'

Avinash was now talking to Rajendra, an archer, who had his event after half-an-hour. He told Rajendra to close his eyes and listen to him carefully. He started by asking him to focus on his breath. Then, he took him through an imaginary exercise where he was aiming at his target. He was surrounded by his competitors on either side, all of them having stern expressions on their faces. Rajendra could see wrinkles of tension on his forehead and feel his heart pounding. Avinash asked him to pull the string looking at the red circle in the centre of the annular rings he was supposed to shoot at. He was about to let go of the arrow when Avinash asked him to hold the string and follow his breath. Then, he took him through a meditation session he had devised, which would result in a firm and more stable posture. He made Rajendra look at the target till he could see only the target and not the people on either sides. Then, he asked him to focus only on the black circles till that time, when he could see nothing but the red circle—the bull's eye. He, now, asked him to hold his breath for three seconds, count, and let go of the string on the count of three. Rajendra could see the arrow rush for the target and land at the bull's eye. He repeated the same again and again and to his surprise all the arrows landed at the centre making the earlier ones fall off. Rajendra did not realize when he went into a deep slumber. Raghav looked at

Avinash from a distance, as he talked to someone on the phone.

'How long has it been?' asked Rajendra, worried, as he opened his eyes. 'Exactly 18 minutes since we walked away from the group,' said Avinash, 'How do you feel?'

'I feel like I have just woken up from a night long sleep—fresh, energized and calm. All the anxiety built up since morning…whether I would be able to live up to the expectation or not…has vanished,' replied Rajendra.

'Did our new coach tell you something that I missed in the last three years?' asked Acharya, Rajendra's coach, walking towards them with Ramdas. Rajendra smiled and walked towards the archery fencing…cool and confident.

Next in line was Kuldeep, wrestler in 'light weight' category, who was to take on the mighty Ukranian, Gomez, having world no. 2 ranking. 'What is your strategy, young boy?' asked Avinash.

'I have watched Gomez's videos and observed his style, strengths and weaknesses. It is almost impossible to overcome his brawn and toughness. He has never been knocked-out no matter how much physical abuse he faced in a match. He used to be a war soldier. The Russians once got hold of him, removed his nails, cut one of his earlobes and two fingers from his feet, and held him prisoner at one of their camps. They left him lying on the floor of their torture dungeon, writhing in pain. This was their greatest blunder! Even in this state of agony, he escaped, killing all of them at night with their own guns. I have planned to exhaust him and then trap him down, that's what Ustad Nemichand ji has also advised me to do.'

'And how will you do that, Son?' asked Avinash.

'I have practiced for 14 hours a day. Ustad ji has put me through intense pain-inducing isostatic postures, such as pulling my arm backwards and holding it there till one would faint of pain. Gomez may be a bit stronger, but I will outsmart him.'

'Very good, I am sure you can do it,' said Avinash, 'Now, I want you to loosen yourself, close your eyes and picturise what I say, in your mind.' Like Rajendra, he took Kuldeep through a hypnotic meditation session. Raghav had now joined him and was observing him very carefully. After all it was an experiment he would be answerable for. Nemichand, who was also very curious, had joined them too. As Kuldeep opened his eyes, he kept silent for another two minutes as if basking in the after-effect of the session and looking at his ustad ji intermittently before he asked Avinash, 'Sir ji, I already feel like a winner. You covered almost every possible situation in the imaginary fight in which you led me to victory. However, I want to ask why you adopted the reverse style? You made me attack Gomez the moment I stepped in the ring and kept me on the aggressive mode till the last.

Avinash turned to Nemichand and said, 'Ustad ji, first of all I must say that you have trained Kuldeep really well; especially the endurance, it is unbreakable. Just one small alteration is required. With your training Kuldeep can take on the world's best, given his stamina, resistance to pain and advanced combat techniques. But when he already has everything, what is the benefit of being defensive? Statistics say that chances of victory in defensive combat are only 41 per cent. Also, the chances of winning when a wrestler trained in defensive style but fights in an aggressive one are doubled. Now, I leave it to you to guide him for the best.'

He knew his job was half done. The inner calmness had been established as he had aligned Kuldeep's consciousness with the centre of his being through the meditation session. The chakras were perfectly aligned. This technique was Avinash's own invention, developed through the years of meditation in the Himalayas with the saints and tapaswis. He had combined the techniques of the spiritual world with science and logic. For years, he had researched combat techniques by watching videos, studying literature, interacting with the best trainers across the world during the Olymics, Asiads, Commonwealth and other games that he visited over the last twenty years. But this may just not be enough, Avinash's instincts told him…not against Gomez!

He asked Raghav for a minute and they went inside a meeting chamber, a few yards away. Avinash delicately put his decorated briefcase on the table and opened it. Raghav who had been wondering ever since they boarded the plane what it contained, could see it had a diary, some tools, a very old looking book with an antique wooden cover and many tiny bottles, almost like ampoules with different colours. He took out one of those bottles, turned towards Raghav and said, 'I need your permission to give this to Kuldeep. It has to be taken exactly 20 minutes before the fight…that is now!'

'I may agree to your uncanny ideas and strategies, but how can an experienced person like you even think of giving any such drug to an Olympic player?' said Raghav. 'Any kind of booster medicine could not only ruin our dream but also bring shame to the country. I will not allow you to do anything like that!'

'But, this is not a steroid, it is a herbal extract from a rare plant species that is found in the mountain ranges of the Himachal. It catalyzes certain complex reactions within the body, sharpening one's reflexes and multiplying one's the strength,' said Avinash. 'I came across this formulation when I was living in the interiors near Kasni village. The villagers told me that their ancestors used it when they used to go for hunting. Sometimes, they would even fight a bear and manage to escape alive.'

Now, Raghav was wondering whether he had made a mistake. What was this crap about 'Popeye and the magic spinach'? He was not expecting such gimmicks from a person like Avinash.

Avinash continued very seriously, 'Then, I secretly tried it on some of my students in the 1997 Asian Games. They performed unbelievably well and even came out clean in dope tests.'

'But you have accompanied the Indian troop to the Olympic games on several occasions. Why did you not use it there till now? Our performance has always been dismal,' said Raghav.

'Because no Sports Minister ever came to pick me up from my home! No one ever placed in me the kind of trust that you did. I would have been ridiculed. This is probably the one ayurvedic recipe that our country must guard closely... Something we have inherited from our rich ancient culture that has yet not been stolen.'

'But the dope tests are much more advanced now,' said Raghav, 'and, as the Sports Minister, for me, it is more important to safeguard national dignity than winning a medal.'

'I have lived my life for this day and here I am, at the right place, right time and with the right person who has the courage to take a bold decision. Do you think I would do something that irresponsible? You need to take this decision, now, as there are only five minutes left,' said Avinash.

'Okay, go ahead,' said Raghav. He was not sure he had taken the right decision, but the wait to know wouldn't be too long and he could continue with or discard the Dronacharya accordingly. Today was only the second day, anyway.

Avinash quickly injected the wonder-drug into a Yakult prebiotic bottle, keeping the foil seal intact and gently shook the contents. The 50 ml pre-biotic drink was taken by the wrestler. No one, except Raghav and Avinash, knew about this experiment.

Raghav's mobile rang and he answered. 'Hi Neha! Is all well there?' After that there was a long silence as Raghav listened carefully to what the person on the other side was saying, his expression becoming more and more worried. 'All right, call me back once all the reports come.'

'I may have to leave for India, today,' he told Ramdas and Avinash after hanging up. 'Take good care of the crew and the mission in case I have to go.'

Raghav could see the scoreboard behind the judges. Gomez was leading after two rounds. Although Kuldeep was giving him a tough fight with his new-found poise and aggression, Gomez was too swift and sturdy. He stopped to watch the conclusion as the match was about to be over. Gomez pinned down Kuldeep to an immovable position and held him there for a few seconds as the referee started the counting. Obviously, the medicine thing was a hoax. He looked gloomily at Avinash and Ramdas, not sure whether it was safe to leave his crew in the hands of Avinash.

'Don't worry,' said Avinash, smiling at him.

Suddenly, he heard a loud roar behind him. Kuldeep was holding Gomez over his head, both arms stretched above, he spun himself one full round and tossed Gomez a good eight feet away to the other side of the ring. The impact of the thud was paralyzing and Kuldeep rushed to plunge himself over Gomez, pinning both his shoulders to the ground. The referee counted till three and the match was won.

'What was this? Was Kuldeep intentionally holding his strength for the last?' asked Raghav.

Avinash looked at him with the same serenity and replied,

'Didn't I tell you the medicine would take twenty minutes to gain its full effect? Since we were few minutes late due to our dilemma over using it or not, its effect came towards the end of the match.'

'This cannot be a coincidence', he thought.' 'And if this is not a coincidence, then this supplement of Avinash is really a wonder-drug.' He wondered if there were many similar secrets in our country, waiting to reach the right hands or be lost forever.

While Raghav was still chewing on what he had seen happening, a few minutes ago, he saw Rajendra being carried towards the Indian pavilion on his team's shoulders. He too had won a gold in the archery event.

'No wonder, our country is looked upon as the land of unconventional medicine, spiritualism and the supernatural,' he told Ramdas who was standing next to him.

Raghav saw the swimming coach approach Ramdas with a worried expression. 'One of our swimmers is in critical condition. He has had food poisoning. We had put him on antibiotics, but he can't even stand properly, let alone participate…'

'Which event?' asked Ramdas.

'Underwater swimming,' came the reply.

'Never heard of this before?' said Avinash.

'That's the problem. This event has been added for the first time after the 1990 Olympics. So none of our swimmers have practiced for this one, except Viraat. He can swim underwater for almost three minutes,' said the coach.

'So, I guess, we have no option but to abandon this event,' said Ramdas, looking at Raghav to seek his consent.

Raghav was silent, gazing inward, once again. He took out his purse and opened it. Then, he kept staring at a picture of two ladies for a few minutes. One of them was Chachi ji. The other also seemed to be a lady of royal descent. Ramdas had seen her portrait in the Education Ministry conference hall a few years ago. His boss would keep looking at...crestfallen. She was Raghav's mother, Sakshi. There was more that happened on that fateful day when Raghav had lost his mother to the Sangam waters.

◆

As Raghav saw his mother go down in the water, he immediately rushed towards her. She was underwater and flowing with the stream, moving her hands and legs frantically as the water filled her lungs. As he came close to her and she clung to him, unaware of the impact it would have. Raghav found himself helpless. He had been told many things by the gotakhors about how to save a drowning person, but this was his first time in practice. Water started to enter his nose and mouth. He could clearly see his mother's face. Her expression was one of horror mixed with hope—her son was there and would save her. She knew he was a good swimmer. Raghav felt his sensibility giving way.

Suddenly, it struck him. In such cases, he had been told, the best way was to knock the person, to be saved, unconscious, and then pull them by the hair to the shore. He acted immediately. He hit her in the stomach with his knee, again and again, till she loosened her grip. He could still see her expression. It was beyond description. Was she feeling betrayed or had she realized that she was drowning her own son in an attempt to save her life. He could never figure out. He held a corner of her saree and came to the surface to gasp in some air.

He coughed and pulled in some deep breaths and went in again only to find his mother gone, while a piece of her saree still remained in his hand. He looked for her as far as he could, kept underwater longer than he had imagined he could, but he could not find her. Her body was, in fact, never found. It was as if she had gone to another world, to join her husband Virendra, to save her son's life and to save him from further trouble and embarrassment with her last rites.

♦

Raghav had lived with this guilt for long. His mother's expression, when he hit her, continued to haunt him. The thought that she would have died thinking that her son hit her to save his own life pierced his heart. What would he not have given to tell her once what his real intention had been! He would have happily bartered his life for his mother's that day...God only knew. Almost every day of his life, he had opened his purse, looked at his mother's picture and begged for forgiveness.

'I will go in his place,' Raghav said, sotto voce. His mother wanted him to. The picture in his purse that had remained mum for years, had come alive today and asked him to fight for the country's honour...for the pride of Sumerpur.

'But, Sir, I have never seen you swim. Are you sure?' said Ramdas.

'Yes, it has been a while. But I have been underwater earlier...,' Raghav said, in a barely audible voice, as if speaking to himself.

'This is Olympics and the world's best divers would be in the race. It's better not to attempt rather than have people talk about India's Sports Minister taking an impulsive plunge and surfacing one-third of the way through,' said Avinash.

'Just pull me out in time, if I don't surface,' said Raghav, as he took off his suit and changed into trunks. There was a lost expression on his face...as if he was having a hallucination.

Ramdas, Avinash and everyone else in the team was still too shocked to understand what was going on. The permissions to change participant were quickly obtained with some additional diplomatic effort, as his name had not been on the list.

The official name-change formalities were completed just in time for Raghav to be standing on the edge of the pool as the 'start' shot was fired. There were nine finalists, including two from Australia, one each from Cuba, the USA, South Africa, China, Germany, India and Brazil. All of them, except Raghav, had excellent physiques, the elevated trapezius making them stand apart as swimmers. Raghav's posture gave away his non-swimmer status though he still had an athletic built.

As Raghav's body touched the water, a shiver went down his spine. He could see his mother…just a few yards ahead of him. She was at the bottom of the pool, both her hands stretched out towards him, expecting her son to get hold of her and save her. He darted forward to catch hold of her but the flowing river water carried her away. He went after her, sure not to let her go this time. There were four laps of 50 meters each, the swimmers being allowed to come up for breath, after each lap.

Avinash and Ramdas watched intently, not flashing an eyelid. Raghav was far behind his competitors. As the other contestants surfaced with barely fractions of seconds separating their emergence, at the end of the first lap, Raghav still had a fifth of the length to cover. They waited intently for him to surface but he didn't.

Not only Avinash and Ramdas but the entire crowd noticed this and stood up to see what was happening. Had the Indian swimmer drowned? Back home, millions of Indians, who watched this on the TV, noticed what was happening much faster. The underwater cameras and the commentators described it vividly,

'I can't believe this! Swimmer no. 6 has not come up to breathe at all. Does he realize that he cannot come out for another 50 meters, now? Is it possible? Is this a gimmick or can he really pull it off? Well, let us see...'

The commentators did not know yet that the Indian swimmer was none other than their Sports Minister.

Raghav was in a state of subconscious control. He had to save his mother. The second lap had finished and this time the other swimmers came out, pausing for a little longer, to take in a few extra lungfulls of air as the oxygen levels in their bloodstreams went down. Every eye in the stadium was glued to track no. 6.

'This is crazy...unbelievable! The Indian swimmer has not surfaced yet again. He has turned back and is now in the sixth position. This has to be it. He has to come out anytime now. The third lap is halfway through,' said a commentator.

'We don't have any existing world champions in this contest. This is the first time after 30 years that this event has been added to the Olympics. And lo! The third lap is now over and we can see the Australian Swimmer in track no. 3 is the first to come out. And here comes track no. 2, the USA, track no. 7 Brazil... We can still see them holding on to the edge, gasping for extra shots of oxygen. And the Australian contestant is on his way back. Last lap! I am sure the Indian will have to come out this time. It is not humanly possible to hold breath for such a long time while you are swimming. The current record is held by Stig Severinsen, a meditation teacher from Australia, who swam 500 ft in 2 minutes and 12 seconds, and that too, when he was not competing,' said another commentator.

The rare few who watched the Olympics in India on the TV were going mad. The mobile networks got congested as people called each other to switch on the TV and see what was happening.

'Oh no… No way! He has not come out yet another time,' continued the commentator. 'This is the last lap and we can see him in the third position now, closely following the Australian in track no. 3 and the Brazilian in track no. 7. What a vibrant example of the mystique that surrounds the land called India! The Brazilian seems to be disturbed. He is looking sideways at lane no. 6, again and again, retarding his speed with each turn of his head. We can't blame him! Even we, who are sitting here, are flabbergasted, it is not difficult to understand the state of mind of the swimmers. Oh God, the Indian just overtook the Brazilian! Just 20 meters left and there is a good 10 meters gap between track no. 3 and 6. The Australians seem to have bagged this medal,' the commentator bent his head down to take a sip of water, when a sudden outcry from the spectators made him spill the water over himself as he attempted to look back up, without losing a second.

'What did I just see! The Australian has surfaced just five meters from the finishing line. Does that mean the Indian in track no. 6 has won the Gold here? Two minutes and fifty seconds! A new world record, not only for this event in Olympics, but also for the Guinness Book! 666 feet underwater at one go! The last record was 500 feet,' said the commentator.

'Wait…Something is wrong here. Is this guy a male mermaid or something? He has turned back! I am not sure whether they are going to send the rescue team or allow this to become an unbreakable record of sorts,' he added.

Raghav's mother smiled at him as his hand touched hers and he held it tightly, swimming with all his might to reach the shore. He had finally been able to save his mother. He reached the shore, only to find himself surrounded by thousands of people giving him a standing ovation. His mother was nowhere in sight. He was barely breathing as he stepped out. His bloodshot eyes were looking around for his mother. He came back to consciousness as Avinash came up to him and held his hand. Avinash put a towel around Raghav and escorted him to the changing room, away from all the noise. He had some idea what Raghav was going through. He left him alone and closed the door behind him.

Raghav sat on a bench and cried like his heart would burst. 'Hold my hand and I will lead you to safety, to glory!' He now knew what his mother had meant. He had betrayed her and she led him to glory even from the other world.

'I did not betray you, Mother. I just hope you know that! Your face that day inside the water, I can't put it out of my mind. You were surprised when I hit you…hit you again and again… with my knee. What kind of a son would do that? Where did you go Mother? It was too big a punishment. My guilt gnaws into me, taking a piece of me every day. I did not hurt you to save myself, Mother. I only wanted to save you. I just hope you would have taken me with you that day,' Raghav said, as he sobbed. He had a vision of Sakshi standing in front of him, smiling. The smile of salvation told him that she knew! This rescued his soul and washed away all his guilt after a long gap of 26 years. Souls have that power, don't they!

The snap of the latch being removed brought him back to the present. Avinash walked in and put his hand on Raghav's shoulder comfortingly. Ramdas was standing behind him. Raghav sat there for a while gaining his stability. His phone rang. He picked it up and heard the voice from the other side for a while. 'Ok, fine. I will be there in seven to eight hours. I am starting right away,' he replied in a worried tone.

'What happened?' asked Avinash.

'It is an emergency. Remember, I told you that I may have to go back. It is confirmed now, I have to rush back,' he said. 'Thank you Avinash and all the best for the days to come.'

'Jai Hind!' said Avinash and they looked into each other's eyes for a split second which was sufficient to understand each other's expectations and responsibilities. The turmoil in Raghav's mind ended as he knew the decision had been correct and that he could leave to attend the emergency at home, peacefully.

◆

'That brings us to six golds, eight silvers and three bronze medals,' said Ramdas, 'against our target of 30 golds and 75 medals in all. Great show Indians!' The entire crew was together for the daily closing and briefing session.

Later during the night, as they were driving back to the hotel, Ramdas and Avinash were discussing about mission 'Golden Bird', the most expensive sports mission in Indian history. The last Indian Olympics Association under Sports Minister Narayan Ghatge had been allocated ₹250 crore for fifteen sports in which India had participated. The government felt that spending more on medals would not be justified in a country where many could not afford basic necessities. Raghav vehemently opposed this philosophy giving examples of numerous scams which had cost many times more. Then why not spend on something which was the only non-military way for a nation to prove its strength and superiority—a matter of national dignity, strength and pride, he had argued.

His predecessors strategized fund raising from corporates and business houses as the main way to fund the training of participants for Olympics. Raghav had realized that this would never be enough and charity or CSR-spending by corporates would only be a drop in the ocean. It was the government's responsibility to safeguard national pride. He increased the budget to ₹4,000 crore, making every possible state of the art facility available in the four new sports complexes in four corners of the country, apart from the Neta ji Subhash Institute of Sports in Patiala that had been the only Olympic training institute in the country until now. He named them 'Udghosh'. He floated the idea of sports schools amongst the business houses and promoted it till sports became an industry. People started sending their children to schools that focused on sports skills development. They started churning out sportsmen, who were raw material for the four Udghoshs as well as the sports clubs and leagues that had by now mushroomed across the country.

Unlike his predecessors, he planned participation in all the sports in Olympics, including even the most obscure ones like beach-volleyball and water-polo. His logic was that even if they would not qualify, at least the foundation would be laid for a broad-base Olympic participation. The launch of events, like National Beach Volleyball Championship at Goa, basketball at Amritsar, canoeing at Kullu, mountain-biking in Ooty and sailing in Mumbai, led to a sudden outburst of constructive energy amongst the youth.

He also started a helpline, widely advertised over national television, through which even the poorest person with talent could call or be reported. He/she would soon be visited by the nearest State Olympic Association officers.

That is how they picked up Tejkumari, a 14-year-old girl from the streets (the gypsies or 'nats' as they are called in India, who ropewalk for money) and turned her into a gymnastics contender.

The famous diver, Ajaymohan, spent his childhood trying to impress his friends by jumping off and somersaulting from the pillars of a temple on the banks of the Ganga in Varanasi, till his father used the helpline.

Some rumours even said that Raju, India's hope in the pistol event, used to be a dreaded sharp shooter from Azamgarh, till a police officer used the helpline to get rid of him. They say that the gang he worked for gave him a tear-laden farewell, though they would normally kill a person wanting to leave the gang.

'Where else would you find such patriotic mafia other than our beloved India?' Avinash laughed.

'Any idea how the Chief did it?' Ramdas asked Avinash, sure that he would have some insight to the superhuman feat Raghav had performed.

'He went into a meditative state. Sometimes, it is trauma triggered. Your heart rate drops, the blood pressure goes down and activity of the brain gets altered. It is something like an anaerobic state, like the Samadhi. Your chief must have had a really eventful past,' said Anivash.

'Sure thing! No one would know that better than me,' Ramdas replied.

♦

'This is not good Neha. You know how important it was for me to be present with the team! I never expected you to behave so irresponsibly. And you should not have lied about Vikram at least. How much we love our little boy! You should have thought about the stress I would go through on hearing about Vikram's health,' said Raghav, standing firmly with his face turned away from Neha.

'Sorry! But you also need some time for yourself. And I have this responsibility to ensure that you get it. It's Vikram's birthday today and he was sad that you were not here. I don't want our children to undergo the deprivation of love we had to go through,' said Neha, as a tear rolled down her cheek, sufficient to melt Raghav's heart.

'My life would be single-flavoured, had it not been for you. From the time we were separated by our families, till destiny brought us back together after the death of your father-in-law, Arunesh ji…I lived each day mechanically. I was aggressive, I was doing what life expected me to do, but there was no joy inside. You brought contentment to my life,' he said, as he held Neha and kissed her.

Later that night, leaving the security behind, they sneaked out for dinner to a small rustic restaurant, where they used to meet during their courtship days. This one was on the outskirts of the city, not very crowded and provided separate cottages to its guests, so there would be no privacy issues, they reckoned.

'Papa, you love me so much,' said Vikram, 'that you came back from Tokyo just for my birthday!' He asked Raghav to bend towards him as if we wanted to whisper something in his ears. Then, he kissed him on the cheek and hugged him tightly. Raghav's eyes became watery and he looked thankfully towards Neha.

Before he could say anything Vikram rushed towards the swings where his elder sister, Mohini, was playing.

'The world doesn't yet know about the romantic Raghav. They must think of you as a stern person, who likes the same discipline at his home as in the office,' said Neha as they held hands, looking at each other in the candlelight, sitting in a small cottage with a thatched roof.

'Yes, how would they know I waited for ten years to be with you! said Raghav. 'I felt so bad for you. At least I was busy with my work; I can never match the trauma you must have gone through.'

Raghav got up and sat beside Neha. They could see the children playing at the swings from the little window in the bamboo framed door of the cottage. Emotions flooded them and they kissed passionately, as if it was their first kiss. There are moments when you feel you should reach as close to your loved one as possible, lest the world may snatch them from you the next moment. They were re-living their past, basking in togetherness.

The ringing of Raghav's phone interrupted them. 'How are you Siddhartha? …hmm…umm…great. But how did you find out that I am here? ...anhaan…okay. I will come and get you, stay there.' Raghav walked across the lawn smiling at the children playing on the swings. Siddhartha was an old college friend whom he had met, again, about two years ago. He walked down the narrow dark street, next to the restaurant, where the customers parked their cars. He could see his driver standing near the car, awkwardly. He had an intuition that something was wrong… very wrong. Worried about the safety of this family, he started to turn back. But it was too late! He heard a gunshot and blacked out.

Operation*

Unknown Location, July 2020

Raghav woke up in a dark room. 'How are Neha and the children? I hope they are safe,' he said to himself, as he started recollecting what had happened...He could remember the children playing on the swings...and then him...out on the dark road...after which he had gone blank.

His mind started racing at the options. 'Am I in China, the communists obviously do not like strong neighbours! Or maybe it's England... After ruling us for centuries, our Olympics rise may be hurting the tall British egos. Have I been put in this black hole for a lifetime? Or do they want something from me and will negotiate.' He could not think of any other reason why he could be kidnapped except the meteoric rise of India's Olympic performance upsetting the digestion of many.

He tried hard to remember exactly what had happened. The gunshot he had heard had hit his driver in the shoulder bringing him down instantly. He had immediately realized that he had finally fallen into the trap he had been avoiding for a long time. He just had time to press the '*' button on his mobile, before two people caught him from behind, put a handkerchief to his nose and he had blacked out.

After what seemed like three hours, two men opened the door through which some light came in. They were dressed in plain shirts, trousers and slippers with sleeveless sweaters and mufflers, and looked more like teachers than kidnappers, except for the Mausers they carried. 'Thank God, I am in India', thought Raghav.

'What do you want?' he asked.

'Don't be so impatient, Minister,' answered one of them as they led him to a lit-up room where a TV set was kept. Many people, similarly dressed, had gathered in the room and were sitting on a carpet on the floor. They made Raghav sit on a chair in front of the TV. He looked around to find a window so that he could get some idea where he was, but all he could see was rifles and machine guns adorning the walls. He could make out from the mud walls that either he was in a small town, or village, or a slum in the city.

As they switched on the TV, a news channel was showing people on the streets of various Indian towns dancing with joy, hoisting the tricolour, shouting patriotic slogans. Sumit Bakshi, the reporter with the twitchy face from Indian TV was giving his byte, 'Look at these people, isn't this phenomenal? Like another Anna movement, or even bigger! Sports and not cricket alone has become the medium that has once again bound together the people of this country. We have won 66 medals, including 26 golds, 18 silvers and 22 bronzes, and ranked fourth with only the USA, China and Russia ahead of us. Even Germany and the Great Britain are behind us. It seems like a dream. It feels like the nation has won back its pride. It will be worthwhile to mention that last time India won only a silver and a bronze medal. This dream came true due to the vision and extra-ordinary efforts of one man, Raghav Chandel, the Sports Minister of India, who had been facing tremendous criticism for the huge budget he spent on this. Let us hear what people have to say.'

'How do you feel?' Sumit Bakshi asked a young boy. 'What would you like to say about Minister Raghav's strategy?'

'It's like asking a rape victim how she would feel when she got justice!' replied the boy. 'We have been returned our honour, our dignity. And as far as Mr Raghav is concerned, he is one of the most revered person in the country, today. When we come into the mainstream, we will try to be like him.'

Back at the hotel in Tokyo where the Indian team was staying, the atmosphere was ecstatic. While the players were reveling in the cocktails and mocktails and dancing to Shakira's 'Hips don't lie', one man was sitting on the table in a less illuminated corner of the hall, clearly not in sync with the mood of the party. He was not here, he was in the past. He was kneeling down outside the classroom at a municipal school, head hung down. Girls were laughing at him. Would he ever be able to break free from this life of humiliation? He was the one who swept the leaves in the playground, mopped the classroom floor, and even cleaned the bathroom. Why did Dubey ji, his class teacher hate him so much? Was it because of his family? For generations his family had been cleaning the drains and septic pits in the village. Was it because he belonged to the 'untouchable' community?

'Come in!' He shivered at the thundering voice of Dubey ji. 'I hope this will make you listen to me more carefully in the future.' Dubey ji took off his slippers, looked at them and then at the boy. The boy instantly picked them up, took out a handkerchief from his pocket and started wiping the dust off the black leather slippers. Just then, a young boy, seemingly from one of the senior classes walked into the room and stood there watching what was going on.

'Get out!' screamed Dubey ji, 'How dare you enter my classroom without my permission... Where is your school dress? Stupid villagers! Always giving me a sore throat!'

The boy promptly followed his instructions and rushed out. But only to return with his Uncle, Krishan Singh Chandel, the MP, who was inaugurating a function in the adjacent building. He had accompanied Uncle Krishan and bored with the humdrum, thought of going around the primary school. He used to pass these white buildings with green borders, the government primary schools, often, and always wondered how they were from the inside.

Dubey ji was suspended and the boy was made the class monitor. Not because his saviour wanted to uplift his status, but because he was the most intelligent student of the class and used to get the highest marks, always. This was the turning point in his life. The 'untouchable' boy went on to graduate from IIM Lucknow and cracked civil services examination. His name was Ramdas Sahu. He was now Special Secretary to his saviour, Raghav Chandel, earlier also having served as his Secretary in the Education Ministry of Uttar Pradesh.

The alert message on his mobile shook him from his trance. He pressed the 'show message' button and was horrified to see the solitary '*' on the screen. His worst nightmare had come true. Raghav had been hit. A bouncer had finally hit this ace batsman, who had been standing on the pitch for the last fifteen years, hitting six after six. Time for operation '*' (Star).

◆

'We have been trying to contact Mr Raghav, but he is not available and his office has refused to disclose his whereabouts.

The whole country is waiting for his return, to hear from him about how he feels at this great victory,' continued Mandy, the most popular face in the sports reporting airspace.

Raghav was confused why the kidnappers were showing him this. Was it out of kindness or some specific purpose. The simplicity and discipline had already ruled out their being professional kidnappers. Normal gangsters wouldn't dare to lay hands on him. They did not look like terrorists either. He had been suspecting attack from some of his opponents, but what could be their purpose of kidnapping him?

A man with a heavy beard switched off the TV and pulled a chair opposite Raghav. He signaled the other men to leave. 'What do you want from me?' asked Raghav, looking at him firmly in the eye.

'₹2,000 crore,' said the man without a second's lag. So he was right. They were not normal gangsters, they were some kind of organized mafia!

'I am an honest elected representative and I don't even have one crore in my account. How can I arrange that kind of money?' said Raghav.

'Why? If you can spend 4,000 crore on some stupid games, then why can't you spare half that amount for our starving people?'

Oh! So, they were naxalites. He had never imagined that as a possibility. Immediately the irony of fate struck him. He was in the clutches of contemporary Robinhoods, just like the dacoits who had claimed his father's life. The thought of being faced with almost certain death, strangely, did not intimidate him.

'Because that is the government's job,' he said. 'Taking care of its people is the job of the state and not that of a group of armed citizens.'

'Do you have any idea what they have done to us all these years? Our democracy is of the rich, by the rich and for the rich. In its current form, the poor man is no better than an animal meant to be exploited, molested and left to rot to death.'

'And what better alternative do you offer to these people with your guns and private army?' asked Raghav.

'We are not just a bunch of outlaws with machine guns, Minister! We are patriots, who love the country and plan to give a much better governance—one with human values and justice for the poor. We have some of the most intelligent people working with us, I am an engineer, but I sacrificed my career for the cause.'

'If you are really that patriotic and intelligent, why didn't you become an IAS and work for your people?' asked Raghav.

'Because in this system, I would become a puppet in the hands of some corrupt politicians...a castrated eunuch with a dead soul!'

'So you feel that everyone having a grudge against the system, or who has faced exploitation, should pick up a gun and start a war,' said Raghav.

'You are not on a TV talk show, damn it!' He got up and pushed Raghav's chair roughly with his foot, almost making the chair stumble. 'Get a taste of our people's life for a few days, now, then let us talk again.'

The next few days were hell redefined for Raghav. He realized these people weren't as civilized as he had initially felt. Arun, the bearded leader of the group had a well-defined torture schedule to mentally and physically break down his kidnapped victims. Raghav was put in a dark cell with an open toilet in one corner. The eight feet by eight feet room was infested with mice, cockroaches and spider webs all around. It was dark and damp with little ventilation and he found it difficult to breathe. He started wondering whether they actually intended to keep him alive. He never heard any human voice.

Initially Raghav had spent some time pondering over his options to arrange the ransom. He knew they would torture him till he would break down, succumb to their demands and beg his friends to save his life. Such a huge amount could only come from the state. Was there any such provision? Dr Sabbarwal was too simple to manipulate and put together that kind of fund. Would Salman, Aditya and Varun be able to do something? Was he worth that kind of an amount to the country?

Or maybe they were already in touch with the government and his well-wishers! Surely someone would arrange the amount and free him to resume the good work he had been doing.

Sadly, nothing happened. Days went by and since he never saw the sun, he slowly lost sense of time. He was so weak, now, that he started having hallucinations about black commandos coming to his rescue. Slowly even those went away and he came to terms with the fact that he had been abandoned. How could any public servant be worth ₹2,000 crore to the system?

♦

They were pulling Raghav roughly through the forest. It was a dark night. His eyes felt painfully dazzled with the dim light in the room where he could barely make out Arun sitting on a chair. The men released him as they reached inside the room making him fall to the floor with a thud in front of Arun's chair. Slowly he gathered his strength and lifted his head to look at Arun.

'Any last wish?' Raghav could see a man with a video camera standing behind Arun and shooting him. He realized immediately what was in store for him. They would video tape his beheading, a usual ritual amongst militants, and send it to the TV channels with their message. It would in some way or the other bring them the funding they had demanded. Breaking the quadro, that was leading India's rise to glory, would be worth much more than their demand to many. The deal had probably been struck and they were here just to do the rituals.

'Neha…my wife…talk…' He was surprised he had to put in so much effort to speak two words. He had hardly spoken anything for so many days, even his cheek muscles were wasted.

'Just thirty seconds,' said Arun and handed him a mobile phone. He was given a glass of water and made to sit on a chair.

Raghav fumbled funnily with the buttons trying to remember and type in Neha's mobile number. Strangely he could not even dial the correct number or bring the phone to his ear. His eyes turned watery.

Arun took pity on him and signalled one of his men, who took the mobile from him. 'Speak out the number Minister and don't try to act smart for even a second, else it will be your last.'

'Neha… Raghav here,' he spoke as the mobile was handed back to him.

'Oh my God, Raghav! Where are you?' He could hear her sobbing. 'Are you all right?'

His throat became heavy with emotion and he found it difficult to speak. The voice from the other side seemed to bring divine bliss to his aching soul. At least his family was unharmed.

'Yeah, I'm okay. Listen, I will have to go. I will try to come back to you very soon…But remember, if I can't, I want you to be strong. Take good care of Vikram and Mohini.'

The mobile was snatched from him and thrown into the coal firepot. An unintentional tear rolled down his eye, not because he was afraid of death but because there were so many unaccomplished dreams he wanted to fulfill in this life. He had never thought his life would end like this. That he would be slaughtered like an animal at the sacrifice altar...Mum and miserable.

Raghav felt a sudden spurt of energy erupt from within and he stood on his feet, faced Arun and, burst out, 'You unfair, cowardly hypocrite! You are fooling the illiterate masses and even your own people.'

The three men in the room started to approach him to punish his audacity, but Arun signaled them to stop. He walked upto Raghav, put a gun on his head and said, 'What did I tell you? This is not a talk-show! Who cares for your opinion? Take your last few moments to remember your dear ones and god.' Raghav closed his eyes, but fainting with weakness, he fell down to the floor. Like an ant with wings, having its last wind, his flame was about to extinguish.

One of the naxalites splashed some water over his face. Raghav slowly regained consciousness. 'Don't worry, Minister. We are not going to kill you now, not till our chief comes and records his message for the government.'

Raghav had never imagined that each second of life gained could mean so much to him. He never really could follow the wise men's advice to 'Live every day like it's your last', while he had had time.

He was blindfolded and made to sit in a corner. He heard the men talking about how they would kidnap his friend Aditya next. He drifted into memories of the past. How he had met Aditya, Varun and Salman at the Naya Bharat training camps. Their bond had grown stronger day by day, till they became close friends. Being the eldest amongst them, he loved them

The Four Patriots ▪ 233

like younger brothers.

He was jolted out of his reverie by a gentle voice. As his blindfold was removed he could see a thin tall man in his early sixties, with henna-coloured hair, sparkling brown eyes and a professor-like look standing in front of him. However, this 'professor-like' look was that of a cruel and tyrannical one… the kind who take sadistic pleasure in torturing his students. Raghav immediately recognized him as Imran, the infamous mastermind behind the naxalite movement in Bihar, Orissa and Jharkhand. He was on the country's 'Most Wanted' list, with a cross-border network. He was talking to someone on his mobile.

'It's a pity you have to die, Minister… but I have no sympathy for you. People like you must die. Arun tells me you have a big mouth and consider yourself very intelligent,' the tall man said, bringing down his mobile from his temple.

'No. I just wanted to understand why you are sacrificing so many lives, of our policemen and soldiers, as well as your own members and innocent people, for something that can be solved by dialogue. You are not criminals, you have the most intelligent minds leading this movement. In fact I am lucky that I could meet you, Imran Ali, the icon of strength and the very life and soul of the naxalite movement…' said Raghav.

'Tch..tch..tch. I can understand your desperation, Minister, everyone is afraid of death but I am sorry. I don't have time for flattery, debates or explanations. In the next two minutes I will record my message and then you have to die. Try to derive meaning from my message. That's the best I can do for you.'

'Maybe I will also record an appeal to them justifying the naxalites' position! But only if you give me a few minutes of honest discussion to clear my mind,' said Raghav.

'Look, how the national hero of the Olympic mission is

behaving like a fool, trying to buy a few minutes of life with stupid gimmicks!' said Imran into his mobile to the listener on the other side and they all burst out in laughter. 'That's what the fear of death can do to people like you, Minister, who live a life of luxury. Only the brave like us know how to embrace death gracefully. Now shut up, or we will have to kill you first and record our message later.' He disconnected the mobile he had been talking into and threw it into the firepot too.

Raghav did not hear a word of the message Imran recorded. He opened his eyes as he felt the gun touch his forehead. All his desperate attempts to buy few more minutes of precious life, by acting like a 'fool' to instigate them for a debate on the logic of naxalite movement in his last moments, had borne no fruit. He could see Arun and Imran standing on his sides, as he was made to kneel down on the floor. He could see the finger of the man holding the gun start to press the trigger. He closed his eyes and memorable moments of his life flashed before him in microseconds.

The bioscope ended as he heard the gunshot. But he did not feel any pain. Was death really so painless? He realized he was still alive. The man with the gun started to fall towards him like a stone pillar, blood showering from his forehead. Raghav pushed him back and stood up energetically, as if he had been feigning the weakness all along. The oxygen outside the dungeon was all his body had needed to revive. As bullets showered the room he could see Avinash leading his rescue troop. He saw Arun fall to the ground as Avinash sent a bullet through his shoulder. Imran also crumpled as Avinash's impeccable aim hit his calf muscle. Within a few seconds, the team of commandos had taken control, either killing the militants or injuring them to immobility.

Raghav looked angrily at Ramdas emerging from behind the troops and standing next to him now.

'Sorry, Boss. We are a bit late but thank god you kept them occupied,' said Ramdas. 'I know I almost got you killed, sorry!'

'You should not have come here, Ramdas. These people are dangerous. You could have got yourself killed.'

Ramdas was standing with his head bowed down. Raghav stepped forward and hugged him and Avinash.

'I was with our Olympics team when I got your "*" SMS chief, the day you were kidnapped. Me and Avinash, we had no option but to remain with the team as per the task you had entrusted us. The message also reached the surveillance control room, who were on alert. We were on hotline with them. As soon as the Olympic games were over, we joined the surveillance team. Although days had passed, we were sure that we would get some indication from you and we were on our toes, waiting for that signal. When we got your second "**" SMS, two hours back, we immediately boarded the choppers with the commandos, while the ground team was still tracing out the place from where the SMS was sent,' said Ramdas.

'You arrived in the nick of time. When they gave me the mobile to call Neha, as my last wish, I had to act I was so weak that I couldn't press the right buttons. While they thought I was fumbling with the mobile, I managed to sms "**" to the control room. And after that I knew I just had to buy around an hour-and-a-half, for the rescue team to come around,' said Raghav.

'But, Sir, I have seen in the movies that you have to hold the caller for a few minutes to trace their location. How was it possible with just a mobile message?' asked Manoj, the head of the commandos.

'It is! And it is very fast with our current system, which

was specially designed by experts from Israel. Our surveillance team in the control room was also trained by them. It takes about ten minutes to trace a message from within the state and around twenty minutes for another network in some different state and the time required for the rescue team to fly to this location would not be more than an hour or so. So, I knew that I had to hold on to my life for an hour-and-a-half and that's what I did,' said Raghav.

'I have heard people plan their wedding, their bankruptcy, their medical emergencies, their funeral, but who plans for his own kidnapping, Boss! I must say you were really really foresighted to have this 'Operation Star' with the tracking system developed two years back,' Avinash said, with genuine admiration.

'It was not me alone, Avinash! Me and my friends, Aditya, Salman and Varun, got this designed the day we started working on our plans to change the country. We knew one of us may have to face this situation some day or the other.'

'Who were you talking to?' Raghav asked Imran, who was writhing with pain from the torn calf muscles.

'Why? You think we are alone? You think this is your ultimate victory? Weren't you telling me, we have some of the most intelligent minds in this movement? Why should I tell you?' Imran said with a treacherous expression.

'Sir, what to do with these people now, I think we should finish them, they are too dangerous. We can say they got killed in the rescue operation,' asked Manoj.

Flashes of his father's blood-soaked dead body, being brought to the haveli and him hiding behind his mother as he watched in fear, played before Raghav's eyes once again. This memory had haunted him, through entire childhood, taking away a part of his innocence. God had finally granted him justice. He could not punish Abhay Singh, but finishing off these people would be a much more soothing soul salvation.

Raghav took the mouser from one of the commandos and roughly pushed it into Imran's mouth. 'Brave man, say your final prayers,' he said and started to pull the trigger. He stopped and looked down at the pool of water between Imran's feet. Knowing he had made his point, he pulled the gun back.

'So, this is how brave men embrace death? Gracefully… huh?' Imran's head was hanging down in disgrace.

'Why don't you kill the bastard?' retorted Avinash.

'No officer. What kind of a country fights against and kills its own people? We have so many external enemies to kill, if we have to. It is our failure that this movement sustains and we will deal with it. When our government is through with its anti-corruption programme, there will be wellbeing, even in the remotest and most backward areas. Then, they won't have to fight the system. Till then, we will try to make these people our link with the naxalites to establish mutual faith. Send them to the rehabilitation centre for naxalites, being jointly run by the military and Swami Ramdev.'

'Jai Naya Bharat!' Raghav saluted the commandos who dittoed instantly. They could see Arun holding his hand to his forehead in the same saluting posture, before being taken to the chopper by two commandos. He had been given a gift which even the President of India would have denied against his mercy petition.

Imran bit into the pearl in the ring on his index finger and fell to the ground lifeless. The pearl was cyanide.

Aditya and Mrs Parker
New Delhi, December 2020

It was going to be a busy day. Aditya, Cabinet Minister for Industry, HRD and Social Justice and Empowerment, had many important meetings and would have to get back home early for dinner with some old friends. Prachi hadn't seen him so excited to meet anybody in all these years.

He reached his office at the Ministry of Industry at 10 am sharp. Mr Bharat Mittal, the Chairman of the largest Indian mobile communications company, a first generation entrepreneur, would arrive in five minutes, his secretary told him. Aditya quickly flipped through a thick file kept on his table.

Mr Mittal was accompanied by three of his most important team members. The team members were about to take a seat outside, as expected during high-level confidential meetings, but were ushered in with Mr Mittal.

'Good morning, Mr Aditya. It was a pleasant surprise to receive your invitation in person, yesterday, but why were you so discreet about the purpose?' asked Mittal.

'Nothing Mr Mittal! *Khane-peene ke maamle phone par to discuss nahin kar sakte,*' said Aditya, as they all took seats around an oval conference table. Mr Mittal tried hard to conceal the surprise. He had not been prepared for this. The Naya Bharat government was known to be corruption-free, although the opposition claimed they took mind-boggling amounts at the highest levels, sometimes as donations to party fund and sometimes just unaccounted-for bribes.

He wondered whether it would be a barter deal or simply a demand. A look at the conference room full of people made him quickly rule out the latter.

'I am sorry for putting you through the inconvenience. I would have come to your office, but there are many people I would like you to meet and some papers I would like us to sign, if the meeting is successful,' said Aditya.

'No problem,' Mr Mittal said calmly. At 45, he looked younger than his age and exuded the confidence and maturity of a seasoned tycoon.

'Our ministry is coming up with a new project. It's called "Make Outside India". We would like Indian companies to set up more and more businesses in every corner of the world. And I want you to take up our first flagship project,' said Aditya.

'This has been something very close to my heart since a long time,' he continued. 'Whenever I used to eat at a McDonald's or a Pizza Hut or a Subway, I used to wonder why no Indian company has ever tried a similar thing. We have such delicious preparations! We should have a chain like "Samosas and more!" or *"Murugan* Dosas" with several lakhs of outlets worldwide...'

Mr Mittal nodded his head, listening carefully. 'Oh! so this was what *'khane-peene ki baat'* meant, an involuntary smile appeared on his face, in appreciation of Aditya's sense of humour. He, however, stopped shaking his head in agreement as soon as it sunk in that he could be in a bigger soup here than some financial demand. This was too impulsive on part of the

Minister. They were asking him to venture into something that was not his forte. The Minister sounded like a child.

'Of course you can give it whatever name you wish and choose what to offer on the platter,' said Aditya, as he could read from Mittal's expressions that he was not taking the proposal well.

'But we don't have any experience with the catering industry! What you are talking about, requires huge resources, much more than we can muster from any equity offer we throw open to public. Besides, the chances of success are really feeble. Sorry to say, but maybe you should discuss this with Haldiram's or Taj Foods, or someone more related to this industry,' said Mittal.

'Mr Mittal, we chose you after a lot of homework and research. If you can establish Airtalk above international brands like Crodacell and Easycon in such a short span of time, starting from ground zero, tell me, who else could be more appropriate for this project?' said Aditya.

Mr Mittal was somewhat pleased with the appreciation, but was determined that no one could take him for a ride. 'Sorry, Minister Sahab! The Bharat Group thanks you for choosing us and showing your confidence in us, but I am really sorry, we have no plans to get into this line of business.'

Aditya laughed softly, able to sense how Mr Mittal was feeling trapped and wanted to end the discussion. 'At least hear me out. Listen to the full proposal Mr Mittal and then you can decide for yourself. Relax! We will not pressurize you.'

Mr Mittal again nodded his head, somewhat relieved. He knew the power Aditya yielded as a member of the quadro. Had any earlier industry minister invited him, he would not have cared to come personally on such short notice.

'Our embassies all over the world will help you find suitable locations. That will be our responsibility. And the space will come to the new enterprise at a substantially lower than normal rate, as we shall use our ties to get subsidized or special prices.' Aditya could now see Mittal's expressions change. He was listening intently now. He would not have expected this kind of support from the government. So much realty all over the world would have taken them generations to acquire. He knew this because the Bharat Group was also into real estate and construction business in a big way.

'Our HRD ministry will train the required staff and help fast track their visas so that the outlets become functional in the shortest span of time. Suppose, we start with say 2,000 outlets in the first year, we will need to train around 50,000 young managers and workers. Our new skill development centres are already churning out a whole new generation of result-oriented, digitally active, cultured workforce for all arenas of national development. We will easily have those numbers.'

'I was honestly not expecting this kind of fervent support,' said Mr Mittal, unable to hide the excitement in his voice now. 'Once the properties and manpower is taken care of, putting our core strength of enterprise management to play, driving it to profitability, would not be too difficult. It's our core strength.'

'I know. That's why we zeroed in on you,' said Aditya.

'But why is the government taking so much pain, even when the profits shall come to us, and taxes shall go to the country we operate in?' he asked.

'Let me explain. We derive several benefits—firstly the HRD Ministry generates employment, enabling us to achieve our targets. Secondly, we gain presence and respect all over the world. We spread our culture and cuisine. Thirdly, just like your enterprise values learning and experience, we also gain the same when working on this project, with a company like yours. Our same machinery can be put to similar jobs to execute more and more "Make Outside India" projects. And lastly, we will charge a marginal 3 per cent tax deduction at source, that shall come to the treasury and help in national development.'

Mr Mittal saw sufficient value addition in the model, the 3 per cent TDS didn't hurt. 'But what if the government walks out of this at any stage leaving us alone? We will be finished, given the mammoth size of this project.'

'That's what I told you initially, Mr Mittal,' Aditya signaled the Secretary of the department, who presented a folder to Mr Mittal and each of his team members. 'Here's the full agreement that clearly states the government's responsibilities and that you can make the entire claim upon us, in case we fail to execute our part and vice versa. That's why we wanted your team to be present during the meeting. Go through the agreement and discuss it… Take your time.'

'That is really well planned!' Mr Mittal smiled at Aditya, 'That's what I would call a true PPP…maybe the largest Public–Private Partnership in the history of India and maybe the world too.' He was still trying to absorb what had just happened. Bubbles of appreciation and joy popped around in his mind. Appreciation of the uncommon vision and commitment of this man and joy at the bright future of the country and his company, which he could foresee.'

The agreement was signed after detailed discussions on the nitty-gritty between their teams, during the next two hours. Aditya had a quick working lunch and proceeded for the next meeting with the HRD Ministry team working on a joint project with the Ministry of Environment and Forests.

Hari Mohan, the Cabinet Minister for Environment and

Forests (MOEF) jointly chaired the meeting with him. Hari Mohan was from Jharkhand, a civil engineer by qualification. Aditya and Mohan got along very well, right from the Naya Bharat training camp days. They had 14 full-time scientists (horticulture) working under an Additional Secretary, who co-ordinated between both the ministries. Training was provided by these horticulturists to these 'Green Teams' set up in each city in co-ordination with the MOEF. There were online video conferences with each city team. These teams comprised recruits trained by Aditya's ministry to ensure everything was fast track and done with a long term view as the greenery is vulnerable in the initial phases. The scientists took frequent training at Municipal Corporations in Thailand and Singapore, to keep abreast of the latest technologies in road plantations.

Aditya and Mohan saw video rushes from some of the cities they selected. Every week each team was supposed to send in the footage of the plantation work being done—a motorcycle shoot of the plantations all along the dividers and on both sides of the major roads in each city. Underground drip irrigation system with sprinklers had been laid out and the workers were equipped with latest power tools to increase their efficiency.

Aditya was happy... He seemed to be getting there. He remembered how Pappu, the Khalifa, had destroyed his roadside plantation mercilessly. No one could do it now, as the law against causing damage to any kind of greenery was strict and implemented aggressively. Once the government respects something, the people automatically do it too. No one wants to spoil a good looking picture, but most wouldn't mind splashing some colour on an already tainted one.

'How far are we from our target, Mr Chaturvedi?' he asked the Secretary in charge of this programme, as the projector was switched off.

'Sir, in another three to four years we will be at par with the levels of urban greenery in China, eight years for Singapore and by 2035, we will be the greenest country on earth, that is assuming this programme continues at the same pace,' replied Chaturvedi.

Aditya took leave from Hari Mohan, as he had to address a meeting with the largest corporate houses of the country at 5 pm, organized by the ministry of Social Justice and Empowerment.

'The journey to a welfare state, my friends, is not an easy one, considering our size and population. We are trying to provide social security to our women, children and the aged; rehabilitation to the victims of substance abuse whether from alcohol or drugs. We already have all our cities and about 2,000 towns covered in just the last two years. One of the most ambitious projects the Ministry of Social Welfare and Empowerment has ever undertaken. And this journey my friends would not have been possible without your unrelenting support,' said Aditya, addressing this meeting of FICCI, where almost every large corporate house of the country was present. Many of them had contributed generously to the help-homes programme out of their CSR budgets, others were patronizing it through PPP. Each city and town was being equipped with an old-age home, women-in-distress home, children-in-distress home and rehabilitation centre. Each of these had a capacity of about 800 inmates in the cities, huge buildings with a ratio of almost four inmates per staff.

The floor was thrown open for interaction.

'Aditya Sir, I am a big fan of this project. Especially the nationwide separate helpline numbers that have been introduced for the aged, children, women and addicts. They are really effective. I want to ask you: when did this idea of such a massive social security system germinate in your mind? What made you perceive its need, when no one ever considered it important?' asked Kanu Patel, the young Director of ROAM-INDIA, a Public–Private Partnership company that was running guided tours in double-decker buses in all major cities of India. The spots of tourist attraction in various cities had been refurbished by the Ministry of Tourism. Glossy, colourful buses spanned the cities. Maps giving details about these spots had been printed to go with the tickets. It had been a huge success and the tourist count had grown five-folds over the last two years. The foreign exchange was pouring in and Kanu did not mind contributing, generously. The guides again had been provided by Aditya's HRD ministry.

'Whoosh! To answer your question, I have to go back a long time…to my Institute days. Someone saw a kid working at a tea stall and it changed the course of my entire life. Someone put me in a situation that had me thinking—what kind of a governance do we have that does not take care of its children, aged or its women! No wonder, there is so much crime all around. The morning newspapers are just full of crimes and scandals and negative things. What if my wife-to-be would go out shopping and someone would loot her…' he said.

'That's a lot of forward thinking!' Kanu remarked, amused, as the crowd burst into laughter.

Aditya laughed with them. Of course, this was not the sole reason, but it surely had been the first time he had realized the ghastly consequences of a poor social security system. The crowd did not know the tale of the Austrian fiasco and they didn't need to!

'But don't you think these help homes are in contradiction of Naya Bharat philosophy to do away with free benefits?' asked Jagat Bindra, with his signature mannerism.

'There is a difference between "needy" and "helpless." While we condemn doling out free benefits to the needy, we have to assist the helpless get their lives back on track. These people cannot help themselves. I feel the government has to make its people feel that the country cares for them and then they will respond with double fervor. Help must reach out to those who need it most...the people in distress. No one should be living in fear or in oppressive conditions. Hence, these helplines and help-homes! These helplines are not just private call-centres that register and pass on information to the concerned departments. They comprise highly dedicated people trained by our ministry. They are responsible to track the progress, till each case is closed. The help-homes work towards rehabilitation and putting the inhabitants back into the mainstream wherever possible.'

'You just mentioned private call-centres as if there is something wrong with private? Hasn't privatization resulted in the highest efficiencies in so many areas?' asked Sumit Bakshi, not to be left behind his arch rival Jagat.

'Yes, privatization is good...but not everywhere! Public services like the municipal work, education, health are some areas where our government believes in providing top class facilities to every citizen. Excessive commercialization of education and health over the past few decades had done tremendous damage to our society. It has taken us a herculean effort to reverse that damage. This one too is an area which is a basic necessity with no scope of profit making. Hence, no scope of privatization here,' replied Aditya.

'Don't you face any threat from the narcotics mafia, in

the face of the drugs eradication drive that you are running countrywide?' asked Jagat Bindra.

'We are the government... I repeat, the government of India. Do you think a group of a few thousand people can dare to threaten a country of 140 crore? No mafia would dare to challenge a government representative unless they have some direct or indirect links or overlapping interests. Our government does not have any soft approach to this, we believe in crushing... obliterating anything or anybody damaging national interest. A few years back, our pride, our Punjab was under this threat. Drugs had become a mania amongst youth. It took us just six months, after coming to power, to eradicate this epidemic. Not only Punjab, three years back, was there any city where you would not find such drug addicts sitting on footpaths, parks etc., including our Karol Bagh/Paharganj juncture near the New Delhi Railway Station, in the very heart of our capital city. Could you have helped these addicts, even if you felt mercy for them? Of course not, they require special care and treatment, and it is the government's responsibility to provide it. Are these addicts criminals? Again no, then what did they do to deserve a life worse than that of street dogs? Forcing someone into drug addiction is like stabbing a corpse every day, it is the most detestable crime. We have a no-tolerance policy towards such mafia. Extermination is the only punishment for them.'

◆

As Aditya drove back home, his heart was pounding in anticipation.

'I hate this Aditya, these weird surprises that you keep throwing at me! At least I should know who is coming!' said Prachi, not very happy about this date with the unknown couple.

The doorbell rang and Aditya walked towards the door of the drawing room, accompanied by Prachi. A couple was soon ushered in.

'Hello, Mrs Parker!' Aditya stepped forward and shook the lady's hand. They came cheek-to-cheek and exchanged synchronized kisses. As their eyes met, a treasure-chest of evocative moments was flung open. Memories rushed out like bees from a broken beehive.

'Meet my better-half, Prachi,' he said.

Prachi sighed in relief as Mrs Parker exchanged kisses-in-the-air with her too. So, it was just their style of greeting. 'Is she a foreign diplomat?' Prachi wondered, as Aditya had never mentioned having a female friend and their intimacy was in the air.

Mrs Parker turned to the man standing just a step behind, smiling at them, 'Meet my husband, Brian. He too is coming to India after a long gap of eight years.' Aditya shook hands warmly with him, while Prachi promptly folded her hands in a namaste, lest Brian steps forward for the cheek-to-cheek greeting.

They took their seats on the elegant sofa sets placed peripherally on a maroon floral carpet, as snacks were laid out on the centre table.

'Thanks for inviting us. Brian wanted to see the Institute where I studied. Thanks to Facebook, I could locate you. So, am I one of the reasons behind this huge transformation India has seen?' Mrs Parker said, cheerfully.

'Yes, I can't deny that Elena! I was a big-time patriot anyway, but when your father denied me your hand, it was an eye-opener,' said Aditya, opening a bottle of chilled Perrier Jouet. They raised a toast to their reunion.

'Denied me your hand? What's going on? Aditya never

mentioned this to me?' Prachi watched the transformed Aditya as she sipped soft drink. She had not seen him this comfortable with any other woman.

'You really are some Superman, Aditya!' Elena giggled, 'I mean. Look at the roads, the greenery, the cleanliness, the hospitality, it's unbelievable! This is not the India where I spent four years, almost fifteen years ago!'

'I remember Uncle especially noticed the pathetic condition of the Ganges. Did you get any chance to go to the river banks?' he asked.

'Of course, we did,' said Brian. 'We landed in Mumbai, then took the "Samrat Ashoka" river-cruise starting from Tapti river to Narmada, then Son river, Ganga and finally Yamuna. The cruise stopped by the cities of Jabalpur, Patna, Allahabad, Varanasi and Agra. One of our most enjoyable river journeys ever! The water traffic was so well managed. There were separate lanes for the cargo ships, passenger boats and cruises. I have never seen so much water in the rivers, here or anywhere. It's amazing! Few years back they were dwindling and now they seem to be inundated. It's difficult to imagine how so many rivers could be linked in such a short span of time.'

'Oh! It was pretty simple,' Aditya said, as he led them to the dinner table. 'We turned our drawbacks to our advantage. People used to consider our huge population as a curse and a pullback. I just put all those hands to productive work and the results are here, in front of you. Everything that you see around you all the development, could not have been possible without the millions of working hands—our biggest resource—the human resource.'

'Hmm! So, your government must be encouraging families to grow?' laughed Elena.

'Oh yes! We have even banned the production and sale of contraceptives,' said Aditya merrily.

'Why? Doesn't go very well with your name "Copper-T,"' Elena countered immediately, as they all burst into laughter except Prachi, who was not exactly liking how this was shaping up. "Copper Turnings" to "Copper-T." How dare she! She wore a fake, uncomfortable smile.

'On a serious note, we have passed a law last year, whereby any family with more than two children, is restricted from getting most of the government facilities and support. The results have already started showing and we expect to achieve planned results within the next few years,' Aditya added.

Brian and Elena held hands often as they laughed and talked. Aditya was happy to see Elena happy. Her trip had brought back a lot of memories. The past is in the past, as they say, but you can never really get over your first love. It always has a special place in your heart. Aditya and Elena, though happy and committed in their own relationships, would always share that bond, of being special to each other.

'Still play the guitar?' Elena asked Aditya.

'A little bit,' said Aditya. He could see the turmoil going on inside Prachi through her fake smile and hurt expressions.

'This song is dedicated to the love of my life, my wife Prachi,' Aditya said softly, as he plucked at the chords in their sequence. His voice turned resonant and penetrating whenever the strings played in the background. 'It's a country song, called "Unanswered Prayers" by Garth Brooks.'

Just the other night, at a hometown football game,
My wife and I ran into, my old high school flame,
And as I introduced them, the past came back to me,

And I couldn't help but think of, the way things used to be…
She was the one, that I'd wanted for all times,
And each night I'd spend praying, that God would make her mine,
And if he'd only grant me, this wish I wished back then,
I'd never ask, for anything again…
Sometimes I thank God, for unanswered prayers,
Remember when you're talking, to the man upstairs,
And just because he doesn't answer, doesn't mean he don't care,
Some of God's greatest gifts…are unanswered prayers…

All through the song, Aditya was looking into Prachi's eyes. With each word, he could see her anxiety vaporize. Some songs are like that…they convey your feelings better than a thousand… words said aloud.

The Youngest Prime Minister
New Delhi, Feb 2021

'Blood cancer...4th stage.' Dr Sabbarwal pushed forward the files to the quadro who were looking at him, stunned. Dr Sabbarwal was seated on an easy chair and looked weary and feeble. Dr Harsh Goenka, his friend and chief doctor, was sitting right beside him. Dr Sabbarwal had lost a lot of weight recently. Raghav, Aditya, Varun and Salman were seated on the sofas in the drawing room of Dr Sabbarwal's house.

Prachi and Neha were also there. Both the ladies were on the verge of tears. They had accompanied their husbands several times to Dr Sabbarwal's house, but it had always been on some pleasant note, like the Makar-Sankranti dinner just two months back. Dr Sabbarwal had no immediate family as he did not have any children and his wife had died twelve years ago of lymph node carcinoma. He loved Neha and Prachi like his own daughters.

'Are you sure, Doctor? Sir has been fit like an athlete always. Apart from the weight loss, we have never seen any sign of exhaustion or any other symptom, that is, before these last 10 days that he has stopped going to office,' Raghav asked Dr Harsh, as if he was the culprit.

'I have lived a full life, my dear children... No regrets,' Dr

Sabbarwal intervened, 'I will die a peaceful death. So don't shed a tear. I know, I am leaving my country in safe hands.'

'But what about us? What will we do without you?' Varun retorted. Neha, Prachi, Aditya and Salman nodded their heads in agreement.

'You will do well, I will be watching you from up above. And Raghav, who has been an elder brother to you...all this while, will take good care of you. He will take my place.'

'What do you mean take your place? You are not going anywhere Dada!' Raghav walked to him, kneeled in front of his chair and held his hand.

'I wish I could stay, Raghav, but I don't have much time. Just a few months maybe! And Dr Harsh will not allow me to take any further stress,' said Dr Sabharwal.

Dr Harsh nodded his head in agreement.

'What kind of a doctor are you, Sir? How could you diagnose this so late?' asked Salman. He was feeling so angry that he could strangle the doctor with his useless stethoscope.

'Unfortunately, that's how cancer is. Most of the times it does not show up in the health checks that we do. Besides, Dr Sabbarwal had been skipping his wellness checks frequently in the last few quarters.'

'Why Dada?' asked Raghav, as every head turned towards Dr Sabbarwal.

'He was keeping busy with the trouble you people have been in, one after the other. The terrorist attack, Salman's arrest by the CBI and Raghav's kidnapping,' Dr Harsh replied in Dr Sabbarwal's place. 'He used to share everything with me. I did the clinical examinations, but they did not reveal anything alarming until now.'

There was pin-drop silence. The thought that they were

in some way responsible for Dr Sabbarwal's present condition, took a few moments to sink in.

Raghav was still sitting on the floor near Dr Sabbarwal's chair, holding his hand. Dr Sabbarwal felt a tear on his hand. He gestured for the other boys to come near. They kneeled down around him.

'We are not letting you go anywhere,' said Aditya, he felt his thyroid hurt inside his throat. Prachi put her hand comfortingly on his shoulder.

Dr Sabbarwal put his hand over Raghav's and said, 'Why I called you here today, is because I feel too weak. I want you to take over my responsibilities Raghav. I am sure Aditya, Varun and Salman also respect you like an elder brother. You have sufficient experience and everyone in the party will also accept you as their natural leader after me.'

'I would, Sir, but we have much younger and energetic people in our team. You are the one who has always advocated the need of young leadership for this country. I have crossed 40, I think we have the opportunity to present the world with its youngest Prime Minister. My friends here have barely crossed 30,' replied Raghav.

'No doubt, you are unassailable as a team. I have equal trust in each one of you. So take a few minutes, discuss, but let me have a name now, so that I can call a party meeting and propose the name. I could have gone for an internal election, but it would be a time consuming exercise and I may not have that much time. Besides, the outcome would be the same anyway. Whatever time God gives me, I want to utilize that to help the newly appointed Prime Minister discharge his duties perfectly. I will propose this to the party members in the Annual General Meeting that I shall call upon shortly and if there is any resistance, then we will consider elections,' said Dr Sabharwal.

It was not a difficult decision. All three found a perfect balance of poise, competence, sincerity and die-hard attitude in Aditya. Besides he had been a permanent member of Dr Sabbarwal's think tank along with Raghav and had a lot of knowledge on planning and execution required to run the government. He was also probably the most non-controversial name amongst the party cadre.

Aditya looked at Prachi, awaiting the kali zaban verdict. The country's most powerful man to be was just as powerless as any married man in front of his wife.

'Yeah, go ahead! Why are you looking at me?' she chuckled, 'You will make a fabulous PM.'

Aditya let out a sigh of relief and everyone else laughed as they knew the secret behind Aditya's anticipation of Prachi's comments in such situations. The Prime Minister-to-be of a nation that prided itself for being futuristic was still a slave to this queer superstition.

'Great! Stay united like this. People will try to divide you, but hold on to one another. Remember that together you are invincible.' Dr Sabbarwal had an expression of contentment on his face. 'Salman and Varun, will you fulfill my last wish?'

'For sure, Sir! Your wish is our command,' they echoed.

'I want you to get married,' he said.

'But, Sir...' they said.

'No ifs and buts. Just tell me when and to whom.'

'Sir, I think we can advertise on matrimonial sites—"*Sunder, sushil, gori, gharelu kanya chahiye, bharatvarsh ke Home aur Finance Ministers ke liye,*"' said Aditya, teasingly.

'I don't think you will need to do that Aditya, at least for Varun. I have someone in mind for him. In fact, I have called her here and she will be with us any moment,' announced Dr Sabbarwal. He looked at the doctor who nodded in affirmative. 'Oh, so she is here already. Why don't you call her here?' said Dr Harsh.

Prachi looked at Neha in astonishment and so did everybody, trying to figure out what was going on. What was Dr Sabbarwal up to? Varun's heart was pounding like a kettle drum. He was already working on strategies to escape this situation gracefully. He did not want to hurt Dr Sabbarwal and marriage was the last thing on his mind right now.

He was surprised and relieved at the same time to see Radhika walk in with Dr Harsh. Not because a known devil would be better than an unknown one, but because he was sure Radhika would not lead him into an embarrassing situation against his will.

He was, however, totally unprepared for what he saw next. His heart stopped beating for a moment. Floodgates of old memories were thrown open. There she was, standing right in front of him, after eleven long years. Alisha, his love gone sour!

'She heads the City Social Audit Teams for the state of Rajasthan. She was adamant on not seeing you but agreed to come here only once, when she came to know about Dr Sabbarwal's condition,' said Radhika, remembering the chill that had run down her spine when she had first seen Alisha, sitting in front of the interview panel two years back. How she had compared herself with her, felt envious and wanted to reject her candidature till the sense of duty got the better of her.

'Oh, so you have known her for a long time?' Varun made a wry face at Radhika. 'You know this is the one chapter of my life I would not like to revisit.'

Alisha stood there without any change of expression. She did not seem to feel any malice, she was just indifferent. She had put Varun out of her life…out of her mind.

'None of us here knows what happened between the two of you and why you parted, nor will we get into that,' Dr Sabbarwal said. 'But we do know that neither of you married again and that you are both single till date. Life is too short to hold on to grievances and people change with time. We mature, we become less impulsive. I know for sure Alisha, that Varun is not a boy to let go of. And Radhika has a very high opinion about you as well. Life is really too short and who would know this better than me!'

'There is no point, Sir. I…,' Varun started to say.

'We are going to the projector room. I have to show Aditya and Raghav some important video clippings that we received from our overseas embassies,' Dr Sabbarwal cut him in between. He seemed to require a lot of effort to get up and it pained Varun to see him like that. 'I request both of you to give each other a second chance.'

All of them including Dr Harsh and Radhika left the room.

There was what seemed like a never ending silence. 'Please sit,' Varun said, as he perched himself on the arm of a sofa.

'Seems you got the right department, lots of violence, huh!' said Alisha.

'It's called "Defence"! By the way, violence is also a form of self-protection at times, as in our ministry. And ironically, the other ministry I have is "Home". Someone demolished my home twelve years back. How are coolstud_farzan and machoman?'

'Oh…ho! You even remember those names! Must have been really jealous! I did not get the time to chat after I came back to India,' she said.

'You left me in jail and vanished? I would not do that to you even if I hated you. We had something…did the damned computer mean so much to you?'

'Don't poke me, I will not react,' she said.

'Were you having a surreptitious virtual affair or something? Why else would you have left me and rushed back to India?'

Alisha was silent. She was determined not to speak. Her eyes became watery as she struggled hard to keep it all within.

Finally, she erupted, 'It was not about the computer, Varun! Didn't I tell you, I had a tormented childhood? My cousin maternal Uncle and his sons...they used to thrash me all the time. I was only 12 years old. And it went beyond just beating, they exploited me... Did you expect me to tell you all that and beg you to be kind to me? I created a small world of my own, teaching those villagers. Just when I thought I had broken free from the world of abuse and slavery, you came along. I left everything behind for you. I know I did not act maturely, I made some mistakes, but you did not support me during this adjustment period. You stuck to your principles like a bloody headmaster. But when I saw the shattered pieces of glass on the floor, the smashed frame of the monitor and the CPU, all my anguish and fears came back in a tsunami and drowned me. I decided I was not fit to be in a relation with anyone, I was much better-off alone. And I truly am...to this day.'

A regular stream of tears kept flowing as she spoke. Varun softened as what she was saying was probably correct. Dr Sabbarwal was correct. Varun 'Panga' Pandey had matured over time.

His gaze was fixed on those perfectly crafted pink lips that danced to the rhythm of the pent-up feelings. Her flowing black hair were loosely tied along the back with a broad hairclip. She was very fair, with skin so transparent that the redness of the blood flowing below rendered it a fairlytale-ish pink shade. She wore an orange/yellow chiffon saree.

Was he falling in love all over again...or having a déjà vú?

'So, you didn't have any affair even after leaving me?' he asked.

'No,' she said wiping her tears.

'*Jhakaas*'! His instinct told him to grab her and kiss away those tears.

'I was such a fool, Alisha, to ever let you go,' he said.

'And I am still a vegetarian,' she said with a cute smile. 'I thought of going back to the egg-curry and fish I used to have before marriage but I had made you a promise.'

'Me too! I still brush my teeth at night. Remember, you always wanted me to do that before coming to bed.'

'Stupid!' she said sweetly.

It is strange how icebergs of grudge and resentment between two estranged lovers can melt in the warmth of a few moments of togetherness. Love has its own way of dressing old wounds and reconciling.

'I would be a bigger fool, if I don't keep Dr Sabbarwal's wish and let you go this time too,' said Varun.

'It's your habit. You were letting me go the first time you proposed to me, remember?' she said.

They laughed together. The malice and discord had been banished. The reign of love had been re-established.

Varun got up, walked to her, went down on his knees and holding her hand said, 'Please be mine again... forever and ever!'

To the outside world, the Home and Defence Minister of India, one of the most powerful persons on earth, was proposing to an officer, much lower in terms of hierarchy in his own department. To Varun, he was trying to gain back a part of him that he had lost...that would make him stop living in pieces and complete him again. It reminded him of a song Aditya used to sing, one of his own compositions:

'Jee Utha'
Sanson mein jo samaye wo,
Ragon mein ghul jaaye jo,
Haan issi se hai chalta ye jahan,
Ishq ka hai wo jalwa bepanaah.

Rok sake naa koi jo,
Pyaar hai sailaab wo,
Jee utha jo pada iskaa saya,
Khoya jo dil sab kuch hai paya.

They joined everyone on the dinner table. Everyone was sad at Dr Sabbarwal's incurable illness, but he seemed to feel elated. Both his wishes had been fulfilled that day. 'Salman, now that we no longer have a bachelor company in this group, other than you, find yourself a girl quickly.' Everyone laughed.

Varun was seated next to Radhika on the dining table and Alisha was sitting on the opposite side. He turned to Radhika and whispered, 'One thing upsets me, Radhika. If you knew Alisha for almost a year, why did you take so long to bring this up?'

'I knew your side of the story, Varun. So, to me, Alisha was practically the vamp in this story. I slowly got to know her better, as she worked with me and I realized that she was not such a bad woman. Still, I had to make sure she was good enough for you and would not hurt you again.... It took me some time. I got all kinds of checks done on her. She is an upright, strong yet sweet girl. She is perfect for you,' she whispered back in his ear.

'I am blessed to have you in my life, Meerabai!' was all he could manage to say with an emotional lump in his throat. From a corner of his watery left eye, he noticed Salman sitting alone, just opposite to Radhika. A heart-warming idea germinated in his head and it brought an involuntary smile on his face.

The Incineration Plan for the Superbugs
New Delhi, March 2022

'Yes Sumant, what's new?' Salman was on his way to his office. He listened intently, then said, 'Ok, I am coming over to your camp office. Yes, I shall also bring Varun with me.'

Sumant Srivastsan along with Vinod Saxena of CBI had been working on an assignment to dig-up the conspirators behind the gold scam. They had come across some vital information which they wanted to discuss with the Ministers. The Ministers were escorted to the conference room where Sumant and Vinod were waiting for them. The door was shut leaving them alone.

Sumant turned off the lights and switched on the projector. A female face appeared on the screen. Salman went numb and his heart stopped beating.

'Was there someone called Mahi in your life?' asked Srivatsan.

The name that kept echoing in his mind over the last twelve years, taking a piece of him every day, reached his ears today through vibrations in air molecules around him. The name that had never come to his lips all these years, but resonated within his body with each pulse.

'Yes. Why do you ask?'

'How important was she to you? Did you love her?'

'Yes, she was everything to me. But she died twelve years ago. What has this got to do with your investigation?'

'She did not die in a road accident, she was killed... Killed to take revenge upon you!'

'Who was it?' asked Varun as Salman was still too dazed to speak.

'Ganesh Vidarythi, the National Front MP from Navi Mumbai. His men in a mini truck hit her scooty on the highway, then ran over her, making sure she bled to death.'

'Oh God! I am responsible for her death too? I have been living with this guilt of putting her through mental agony till her death, and now this?' Salman wept like a baby, sobbing hysterically as the officers watched him in this condition. He did not want to but it was involuntary. Varun put his arm around his shoulder and held him close, as Salman cupped his palms to cover his face.

'That bastard! He killed Mahi just because I spoke against him at his public address in my chawl! He's so dead!' Salman shook his head determinedly, wiping off his tears.

'Wait, Sir. There's more. He is also the one who got you behind bars, by stashing all that gold in your basement.'

'Why would he do that? It would cost him several times his net worth to do something like that!' said Varun.

'True. He could not have done this alone. But the motive is obvious. Mr Salman took away his MLA seat in the election following Mahi's death. He is a very dangerous man, an iceberg–deep-rooted!...Cold! There is hardly any case against him as he works with a remote control, a wireless one. He has become even more powerful after joining the National Front,' replied Vinod.

'But, how did you find out about Mahi?' asked Varun.

'While digging into Mr Salman's case, we came to know that Ganesh had played a major role in the whole episode, even arranging part of the gold from some of the temple management committees, who were upset with Mr Salman due to the new programme jeopardizing their wealth. Digging deeper into his history and studying files of the crimes that he had been linked to, we came across an old man living an incognito life in a remote village. He had worked for about fifteen years for Ganesh as his right hand before renouncing the life of crime, which was his daughter's last wish, who died of cancer two years back. He specially recalled the Mahi incident as his daughter was almost the same age as Mahi, when she died. He thought it was his retribution for being party to innocent Mahi's murder.

'Tell me seriously, Sumant. You are more of a friend now than just an officer,' said Salman. 'Would you wait for justice if something like this happened to Rukmani? I don't mind having gone to jail for a few weeks in the gold scam. But he should not have killed Mahi. *Usko prasaad chahiye, dena padega! Ganda wala dena padega!* Tell me, if I beat him to death on the road right now with a cricket bat, how many years would it take you to get me out?'

'You are known for your bad temper, Sir. We could prove in the court that you were in a state of mental imbalance and get you minimum or no punishment. We also have adequate evidence against Ganesh in Mahi's accident case. There is a dhaba on the highway, only a few yards from the scene of the accident. The owner of the dhaba yielded during strict interrogation by the STF that he knew the goons driving the mini truck. It was a milk delivery vehicle from Ganesh's friend's dairy company in which Ganesh holds secret stake too. The two goons are in our custody. No one knows when or how they were lifted. We could make them disappear forever if you say.'

'No, just lock them up in a four-by-four dark room till my next instructions. Put a three inch hole in it for air, let them choke and gasp for air,' Salman said, coldly.

'Quite innovative! Wise decision, I would say. I would still advise you not to harm Ganesh because it could make his sponsors wary. We could be real close to laying our hands on them.'

'Sponsors? And who could they be?' asked Varun.

'People who could amass such huge wealth in the form of gold and silver on a few months' notice! Obviously not an industrialist or the underworld, they would reach nowhere close. This has to be a political group with support of some affluent anti-Indian economies,' said Sumant.

'Who are your prime suspects? Don't beat around the bush,' Salman said, visibly vexed.

'Brijmohan Gupta is one of them. He has made several trips to China, Middle East and North Korea, and we have also intercepted some of his calls.'

'Oh, come on! Brijmohan is nothing without Jatin Oberoi's support. Fine, I get it. It is Mr Jatin and company. Who else could hold more grudge against us? We dethroned them, right?' said Salman.

'I would not have told you Mr Varun and Mr Salman, under normal circumstances, till our investigation ended. But I want you and your friends to be extra careful. Put vigilance and RAW on alert. You have already warded off three attacks from them. These guys are desperate. They will go to any extent,' said Sumant.

'What do you mean three attacks?' snapped Salman.

'The terrorist siege and Raghav's kidnapping may also have been their brainchild,' said Sumant.

'Maybe...? The country's intelligence cannot talk in such ambiguous terms, tell me clearly,' Salman demanded.

'Alright! So, here's the truth. Yes, they were involved. The owner of the house from whose basement the tunnel was dug, the one who we arrested soon after the case was opened, has given us information that leads to Ranjit. Ranjit's driver is one of the six people whose fingerprints were found on the trunks in your basement. That's why he was there during your trial, relishing his triumph. The man to whom Imran was talking on his mobile just before the rescue team reached to free Raghav from the naxalites...the one in whose fear Imran bit the cyanide, was Brijmohan Gupta. But we don't have fool-proof evidence yet. It will take some time. So, trust us and do not give out any signals, please! Only the four of you and your very trusted officers should know,' Vinod pleaded.

'Bloody parasites! They are just so desperate to be back in control, to suck on the country's blood,' Salman said in an exasperated tone. He was just thinking aloud, speaking his mind. 'You must have heard of the superbugs. They are like them. I am trying to figure out what to do with them. When I think about what they have done to me and my friends and this country, I can't help gloating over ways to kill them. Should I boil them alive or irradiate them in a large microwave, dehydrate them or freeze them lifeless. Ummm... no no no! I don't think that would be good enough. These germs are too shameless and thick-skinned. The only way to eliminate them is to burn them. Fine, that's what I will do, incineration would be best. Just let me know as soon as you have solid evidence.'

'The country needs you, Sir. I know how you must be feeling but don't take the law in your hands,' Sumant said with folded hands.

'Don't worry, my friend here knows better than that. You just make sure this investigation is concluded at breakneck speed,' said Varun, holding Salman's hand as they walked out together.

'Hi Aditya... Varun and I are coming over to your office. Please call Raghav too. This is top urgent.' Salman spoke over his mobile phone as he signaled the driver to head for the Prime Minister's office.

The Prime Minister's Development Fund

New Delhi, June 2022

'The question is how to bring down corruption in India to a level that we are among the five least-corrupt nations in the world,' said Aditya, talking to his core team of friends. They were sitting together after a long time over scotch that Aditya's house.

'We have implemented the Social Audit Scheme over the last three years and the Janlokpal last year. The CSATs are doing a wonderful job, statistics say that we are down by 30 per cent already,' said Varun. 'The recruitment process for the Town Social Audit Teams (TSATs) is also in full swing.'

The City Social Audit teams (CSATs) used to audit various government departments and upload their reports on a departmental performance portal, which was accessible to every citizen. These reports had to be taken seriously by the state governments as the central government's budget allocation to the state was done on the basis of department-wise performance. Apart from this, the audit was video recorded and any case of intentional neglect or corruption could be directly reported to the Janlokpal. There had been a phenomenal improvement in the performance of government departments countrywide.

'But we don't want to wait another ten years to be in the top-five list. I want the current 30 per cent figure to be 80 per cent. We have to do it within the next six months.'

'Now, that's a bit too ambitious Aditya,' said Varun. 'If we move too fast, many of our own MPs and MLAs will turn against us and we will be faced with a vote of no-confidence in no time.'

'If we want to eradicate corruption, we will have to start top down. Till we have corrupt politicians in power, we cannot expect the bureaucracy and police to become honest. And till the time they are corrupt, our country's poorest population will continue to suffer,' replied Aditya.

'Agreed,' said Salman 'The Janlokpal is only a mechanism to punish wrong people, but if we have the right people, even in the current system, they can take the country to the top.'

'No doubt,' said Varun, 'What I meant is that maybe we should give this two or three years to percolate down. How can we bring in the right people all of a sudden? The elections happen only once in five years and good people still barely come forward.'

Aditya looked at Raghav, the teetotaller of the group, silently listening to the conversation, then said, 'Varun, the purpose of today's meeting is to brainstorm about doing it in the shortest span of time. My personal opinion is that we came in with the determination to make a change, we must not allow our positions to allure us into retarding our passion. What is the worst that could happen? Our government could fall? Let us be ready for that,' said Aditya.

'Alright,' said Varun and after a few seconds of deep thought. 'Let's first have a meeting with all our 18 Chief Ministers to take them into confidence. What do you actually want to do?'

'I want to send out a strong message by taking action against the most corrupt politicians, that looting is no longer allowed in this country,' said Aditya.

'But do you think people like Ujjwal Shinde and Prashant Rajavat will change their ways? They may be our party's Chief Ministers but they are the mafia of sorts in their states,' said Varun.

'There are two types of corrupt politicians. Half of them are corrupt because they know the party allows that. If the party says no to corruption, these people would not sacrifice their image or position in the party for money. They can be corrected. However, half of them as you said will go to any limits against an honest system,' said Raghav.

'Actions do speak louder than words, so Ujjwal Shinde and Prashant Rajavat it will be,' said Aditya. 'We will not have any regular agency working on this, as they are connected to these people's network somewhere or the other. I will put the best officers at RAW to gather evidence against these two and then we will expose them.'

'*Jhakaas*! Let us first finish our country's enemies from within,' said Varun.

'Cheers to "political will-power" as they say,' echoed Salman. '*Ab to line se prasaad bantenge.*' Raghav was smiling in admiration at his younger friends' zeal.

And they raised a toast to the first Prime Minister conspiring against his own Ministers, so ruthlessly.

A week after this, a leading news channel started broadcasting news about the disproportionate wealth that these two Chief Ministers had amassed. They had amazing evidence that stated that Shinde and Rajavat had invested their black money in various corporate houses. They had inside information...right from the INR 1,200 crore rerouted through the Mauritian bank account of Shinde, to the picturesque island Rajavat owned in the middle of the Mediterranean. Very soon the entire media was buzzing with fresh news about them every day, like a swarm of bees after a person who has broken their hive. Within three days, the CBI was questioning them and the Lokpal too initiated proceedings against them.

The party President, Aditya, had no option but to call an image-saving emergency meeting of the cabinet and the party Chief Ministers.

'But the charges against us are still not proven!' objected Rajavat and Shinde. 'We have dedicated our lives for this country. You cannot do this to us.'

'Don't be so upset! Remember, you vouched at the Planning Commission meeting four years back to denounce politics if corruption would be curbed, so there's hardly any time left anyway,' remarked Varun.

There was a vote on whether to support the accused or not, which went against them. The two Chief Ministers were sacked from party membership. Two honest and intelligent MPs with deeply investigated files and clean backgrounds were given charge immediately as the new Chief Ministers.

The people of the country remained glued to their TV sets for these reality shows...unscripted and with more real-life spice than any TV serial they had ever seen. Aditya had made it a policy that even his party meetings would be made transparent. After all they did not have any planning or plotting to do in these meetings against their opponents. It was the country that was in focus in every meeting and it was important for people to know what was going on. It was a new way to bind them together and make them patriotic, while at the same time winning more support for the party.

Another bigger meeting of all the MPs and MLAs was called two days after this.

'The party image has taken a plunge,' said Aditya, addressing the emergency meeting of the 275 MPs and 2,245 MLAs of the party. 'And I will not allow that to happen. We still have so many promises left to fulfill, before the people make up their minds to give us a second chance. So, let us focus our energies on that. Remember, we came in with a promise to take India to the top.'

He looked around the conference hall, from one end to the other, observing the expression on each face. Some of them were listening very carefully, some were whispering to their neighbours, some had a sly grin on their face and some wore an admiring smile, while others acknowledged with a nod.

'And so, I have decided that all our members will be given 60 days to surrender to the Prime Minister's Development Fund, the unaccounted-for money and properties, undeclared shares in private businesses, dollars and euros in overseas bank accounts… anything that could enable anyone to raise a finger on our party. If we have to create a corruption-free nation, we must first purge ourselves. And yes, your identities as renouncers shall be known only to my office and shall not be made public. You can make a new beginning.'

The hall burst into a roar. Everyone seemed to be venting out their surprise.

They suddenly became silent as he continued, 'After which the CBI will have their way. Mr Pramil Kamble, the CBI Head has sought our permission to initiate proceedings against 126 MPs and 978 MLAs, against whom they have evidence pouring in from every corner of the country after this episode.'

'Why don't you bloody sack this Kamble? Have we worked day and night and burnt our blood for the party to see this day? I would rather quit the party...' These were the kind of thoughts that occurred to many. Just that they could not speak it out because the session was being recorded as usual, a part of the transparency policy of the party.

All decisions in the Naya Bharat party were taken democratically. They had made it a point to have internal democracy, unlike many other family-led parties. The Prime Minister was not one to impose his personal decision on them without internal referendum. So an open vote was called, wherein each member had to stand up and say 'yes' or 'no' as the camera moved from person to person. Very few were stupid enough to say 'no' and convict themselves in front of the country, so the motion was passed with a thumping majority.

'And this moment in Indian's history became witness to one of the most brave and unexpected decisions taken by any politician after Independence, one that would be remembered by the future generations as the ending of an era of greed,' reported Sumit Bakshi, live on Indian TV, as people remained glued to their TV sets. 'One that would change the fate of 140 crore people living in a country whose potential had been undermined, whose self-respect had been trodden down upon time and again due to shameless betrayal by its politicians. After 75 years, this nation of 140 crore has finally found an honest, righteous and fearless Prime Minister, who is also a capable implementer and administrator.'

He continued, 'Analysts say that once so many Ministers actually and officially shed their baggage and become honest, it will be almost impossible for corruption to continue in the bureaucracy and public offices down the line. Now, the opposition also has no option but to follow suit. The Prime Minister has already informed them that any MP from any party can renounce his black money to the PM's Development Fund, confidentially.'

'Truth is stranger than fiction,' said Jagat Bindra to his colleague Shazia on the sets of their new chat show 'Khalbali'. The positivity all around had forced him to give up negative reporting as it no longer had the same audience. He retained his style, however—still the audience's favourite. 'We just received a byte from Janardan Singh, the Naya Bharat MP from Rampur. He says, he will surrender ₹80 crore to the development fund. He seemed genuinely happy and relieved as if a burden had been taken off his shoulder.'

'Yes, and truth is also more intriguing and dramatic,' agreed Shazia, 'There couldn't have been a better way to reverse the damage done by all these years of corruption.'

'Good afternoon, Mr Yadav. You will need to step up my security for the next three months. Cut down my travel schedules and inform vigilance to pass the unavoidable ones under double scanner,' Aditya instructed his Chief of Security.

'Anything serious, Sir?'

'Nope! I just have a feeling that by the end of next month our Development Fund will be bigger than the International Monitory Fund and all other funds of the UN put together. Being the signing authority of the world's biggest fund brings with it unforeseen perils. Hope you are convinced!'

'Of course! Yes, Sir,' said Yadav, slightly worried, wondering which beehive his boss had just struck. He was proud to be serving the most powerful yet adorable person he had known till now. 'I think I have lived my life to the fullest, in these last few years of being with Aditya Sir,' he used to tell his family. 'People say I would not wink an eyelid before killing for him… I say, I would not do so even while dying for him.'

◆

'Can you guarantee that the money pouring into the Prime Minister's Fund will be used rightfully? All of us know that hardly 50 per cent of the money the government spends on development really reaches the ground,' said Jatin Oberoi addressing a press conference where reporters wanted to know his views on the step taken by Aditya Garg in Naya Bharat Party.

'But don't you think this is a very good and bold initiative to control corruption in politics? As there is a mad rush to dispose of the dead black money within the stipulated period, the prices of property and gold have already crashed to the ground, bringing them nearer to the reach of the common man,' asked Sumit Bakshi.

'The motive may be good, but the approach is very tyrannical and insulting. I would never do it with my party members. There are better ways to address this issue.'

'What would you have done?' asked anxious reporters, most of them not even caring to wait for their turn.

'I would have got an investigation done and initiated action against the corrupt members rather than threatening them all. These are people who have dedicated their lives for the masses and the country.'

'Then, why was it not done by your party when they were in power?' asked Jagat Bindra, the aggressive reporter from ABCD channel.

'Sir, the public is expecting a similar action in your party. Does that mean you are not going to take any step for the time being?' accosted another reporter.

'Mr Jatin, it is being said that Mr Aditya's next target will be the other parties, what are you going to do?'

'What will I do? Of course, he is free to do what he wants to do. We are not going to support corrupt politician. We will, however, strongly oppose any harassment of our members. That's all gentlemen, it was a pleasure talking to you.' Jatin, surrounded by his bodyguards rushed his way through the swarm of reporters. He got into his car and the fleet drove off.

Soon, he was in his private aircraft with Brijmohan Gupta, Ranjit Shastry and Ganesh Vidyarthi. With access to the best indulgence from the glamour capital of the country, Ganesh had become the favourite of Jatin and Ranjit too.

'This guy has gone mad. We need to set him right,' said Ranjit, sipping scotch with a tense expression.

'Of course! But there is something more important we need to do for which I called you on this emergency trip,' said Jatin.

'What?' both Ranjit and Gupta asked anxiously.

'I have news that CBDT under the Double Tax Avoidance Treaty has made Swiss Bankers Association reveal the names of the Indian account holders. So, we have to shift our money to Morocco, which does not have any such treaty with India. Mark, my fiduciary in Switzerland, will organize everything.'

'Cheers to your prudence,' said Brijmohan Gupta. 'But at least you should have told me beforehand, I seem to have forgotten my account number.'

'Oh, come on Gupta ji, don't tell me. You don't forget anything. But that's not the only purpose. We have a guest with us today, Mr Soumik Dey Mistry.' An attendant escorted Mr Mistry to the meeting room from an adjacent cabin.

'Mr Mistry! How are you? And how are our friends in the

left?' said Brijmohan shaking his hand.

'So, where are we going after Switzerland? We must be having a meeting with the communists in China or Russia?' laughed Ranjit Shastri.

'No, we are going to Sicily. Mr Mistry has the best private resort booked for us there, owned by his Russian friends.'

'Yes! We deserve some relaxation after all the stress we have been through over the last few months. They say, Sicily has one of the best exotic flavours of Italian culture,' said Ranjit.

'Culture I don't give a damn about! I am excited thinking about the hospitality the Russian beauties will extend for their special guests,' grinned Brijmohan.

'Russian! Really?' Ganesh said greedily, sipping his Bloody Mary, his eyes wide open and mouth agape. Everybody laughed.

'Foursome, haan?' teased Gupta.

'Amazing boss! What a plan... A perfect cocktail of business and pleasure! That's why you are the Boss! Cheers!' said Ranjit, as they all looked at Jatin with true appreciation in their eyes.

Dekhna Nahin...Karna hai
New Delhi, Red Fort, 15 August 2022

The Prime Minister of India was addressing the nation on the occasion of its 75th Independence Day. This address was special and had people across the country glued to their TV screens because on this day he gave something very unique to the nation. Something that made people wonder at his intelligence and wisdom.

'No way! How embarrassing, James! Just hold on for half-an-hour,' the annoyed teacher scolded the pleading skinny boy with untidy hair, in a hushed voice. 'Okay, come, I will speak to the security. Just don't sit there for an hour like you do at school.'

As the PM rose to the podium the crowd broke into a frenzy cheering for the country and their leader.

'Today, my friends, I will tell you about a decision of mine, which maybe the most controversial decisions that I have taken for the progress of our country. One, for which we may even have to amend with the Constitution. But I am sure it will have a long-lasting positive impact.'

He looked around and could sense the crowd's excitement. 'Okay, I will give you a hint. After this is implemented, there will be little need for "Right to Recall",' he said.

The boy was back sooner than his teacher would have expected, not intending to miss the action.

The crowd roared and cheered.

'We are going to reduce the tenure of our elected representatives, the MPs and MLAs from five years to two years,' said the Prime Minister.

The crowd rumbled as if India had just hit a six on the last decisive ball against Pakistan. Everybody looked at each other in amazement.

'This man is totally unpredictable!' said Sumit, 'The media had explored all possible options, but no one had dreamt of something so drastic!'

The green-eyed boy was now climbing to a high point in a dense tree with monkey-like adeptness. He removed his blazer, pushed back his hair to a neat stack behind his forehead, then drew a cardboard box from a concealed location and opened it. He took out a carbine and assembled it. He placed the gun on a wooden plank fixed between two strong branches and aimed at his target. The non-flowering tree was carefully chosen so that it was not inhabited by birds. This place was ideal for him. He had a clear view of his target, yet was invisible to anyone looking towards the tree. Finally, he took off his spectacles and put on a pair of dark anti-glare glasses. Now, he looked like a trained assassin. Through the lens on the head of carbine, he could see clearly the forehead of the Prime Minister.

'It was not easy for me, my friends, to take this decision. The politics of looting and doling out lollipops has to stop. The system has to be designed to be performance-driven. This change will, for sure, spur the elected representatives to start working from day one,' he said.

The killer pulled the trigger. His work was not very hard as the PM was not reading out from notes on the desk, his speech was extempore. His head did not move up and down. The sound from the gun drowned in the cacophony of the crowd.

The bullet seemed to have hit right on the mark. The killer saw him fall and immediately started to pack his stuff. He left his ammunition where it was. He converted his looks back to that of the untidy schoolboy and slowly climbed down to a lower branch.

By now, the crowd had realized that something dreadful had happened. Amongst the pandemonium of children shouting and running helter-skelter and with his looks changed back to the untidy school boy, he easily managed to mix in the crowd.

Jagat Bindra and Sumit Bakshi looked at each other in shock and despair. They could not believe their eyes. The damage they had just witnessed was an irreversible one. Had the four patriots finally been defeated? Was this the end of their story and that of India's rise to glory as well?

The killer walked with an expression of tremendous satisfaction. He had put an end to a saga of glory this chaotic country was moving towards. His masters would be very pleased. He had to rush back to Sicily, the place of birth of organized mafia. Sicilian mafia, however, was now controlled by Kosher Nostra, the Russian-Jew mafia. They say, the Sicilians would shoot a bystander outside their rendezvous, just to make sure that they don't leave any loose ends. The Russian Jews would empty their gun into a bystander, just to check that the weapon was working fine. That was the difference! He worked for the same Kosher Nostra, who recently concluded a deal with some powerful leaders from India, at a resort in Sicily, after which he was sent on this mission.

Jatin and team's vacation with Mr Mistry at Sicily was not just for relaxation; it was also strategic.

◆

The nation was shocked. The people who returned from the parade knew something terrible had happened to the Prime Minister. Maybe he had a heart attack, maybe he was poisoned… or murdered. They had seen him fall, after which the stage had been completely surrounded by commandos. Those watching him on the TV encountered an interruption in transmission as the reporters, who had been near the stage to cover his each expression for the TRP and to cross-question him, had been held in custody, both for evidence and to avoid national panic.

'Why is the Prime Minister's core team silent now? Salman Mirza, Raghav Chandel and Varun Pandey must tell the country what has happened to him. Has he been victim of some internal politics, has his team conspired against him?' said Raju Gowda from the Bhartiya Janhit Party, surrounded by the press.

'I have firm reports that intelligence had information that he could be attacked. Why did the Home Minister allow the Prime Minister to address the public without a bullet proof cabin?' said Madhur Singh Chandel, the aggressive new party spokesperson for the Indian National Front. 'We strongly feel the need to declare an emergency and apply President's rule. We cannot leave the country in the hands of immature people, who have no accountability to their people.'

The people were glued once again to their TV sets, to get a glimpse of their hero as his body would be brought out. Many still found it hard to believe that Aditya Garg could be dead but slowly they came to terms with this fact as their mobiles were flooded with a plethora of Facebook and Whatsapp comments about the possible reasons for his fateful end. The success story of the country had come to a jolting halt. Their eyes were filled with tears as they saw crowds of people on the streets lamenting, crying inconsolably as if they had lost a family member. For the first time the assassination of a Prime Minister had not sparked riots, but brought people together in this moment of grief. The heart of each patriot was filled with sorrow, but there was also a sense of determination to make their hero's dream come true...to complete the story of India's glory that he had started writing.

Suddenly, the channels covering the event flickered back to life and they saw Salman, Varun and Raghav walking shoulder to shoulder, in a row, on the parade ground. Reporters, who had been withheld after the assassination, were busy covering them. They walked up the stairs to the podium from where the Prime Minister had been speaking.

A few moments later, Aditya emerged from behind the stage, walked up to the podium and held the mike in his hands. He was smiling. The four patriots were standing tall together.

There was an outcry of sheer joy at that one single moment.

'Thank you for your prayers, my dear countrymen! The Prime Minister of India cannot be killed so easily. Yes, there was an attack on me and I should have been dead by now, but for the security system our scientists have developed. This entire area is under radiation, which can detect motion. As soon as it detects any object moving at above 10 meters per second, it opens the door to the underground mine-proof ballistic cabin on which I am standing right now and within a fraction-of-a-second I am beneath the ground. The killer's bullet could only reach halfway when I was out of its trajectory. Had they even dropped a bomb on me, I would have been safe. However, I lost a trusted officer, Mr Yadav, who was standing behind me.' His eyes were filled with tears.

The tall Sicilian assassin was driving to the airport in a cab. The driver stopped the car, looked back and shot him in the head. The driver had barely moved half-a-kilometer when the cab was ordered to stop at a police check post. There was a high alert after the attack on the PM and the whole area had been sealed. The driver flaunted his ID from the window and the inspector on duty saluted him crisply, forgetting the body he had just seen on the back seat.

It read:

> (License to kill)
> **Avinash Singh**
> Officer on Special Duty
> National Investigation Agency

'Like Yadav, I am also only human,' continued Aditya. 'Tomorrow some other bullet may find its way into me. So, I want to share with you my heart's feelings. I was an ordinary man, running my family business. My love for my country brought me here, in this position. I wanted to change things and I chose to work for it. I am sure almost every young man in this country wants to see things change. But who will do it? You have to stop thinking that someone else, some hero will come and do something to bring about a change. Being patriotic should not end with writing comments on Facebook or participating in candle marches. Unless honest people, who really want the country to change, come forward and offer themselves to run the country, nothing will happen. Yes, if you are really passionate about the country, I am urging you to come forward and contest elections. We don't need more systems, we need the right people in the existing system. And after that I am sure, even if they kill one Aditya, 35 per cent of India's young population...40 crore Adityas will be there in line. *Dekhna nahin...karna hai*,' he added with a pause, as the cameras closed up on his watery eyes.

'With that belief my friends, I welcome you all into India's 76th year of Independence. Jai Hind! Jai Naya Bharat!'

The Reunion

New Delhi, 17 August 2022

'My butt is aching Jatin. When are we going to land?' asked Brijmohan.

'Have patience. Let the good news come. Our friends in Sicily will inform us no sooner than the job is done. We will touch Indian soil only then,' replied Jatin.

'Oh God! That means we are still hovering over the Mediterranean Sea. Are you sure this Romanovich can penetrate all the layers of security arrangements. What if he fails?' Ranjit said, sounding a bit worried.

'Don't worry, even if he fails, the Sicilian mafia will know and they will inform us immediately. He has a GPS implant in his body. As soon as it becomes stationary, they will know that either he is in custody or dead. In any case, no clue would ever lead to us.'

A crew member knocked the door and entered their cabin. He told that there was a call for Mr Mistry from Sicilian air traffic control.

'Yes. There we go!' Jatin slapped his armrest in excitement. A devious smile appeared on his face. 'It's in the Oberoi genes! We are insurmountable. You guys owe me a massage at, 'Nicole

Chocoa Heaven' in Bangkok.

'The Sicilians have told that Romanovich is on the job. He is probably following the target. The GPS is showing him moving on the roads of Delhi. Meanwhile, the Captain says we have to refuel in Sicily before taking off for India. The Sicilians will also change the pilot, as this one is making too much of a fuss.'

'Why don't you join our party, Mr Mistry? Aren't you tired with the discipline in the left? Once you taste the fruits of our company, you will never go back. And don't worry, I have the next plan already worked out. If by any chance Romanovich fails, we have riots planned to push Naya Bharat out of power and get President's rule imposed,' Jatin said, exuding confidence.

'Sure. The pleasure will be all mine, Mr Jatin,' Mistry said with a strange glow in his eyes.

◆

'I am so proud of you Aditya,' said Dr Sabbarwal, watching his Independence Day speech on the BBC. There was a blissful expression on his face.

He was in home-ICU with monitoring devices connected to various parts of his body. The quadro and their spouses were here. They came to meet him twice every week and spent the evening with him.

A 48-inch flat screen television was fixed on the wall opposite his bed. He had successfully transferred the country's governance to the youth. His dream had been fulfilled. God had been very kind, giving more time than he could have asked for. The country was vibrant with a new energy. Not only was there an optimism all around but the development was visible at ground level. Without doubt, it had been a roller coaster ride for his quadro but they had stood up to the test and emerged successful with flying colours.

'We are here to seek your advice on something today,' said Varun.

They called in Sumant Srivatsan and Vinod Saxena who gave Dr Sabbarwal a vivid description of how Jatin and company had made repeated attempts to obliterate the quadro. They also told him how Ganesh Vidyarthi, who had cold bloodedly killed the love of Salman's life, was in Jatin's inner circle now.

'We have sufficient evidence now to arrest and prosecute them,' said Raghav.

'So, what are you waiting for?' asked Dr Sabbarwal.

'They are not in India. They are on their way to India in their private Boeing,' said Salman.

'So?'

'Would it really be wise to put them through trials? We also have a plan B,' said Varun, 'for which we need your permission.'

♦

'What a wonderful island?' Jatin said, looking out of the aircraft window. 'I am sure it's unexplored and uninhabited.' The clear sun and a cloudless sky gave them a clear view of this tiny spec of green in the middle of the deep blue ocean.

'Islands always fascinate you, Jatin. Let us come back to power and maybe you can own a few more,' said Ranjit. 'What do you say, Gupta ji?'

'It has been almost eight hours since the plane took off, we should have landed by now,' said Brijmohan.

'Oh, you were taking a little nap when Mr Mistry told us that the Captain changed the route to avoid some really bad weather, adding some extra hours to our flying time,' replied Jatin. 'And he also said that the mission is accomplished.'

'Really! I can't wait to reach Delhi. Finally...' Brijmohan sighed.

'Did I just hear you own an island, Jatin ji? Please take me there too sometime. Just the four of us, some beer and some hot babes,' said Ganesh.

'Promise!' said Jatin, as all four brought their glasses together for a toast to their great success.

◆

Every eye was glued on to the same breaking news playing on almost every channel.

'The country, today, lost some of its most powerful and promising leaders in a plane crash in the middle of the Pacific Ocean. The private Boeing was being flown by some unknown pilot from Sicily, where apparently Mr Jatin had gone for vacation with his close friends, Ranjit Shastri, Brijmohan Gupta and Ganesh Vidyarthi. Search is on for the plane's debris and the possibility of any survivors has been ruled out,' said Sumit Bakshi from Indian TV, as the camera closed in on him to capture the trademark twitch of his lips and eyebrows.

'A sad end to an era of dynasty politics, where political figures own airplanes and islands. Although he was a very dynamic leader, it is said that Mr Jatin was into all kinds of indulgences, from rave parties to adultery. Why else would a 40-year-old unmarried man travel with his political friends, without their families, to Sicily? There is no official declaration from the Indian National Front about the purpose of this visit. Rest in peace, Mr Jatin and friends! This is Jagat Bindra, signing off from ABCD News,' the short, thin and sly reporter screamed with his orchestrating mannerism.

'So, you finally incinerated the superbugs for good, Mr Salman! *Prasaad de hi diya*,' Sumant said softly to him as they all stood in front of the TV in Dr Sabbarwal's house. 'It is said that the plane turned into a ball of fire before plunging into the ocean. That's why the debris is so difficult to find.'

'Did you really expect that kind of a thing from us, Sumant? Saying something in anger is one thing, but getting someone killed in cold blood is another. We would have had better ways than that to punish them,' Salman said, nodding his head with a wicked smile, as he winked at Varun.

'How did you know about the assassin Romanovich and Jatin's plan?' asked Dr Sabbarwal.

'We were always in control, Sir. From the day Jatin designed this next layer of his master plan, the *"Chakravyuh"*,' said Varun. 'But we did not let it show. Yes, *Chakravyuh*! That's what he proudly used to call it to his gang. A plan no less ingenious and lethal than the *Chakravyuh* of the *Mahabharata*!—designed to besiege and destroy Naya Bharat,' replied Varun.

'It started on our very first day in the Parliament when they tried to stall the proceedings, followed by the terrorist attack, implicating Salman, kidnapping Raghav and finally this attack on me,' added Aditya.

'Sumant and Vinod had already found the threads that led to their involvement long back and when Jatin approached Mr Mistry from the left to organize his meeting with the mafia in Sicily, we intercepted his conversations. We made Mr Mistry our official witness, promising him immunity. He was the one who co-ordinated the entire operation for us—doping their drinks, changing to the pilot of our choice at Sicily and refuelling the plane to cover a long distance before the crash,' said Salman.

'Their deal with the Sicilian mafia was real, but everything else was maneuvered as per our plan. All this time, while Jatin was confident he was pulling the strings, it was us who were in control,' concluded Raghav.

'You too, Raghav? You too were a part of this?' Dr Sabbarwal looked at him in surprise.

'Honestly speaking, this is too small a punishment for the crimes they have committed. You know my philosophy, Sir! Be evil to some if you have to, for the greater good. This is one of those rare situations,' replied Raghav.

'You are right! It was a death trap for me, the Yudhishthira of Naya Bharat,' mused Dr Sabbarwal. 'The only difference was that this time instead of an Abhimanyu, the Pandavas entered the *Chakravyuh* together, holding on to each other and shattered it. Didn't I tell you… Together, you are invincible! What about Mr Mistry and the air crew? Did they also go down with the plane? They did not deserve this.'

'Sir, do you expect this from us? Do you think we would push someone innocent into the jaws of death to punish the guilty?' Aditya said, with a smile. 'Of course, they got off the plane, before the crash.'

'I am proud of you, boys!' said Dr Sabbarwal. 'Where are the girls? Please call them, I want to see you all together. Time is running out for me.'

'They are attending a charity show together,' said Aditya. 'I will call Prachi and ask her to come over with everyone.'

'I have a surprise for you! There is a party at our indoor auditorium to celebrate the success of my young team. To a father, his sons' success brings more happiness than his own.'

'When?'

'Now! Get ready! I too will have to rush, can't go there in this patient's uniform.' Dr Sabbarwal was a strong man even in his weakest physical state. His body was giving up, but his mind was as enthusiastic as ever.

EPILOGUE

Jatin woke up to the roar of the sea waves that lashed out to the shore rhythmically. The orange setting sun in the horizon looked beautiful. The pink and violet sky in its background struck a picturesque contrast to the blue water of the ocean. He got up and sat erect to brush off the sand sticking to his body. His head seemed heavy. He reached into his pocket, for the hashish bidi, but it was missing.

He saw Brijmohan Gupta sitting cross-legged, a few steps away, his forehead supported by his cupped hands.

'Where are we, Gupta ji?'

'On your dream island, maybe the one you were seeing from the aircraft window,' Gupta said, 'uninhabited and unexplored!'

'Where are Ranjit and Ganesh?'

Without looking up, Gupta pointed his finger to a clump of trees, some distance away from the shore. Jatin could see Ranjit's back. He was kneeling down and throwing back scoops of sand dug with his bare hands. As the dim light did not allow him to see clearly what was going on, he got up and started walking towards Ranjit. As he approached closer, he was horrified at the sight. Ganesh was buried neck-deep in the sand which Ranjit was trying to dig out and remove with his hands.

'Gupta ji, come here! What are you doing there?' Jatin

shouted as he scurried to the site of disaster and started helping Ranjit.

'Please save me!' was all Ganesh managed to mumble as the flying sand from the scooping stuck to his face. He kept his eyes and mouth tightly shut to avoid the sand getting into them.

'Why? What were you saying in the aircraft? Didn't you want just the four of us to be on a beautiful island? Foursome? Boss has fulfilled his promise! I'm sure the beer and babes will follow,' Gupta said, slapping him on the back of his head.

Ganesh just gritted his teeth as any other movement would only worsen his condition.

'Stop it, Gupta ji! Just focus on getting him out of here,' said Jatin, as all three sat around the head throwing back scoops of sand.

'Actually I don't think it is a wise idea. Suppose there's going to be just the four of us here, and no women. The thought of what all he could do with us makes me shudder.'

'What non-sense, Gupta ji! Those bastards have committed the biggest mistake of their lives by leaving us alive. Sooner or later we will find our way home... Then, they will know what it means to mess with me,' said Jatin.

'We will chop their balls off,' Ranjit added viciously.

Gupta was shaking his head dismally. Jatin's *Chakravyuh* had boomeranged back onto them and none of them knew the way out.

'What, Gupta ji?' shouted Jatin.

Gupta got up, walked back to the shore and came back with a wooden board. Ranjit peed in his pants as Ganesh twitched his nose in disgust. The board read:

BAT ISLAND

Located 1,500 miles east of the Baker's island, this island is situated in the middle of the Pacific Ocean, almost halfway between the South American and Australian continents. It is off route any sailing track of commercial or tourist ships, one of the most isolated islands on the world map.

Covering an area of just half an acre, the island is totally underwater at high tide. Even if one survives a few high tides by clinging on to the trees, there is no escape from the vampire bats that fly in from South America every full moon and inhabit this island for a week. Hence, the name—Bat Island. You'd better not be here...

Author's Note

This work is an outcome of my burning desire to see my country develop and prosper. I am sure many from our generation would have felt the frustration of seeing our country being left behind and the pathetic condition it is forced to be in, despite having the best brains and the most hardworking people.

When I visit a foreign land like China, Singapore or Europe, I wonder how these people keep their cities so amazingly clean and organized, while we live amidst overflowing containers of garbage. Are these people genetically more intelligent, or do they have better education? Or do these countries have more natural resources, thereby making them richer? The answer is, none, as we all know.

They say that if we keep growing with the current rate of 8-10% for next twenty years, we may reach somewhere near to where China is today. But will I live to see that day? The damage done by the past seven decades of mis-governance will take its toll on me, you and maybe our children too.

I strongly believe that with a positive environment and the right set of people in our governance, we can still march ahead. Our last generation lived in an era where they were busy trying to secure a better future for their families. The current generation is much more secure, comfortable and lives in the Internet Age. I sometimes feel worried to see the apathy of many youngsters towards doing something concrete to translate their patriotism. They have to come out of the virtual patriotism and pitch in to make this country better.

The most important reason why we have not had a truly good governance since Independence is the concept of 'dirty politics'. We stay away from politics as it is not meant for 'good' people. So here we are, governed by the 'not-so-good' people. Why crib then!

Now is the time 'good' people start considering politics as a career option. I hope we will soon see a time when we have to choose the better between educated people with good administrative capabilities and intentions, rather than just good orators with selfish interests. If this story can inspire even a single 'good' person towards this, I shall consider my efforts worthwhile.

Jai Hind.

Made in the USA
Monee, IL
03 May 2026

49438704R00174